MRS. DALLOWAY

"Mrs. Dalloway said she would buy the flowers herself." It's one of the most famous opening lines in literature, that of Virginia Woolf's beloved masterpiece of time, memory, and the city. In the wake of World War I and the 1918 flu pandemic, Clarissa Dalloway, elegant and vivacious, is preparing for a party and remembering those she once loved. In another part of London, Septimus Smith is suffering from shell shock and on the brink of madness. Their days interweave and their lives converge as the party reaches its glittering climax. In this engulfing portrait of one day in a woman's life, in which she perfects the interior monologue and recapitulates the life cycle in the hours of the day, from first light to the dark of night, Woolf achieves an uncanny simulacrum of consciousness, bringing past, present, and future together, and recording, impression by impression, minute by minute, the feel of life itself.

This edition is collated from all known proofs, manuscripts, and impressions to reflect the author's intentions, and includes a catalog of emendations, a stirringly personal foreword by bestselling novelist Jenny Offill, an illuminating introduction and endnotes by the distinguished feminist critic Elaine Showalter, and a map of Mrs. Dalloway's London.

"A revelation . . . A remarkably expansive and an irreducibly strange book. Nothing you might read in a plot summary prepares you for the multitudes it contains."
—Jenny Offill, from the foreword

"One of the most moving, revolutionary artworks of the twentieth century."
—Michael Cunningham

"At a time when our most ordinary acts—shopping, taking a walk—have come to seem momentous, a matter of life or death, Clarissa's vision of everyday shopping as a high-stakes adventure resonates in a peculiar way. We are all Mrs. Dall——

D1268189

PENGUIN CLASSICS (🐧) DELUXE EDITION

MRS. DALLOWAY

VIRGINIA WOOLF was born in London in 1882, the daughter of the editor and critic Leslie Stephen and Julia Stephen, a philanthropist and model for the Pre-Raphaelites. She suffered a traumatic adolescence after the deaths of her mother, in 1895, and her stepsister Stella, in 1897, leaving her subject to breakdowns for the rest of her life. Her father died in 1904, and two years later, her favorite brother Thoby died suddenly of typhoid. With her sister, the painter Vanessa Bell, she was drawn into the company of writers and artists such as Lytton Strachey and Roger Fry, later known as the Bloomsbury Group. Among them she met Leonard Woolf, whom she married in 1912, and together they founded the Hogarth Press in 1917, which was to publish the work of T. S. Eliot, E. M. Forster and Katherine Mansfield as well as the earliest translations of Freud. Woolf lived an energetic life among friends and family, reviewing and writing, and dividing her time between London and the Sussex Downs. In 1941, fearing another attack of mental illness, she drowned herself in the River Ouse.

Her first novel, *The Voyage Out*, appeared in 1915, and she then worked through the transitional *Night and Day* (1919) to the highly experimental and impressionistic *Jacob's Room* (1922). From then on her fiction became a series of brilliant and extraordinarily varied experiments, each one searching for a fresh way of presenting the relationship between individual lives and the forces of society and history. She was particularly concerned with women's experience, not only in her novels but also in her essays and her two books of feminist polemic, *A Room of One's Own* (1929) and *Three Guineas* (1938). Her major novels include *Mrs. Dalloway* (1925); *To the Lighthouse* (1927); the historical fantasy *Orlando* (1928), written for Vita Sackville-West; the extraordinary poetic vision of *The Waves* (1931); the family saga of *The Years* (1937); and *Between the Acts* (1941).

JENNY OFFILL is the author of the *New York Times* bestselling novel *Weather*, which was shortlisted for the Women's Prize; the novel *Dept. of Speculation*, which was one of *The New York*

Times Book Review's Ten Best Books of 2014; and the novel *Last Things*, which was a *New York Times* Notable Book and a finalist for the *Los Angeles Times* Book Prize for First Fiction. She lives in upstate New York and teaches at Bard College and in the low-residency program at Queens University of Charlotte.

ELAINE SHOWALTER is Professor of English, Emerita, at Princeton University and the author of many works of feminist literary criticism, including *A Literature of Their Own: British Women Novelists from Brontë to Lessing*, *The Female Malady: Women, Madness, and English Culture, 1830–1980*, and *A Jury of Her Peers: American Women Writers from Anne Bradstreet to Annie Proulx*.

STELLA McNICHOL was the author of several critical studies on Virginia Woolf and the editor of a volume of Woolf's stories, *Mrs. Dalloway's Party*.

VIRGINIA WOOLF

MRS. DALLOWAY

Foreword by
JENNY OFFILL

Introduction and Notes by
ELAINE SHOWALTER

Edited by
STELLA MCNICHOL

PENGUIN BOOKS

PENGUIN BOOKS

An imprint of Penguin Random House LLC

penguinrandomhouse.com

First published in Great Britain by The Hogarth Press 1925
Annotated edition published in Penguin Books (UK) 1992
This edition with a foreword by Jenny Offill published in
Penguin Books (USA) 2021

Introduction and notes copyright © 1992 by Elaine Showalter
Other editorial matter copyright © 1992 by Stella McNichol
Foreword copyright © 2021 by Jenny Offill

LIBRARY OF CONGRESS CATALOGING-IN-PUBLICATION DATA

Names: Woolf, Virginia, 1882–1941, author. | Offill, Jenny, 1968– writer of foreword. | Showalter, Elaine, writer of introduction. | McNichol, Stella, editor.
Title: Mrs. Dalloway / Virginia Woolf; foreword by Jenny Offill; introduction and notes by Elaine Showalter; edited by Stella McNichol.
Description: Penguin Classics deluxe edition. |
[New York] : Penguin Classics, 2021. | Originally published, 1925. |
Includes bibliographical references.
Identifiers: LCCN 2020048510 | ISBN 9780143136132 (paperback) |
ISBN 9780525507741 (ebook)
Subjects: LCSH: Triangles (Interpersonal relations)—Fiction. |
Middle-aged women—Fiction. | Married women—Fiction. |
Suicide victims—Fiction. | Psychological fiction. | Domestic fiction.
Classification: LCC PR6045.O72 M7 2021c | DDC 823/.912—dc23
LC record available at https://lccn.loc.gov/2020048510

Printed in the United States of America
6th Printing

Set in Sabon LT Pro

Contents

CENTRAL LONDON IN THE MID-TWENTIES

Bibliographical Note

Diary: The Diary of Virginia Woolf, 5 vols., ed. Anne Olivier Bell (Hogarth Press, 1977–84; Penguin Books, 1979–85).

Letters: The Letters of Virginia Woolf, 6 vols., ed. Nigel Nicolson and Joanne Trautmann (Hogarth Press, 1975).

Essays: The Essays of Virginia Woolf, 6 vols., ed. Andrew McNeillie (Hogarth Press, 1986–2011).

CE: Collected Essays: 4 vols., ed. Leonard Woolf (Chatto & Windus, 1966, 1967).

Foreword

In 1915, Virginia Woolf wrote about a peculiarity that runs through all real works of art. The books of certain writers (she was speaking of Charlotte Brontë at the time) seem to shape-shift with each reading. The plot might become comfortingly familiar, but the emotional revelations within it change. Scenes once passed over as unimportant begin to prickle with new meaning, as if time itself had been the missing ingredient for understanding them. Woolf went on to describe the works she returned to again and again:

> At each fresh reading one notices some change in them, as if the sap of life ran in their leaves, and with skies and plants they had the power to alter their shape and colour from season to season. To write down one's impressions of *Hamlet* as one reads it year after year, would be virtually to record one's own autobiography, for as we know more of life, so Shakespeare comments upon what we know.[1]

For me, *Mrs. Dalloway* is such a book, one to which I have mapped the twists and turns of my own autobiography over the years. Each time, I have found shocks of recognition on the page, but they are always new ones, never the ones I was remembering. Instead, some forgotten facet of the story comes to light, and the feeling is always that of having blurred past something that was right in front of me.

This is because *Mrs. Dalloway* is a remarkably expansive and an irreducibly strange book. Nothing you might read in a plot summary prepares you for the multitudes it contains. In fact, on the surface, it sounds suspiciously dull. The novel depicts a single day in June from the perspective of a number of characters. The year is 1923. The Great War is over, but the memory of its unprecedented destruction still hangs over England. In a posh part of London, a middle-aged woman plans a party. She goes out to get flowers. A man she almost married drops by for a visit. She is snubbed by a neighbor. She remembers an alluring girl she once kissed. Later, friends and acquaintances pour into her house for the party. In the midst of all this, she hears news of a stranger's violent death. In between these modest plot points, Clarissa Dalloway wanders around London, lies down for a rest, and takes note of Big Ben striking out the hours again and again.

But wait, I am leaving out everything. Let me go back to the beginning.

The first time I read Virginia Woolf, it was for extraliterary reasons. I knew she had gone mad. I wanted to know how, exactly. Some dark wing was crossing over me that fall. The middle register of experience had abruptly fallen away. I didn't need to sleep anymore, it seemed. My brain buzzed and whirred in terrifying ways. Everything seemed connected to everything else, but in ways I didn't dare try to explain. I was seventeen, I think, eighteen maybe. I worked an early shift at a bakery, and I'd ride there on my bike before dawn, the whoosh of the darkness soft and creaturely around me. *Why are you crying for no reason?* I'd think, brushing my hands across my face.

I suspected I should tell someone about the buzzing and the whirring and the crying, but I couldn't work up the nerve. Instead, I went to the university library one night and checked out books I thought might contain clues about what was in store for me. *Mrs. Dalloway* was one of them. Before I sat down to read it properly, I opened it at random, and this sentence was given occultly to me—*The world wavered and quivered and threatened to burst into flames.*

I could feel my loneliness recede slightly as I read the words.

I backtracked to the first introduction of Septimus Smith, a shell-shocked soldier, loosely tethered to the world, into whom Woolf had poured many of her own experiences of madness. In the first scene, he is standing on the same street as Mrs. Dalloway. They do not know each other (they will never meet), but in this one moment they are briefly connected, both startled by the sound of a car backfiring. Here is our first glimpse of him:

> Septimus Warren Smith, aged about thirty, pale-faced, beak-nosed, wearing brown shoes and a shabby overcoat, with hazel eyes which had that look of apprehension in them which makes complete strangers apprehensive too. The world has raised its whip; where will it descend?

The world has raised its whip; where will it descend? Yes, this. Exactly this, I thought. I started the book over from the beginning and found that the darkness gathering around Septimus was woven into other narrative threads, ones I was less interested in. All these old people talking about houses and parties and hats, what did they have to do with me? I skimmed over these other stories, noting here and there the stunning beauty of the language, then raced ahead to find more Septimus sections. His thoughts, blazingly sad and strange, seemed beautiful to me. I wrapped myself in an old blanket and read through the night, hoping it wouldn't end badly for him.

I didn't return to *Mrs. Dalloway* again until I was in my thirties, and this time I was on a different kind of quest. I was a wife and the mother of a young child, and after years of living alone I found myself suddenly, startlingly mired in the domestic. My days at home with my daughter were full of emotion yet strangely anecdote-less. I wanted to write a novel about this feeling, which was one of want amid plenty, but I worried it would not make a good book, that it would be too trivial. I'd had an idea before my daughter was born that I would keep a diary during the early years. I imagined it structured like a kind of ledger. On one side it would read "In the House" and on the other "In the World."

A poet friend of mine had stamps made up with these phrases imprinted on them and gave them to me just after my daughter was born. But after only a month, I abandoned the idea. I hated to see the blank space where my impressions of life in the world should be. It was February, blizzarding, and I stayed shut inside most days with the baby. But still, I kept wondering how to do it, how to tear down this screen between House and World. *What would a philosophical novel set in a domestic sphere look like?* I wondered. Stupidly, I did not think of *Mrs. Dalloway*, which I remembered narrowly as a book about madness. But then one day I reread Woolf's essay "Modern Novels," from 1919. It is a manifesto of sorts, and this time I found that it spoke directly to me. (Six years later, she would put many of these ideas into play when she wrote *Mrs. Dalloway*.)

> Let us record the atoms as they fall upon the mind in the order in which they fall, let us trace the pattern, however disconnected and incoherent in appearance, which each sight or incident scores upon the consciousness. Let us not take it for granted that life exists more fully in what is commonly thought big than in what is commonly thought small.[2]

I loved this idea of recording the atoms as they fell, of registering each one, however small a moment it seemed to be. Woolf's insight seemed sneakily mystical to me. Many mystic traditions teach that the distinctions between the mundane and the sublime are more porous than we imagine. If one is truly awake, these differences cease to be apparent, they say.

Once I started noticing this idea, I found traces of this collapsing of scale throughout the modernist canon. Robert Walser wrote about how Cezanne's genius lay in "placing in the same 'temple' things both large and small."[3] And Picasso said: "The artist is a receptacle of emotions come from no matter where: from the sky, from the earth, a piece of paper, a cobweb. That is why we must not discriminate between things. There is no rank among them."[4]

But it was in *Mrs. Dalloway* that this radical leveling of high and low found its most thrilling expression for me. I returned to it as a model for the domestic novel that I hoped to write. Woolf's brilliant, soaring sentences were a far cry from my modest, pared-down ones, but the leaps in consciousness, the insistence on the importance of the half-seen, of the subterranean feeling, of the quicksilver joys and sorrows of domestic life was a revelation. This time around, I cared less for Septimus and his grand soliloquies about Human Nature and Death. I knew his story moved deathward at a mighty clip. Instead, I was hungry for signs of life. This time, I lingered over Clarissa's delight in the incidental things that crossed her path, the laughing girls taking their "absurd woolly dogs" for a walk, the old dowagers in motor cars off on "errands of mystery," and on the pond "the slow-swimming happy ducks." This time, I was interested in the old people talking about houses and parties (though the hats still left me cold). I started to ask myself, as I pushed my daughter on a swing or bought pork chops or counted out change at the bodega, *Wait, what is the exact nature of this moment?* Or, in short, *What would Virginia Woolf do?*

And now, fifteen years later, I find myself wandering through the emotional landscape of this novel again. The novelty this time is that I am nearly the same age as Mrs. Dalloway, who has "just broken in to her fifty-second year." This time, I find myself marveling less over the sweeping insights of the novel and more over the intricate delights of its language and form. I keep thinking about the shocking velocity of Woolf's sentences, how they rocket off into the sky, trailing sparks of emotion behind them. I keep thinking about how beautifully, how gracefully, how ecstatically, even, she makes use of dashes and commas and parentheses to capture the halting stutter step of feeling being transmuted into thought. But there are still, of course, the older, uneasier pleasures of reading some biting insight on the page and wondering whether it applies to me.

This time, I am pricked by the passage in which Clarissa's old flame, Peter Walsh, describes how getting older has changed him. He talks about how it is a relief to retreat from the obsessiveness of his youthful passions:

A terrible confession it was (he put his hat on again), but now, at the age of fifty-three, one scarcely needed people any more. Life itself, every moment of it, every drop of it, here, this instant, now, in the sun, in Regent's Park, was enough. Too much, indeed. A whole lifetime was too short to bring out, now that one had acquired the power, the full flavour; to extract every ounce of pleasure, every shade of meaning; which both were so much more solid than they used to be, so much less personal.

"So much less personal"! I will be fifty-three this year, and this phrase needles me. Perhaps this is because I, like Clarissa, have never been good at detachment. I once found my own relationship to entanglements succinctly described in two lines of a Gary Lutz short story. "Are you involved with anybody?" a character is asked. "Everybody," he answers.[5] To become less personal strikes me as a terrible fate, though Peter Walsh speaks of it calmly, as if it is a pleasant thing. But how could it be pleasant to withdraw from this blooming, buzzing world of people? Woolf seems to imply that this desire for distance grows gradually, almost imperceptibly as you get older, until one day you find yourself noticing the petals of the flowers instead of the person holding the bouquet. I'd like to think she's wrong about this, that for once her insights do not apply to me. (Then I remember how one paragraph ago I was lingering not on the vivid characters in *Mrs. Dalloway*, but on the suppleness of its dashes, the beauty of its commas, the grace of its parentheses.)

JENNY OFFILL

NOTES

1. Virginia Woolf, *The Common Reader, First Series* (Boston: Houghton Mifflin Harcourt, 2002).
2. Virginia Woolf, "Modern Novels," *The Times Literary Supplement*, April 10, 1919.
3. Robert Walser, "Thoughts on Cezanne," *Selected Stories* (New York: New York Review of Books, 2002), 189.

4. Alfred H. Barr, Jr., *Picasso, Fifty Years of His Art* (New York: The Museum of Modern Art, dist. by Simon and Schuster, 1946), 273.

5. Gary Lutz, "Certain Riddances," *Stories in the Worst Way* (New York: Alfred A. Knopf, 1996).

Introduction

In 1961, when I first read *Mrs. Dalloway* as a student at Bryn Mawr College, Virginia Woolf's place in twentieth-century fiction was disgracefully underestimated and her feminist concerns were largely unrecognized. My lecture notes begin: 'March 8: Virginia Woolf. More limited intellectually than James Joyce. Interested in the moment and in certain philosophic theories of time. In *Mrs. Dalloway* we are immediately confronted with Clarissa and must face haunting questions concerning her. Has she made the right decisions in life? Is she a support to her husband?' Clearly these ladylike questions were the ones our professor believed *should* haunt respectable young women thinking about their own decisions in life.

Woolf's literary standing has changed drastically, yet the character of Clarissa Dalloway remains puzzling.[1] As Margaret Drabble has pointed out, like her predecessors Jane Austen and George Eliot, Woolf 'chose on the whole to describe women less gifted, intellectually less audacious, more conventional than herself.'[2] Indeed, in writing her fourth novel, at a moment that marked her own sense of artistic independence and maturity, Woolf chose as her heroine a London society lady whom even she thought 'too glittering & tinsely.'[3] Woolf's contemporaries found Clarissa class-bound and slight.

Furthermore, *Mrs. Dalloway* demands our judgment of its heroine from the moment we encounter its eponymous title. By her emphatic use of 'Mrs.', Woolf draws our attention to the way

in which the central woman character is socially defined by her
marriage and masked by her marital signature. Walking in London, Clarissa Parry Dalloway experiences 'the oddest sense of
being herself invisible; unseen; unknown . . . this being Mrs.
Dalloway; not even Clarissa any more; this being Mrs. Richard
Dalloway' (p. 7). Woolf was well aware that, as feminist theory
now puts it, 'the name of the husband is one of the strongest
insignia of patriarchal power.'[4] Is Mrs. Dalloway a sad example
of the way women have been rendered invisible by the state and
the law; or is she perhaps rather a defiant figure who offers a
critique of patriarchal power? Critics have strongly disagreed in
the way they see Clarissa. At one extreme, the novelist Paul
Bailey argues that 'at her most interesting she is a snobbish, vain,
repressed lesbian who has dabbled in culture, but for the greater
part of the novel she is only a shadow, poetically enshrined.'[5] At
the opposite extreme, the feminist critics Sandra Gilbert and
Susan Gubar describe her as 'a kind of queen' who 'with a divine
grace . . . regenerates the post-war world.'[6]

Yet a contemporary feminist reading which would substitute
a liberated Ms. Dalloway for Woolf's ambiguous heroine, or
would make Clarissa a priestess or goddess, seems to miss the
point as well. Woolf's deliberately realistic title places *Mrs. Dalloway* in sharp contrast to James Joyce's mythically titled and
structured *Ulysses* which she was reading when she began her
own novel. Clarissa is not Penelope or Athena, but rather an
ordinary woman on an ordinary day. Indeed, what is so moving
and profound about the book is the way Woolf sees behind people's social masks to their deepest human concerns, without el-
evating them to the level of myth. Virtually all the characters in
the novel have failed to live up to their early dreams and ambitions. Clarissa fears that her life has been superficial and passion-
less. Richard Dalloway has not succeeded in politics as he had
hoped. Peter Walsh, a Socialist and would-be writer, has not
fulfilled any of his literary ambitions. The most rebellious character, the 'wild, the daring, the romantic' Sally Seton has married
a bald manufacturer from Manchester. The intellectual Doris
Kilman has become an embittered religious fanatic. Septimus

Smith, who had dreamed of being a poet, suffers from an inability to love. Yet the meaning of each life is larger, more diffuse, and less predictable than these simple statements will allow. Clarissa will not label people as successes or failures, or say 'of any one in the world now that they were this or were that' (p. 5).

Like *Ulysses*, *Mrs. Dalloway* takes place on a single day, Wednesday, 13 June 1923.[7] It follows the heroine from early morning through to night of a London day on which she gives a large formal party. Although she has just turned fifty-two, Clarissa's mind keeps returning to the past, to another June day in 1889 when she was eighteen, and involved in an adolescent romance with Peter Walsh. She is obsessed with these memories, and with her decision not to marry him, in part because Walsh is due to return to London after a long absence in India, and in part because her own daughter Elizabeth is turning eighteen. Thus the female life cycle of sexual flowering and marital decision is about to repeat itself in another generation. At the beginning of the novel, Clarissa is convinced that the drama of her own life has come to an end; 'the five acts of a play . . . were now over' (p. 39). As a woman who has come to the end of her childbearing years, Clarissa finds herself constantly aware of mortality and loss. But by the novel's end, she has come, if only fleetingly, to accept the loss of the 'triumphs of youth' and to face the next stage of her life.

Woolf contrasts Clarissa's meditations on ageing and death with those of Peter Walsh. Walsh is six months older than Clarissa; indeed, when he comes to see her, the young maid Lucy perceives him as 'elderly' (p. 32). But as a man he responds to ageing very differently, with a defiant attempt to recapture his sense of youth and virility in a romance with a married woman in India, a woman young enough to be his daughter. Constantly fiddling with the pocket-knife which symbolizes his masculinity, Walsh fantasizes about sexual adventures, and even follows women in the streets. His sense of the social changes in England since the war is primarily sexual – the newspapers are freer in their language, women use make-up in public, and couples are seen embracing. While women relive their lives vicariously through their daughters, men have the chance to renew their lives through action; if women, as Walsh muses, seem to live more in the past, it is because their lives are more bounded and determined by choices made early in youth. Yet Walsh is more deeply scarred by Clarissa's rejection than he wants to admit, and surely more deeply affected by the past than she has been. Behind his mask of masculine bravado is an immature man who cannot reconcile his alleged ideals with his real feelings and acts.

Woolf merges these narratives with a more sensational story: the suicide of a disturbed young war veteran, Septimus Warren Smith. His day, juxtaposed with that of Clarissa and her friends, intersects with it at the party when she hears of his death. Septimus bears much of the novel's weight of social consciousness, and is the vehicle through which Woolf explored some of the meaning of her own bouts of psychosis which corresponded with the war years 1914–18. Through Septimus, and through the character of Doris Kilman, Woolf also considers the nature of fanaticism, both in its mad form of hallucination and delusions of grandeur, and in its socially approved manifestations as Proportion and Conversion.

In planning the novel, Woolf had wished 'to criticise the social system, & to show it at work, at its most intense.'[8] Five years have passed since the Armistice, and Peter Walsh, returning for the first time since the war, is struck by the changes. 'People looked different. Newspapers seemed different.' There are major changes in English society as well. Alex Zwerdling has argued that indeed *Mrs. Dalloway* is a 'sharply critical' examination of the 'governing class' at the turning point of its power. In 1923, there were two Conservative Prime Ministers – Bonar Law, who resigned because of ill health, and Stanley Baldwin, who succeeded him in May – but in January 1924 the party was voted out, and Ramsay MacDonald would become the first Labour Prime Minister. Clarissa's class 'is living on borrowed time. Its values . . . are under attack . . . the empire was crumbling fast.'[9] *Mrs. Dalloway* thus deals on several levels with people's ability to cope with change – Clarissa's experience of the 'change of life'; the change from war to peace; the inevitable changes in the class system and the family wrought by the passage of time.

Mrs. Dalloway also represents Virginia Woolf's farewell to the dreams of youth, and the beginning of her sense of artistic maturity. During 1922 and 1923, as she was working on the various drafts of the novel, Woolf came to feel that she had defined her own literary project in such an exhilarating way that its challenge could sustain her even in the face of critical attack. On 18 February 1922, she writes in her *Diary*, 'I have made up my mind that I'm not going to be popular, & so genuinely that I look upon disregard or abuse as part of my bargain. I'm to write what I like; & they're to say what they like.'[10] Six months later she feels even more certain: 'There's no doubt in my mind that I have found out how to begin (at 40) to say something in my own voice; & that interests me so that I feel I can go ahead without praise.'[11]

Finding her own voice meant pursuing the ideas about fiction that Woolf was also exploring in her reviews and critical essays, marking the difference of her generation of novelists, including Forster, Lawrence, and Joyce, from their Edwardian predecessors Bennett, Galsworthy, and Wells. In a famous essay called 'Mr. Bennett and Mrs. Brown' (1924),[12] Woolf argued that since 1910, 'all human relations have shifted – those between masters and servants, husbands and wives, parents and children. And when human relations change, there is at the same time a change in religion, conduct, politics, and literature.' Neither character nor these relationships, she maintained, could be sufficiently represented by the literary conventions of the Edwardians, such as reliance on material evidence and external fact. 'For us,' she dramatically asserts, 'those conventions are ruin, those tools are death.' Speculating on the story of a 'clean, threadbare' old lady she saw on a train, whom she calls 'Mrs. Brown,' Woolf imagines how the Edwardians would have advised a young writer to describe her character:

And they said: 'Begin by saying that her father kept a shop in Harrogate. Ascertain the rent. Ascertain the wages of shop assistants in the year 1878. Discover what her mother died of. Describe cancer. Describe calico. Describe' – But I cried 'Stop! Stop!' And I regret to say that I threw that ugly, that clumsy, that incongruous tool out of the window, for I knew that if I began describing the cancer and the calico, my Mrs. Brown, that vision to which I cling though I know no way of imparting it to you, would have been dulled and tarnished and vanished for ever.

As her own generation of writers struggled with a new way of capturing character, Woolf warned, readers would have to get used to 'a season of fragments or failures.' They would have to be patient, to tolerate the 'spasmodic, the obscure.' But their patience would be rewarded, for, she predicted, 'we are trembling on the verge of one of the great ages of English literature.'

It's tempting to see Mrs. Brown as a poor relation of Mrs. Dalloway, and to read the essay as a manifesto for Woolf's own work in progress, in which external facts are thin upon the ground (for example, we have no idea when or how Clarissa's mother died), and consciousness is everything. It's also striking that while Woolf omits gender from her list of the variables affecting the novelist's point of view – 'age, country, and temperament' – she names both her adversaries and her allies as male novelists wielding clumsy or violent tools, while their mutual object is imagined as an obscure and enigmatic old woman. Although she does not discuss her quarrel with the Edwardians in feminist terms, the clumsiness and incongruity of the literary conventions she deplored seem connected to the problem of representing the feminine character. In her review of Dorothy Richardson's experimental novel, *The Tunnel* (1919),[13] Woolf had noted Richardson's 'genuine conviction of the discrepancy between what she has to say and the form provided by tradition for her to say it in.' Gradually, Woolf's aesthetic theories came to incorporate gender as well as genre, feminism as well as modernism; and in *A Room of One's Own* (1929), she specifically addressed the problems of the woman novelist having to revise the language, syntax, sentence structure, literary conventions, and value system of the novel created by men.[14]

Not only the conventions for representing character had changed for Woolf's generation, but also the very concept of character and personality. The human personality was not one given fixed monolithic entity, but a shifting conglomerate of impressions and emotions. Psychoanalysis was uncovering a multi-layered self, in which dreams, memories, and fantasies were as important as actions and thoughts. Philosophers were describing the self as a receiver of a tumult of sensations. Artists and painters were experimenting with versions of perception and reality. The Woolfs' Hogarth Press began to publish Freud's works in 1921, and although she was overtly dismissive of psychoanalysis, Woolf developed her own acute psychological method of explaining sensation, memory and repression, one which resembles Freud's in many respects and which uses a similar model of the levels of human consciousness.

Like Freud, Woolf believed that much in adult identity was formed in early childhood. In her novels, and especially in *Mrs. Dalloway*, she made brilliant use of flashbacks and fragments from childhood experience, images that have stayed in a character's consciousness, preserved and frozen like photographs or snapshots, and that come up in unexpected contexts. Clarissa, for example, when she feels most deserted, jealous, and excluded, climbs the stairs to her room and thinks of herself as 'a child exploring a tower' (p. 25). Later, the reader learns that this odd image, with its Freudian hint of the little girl's discovery of sexuality and the phallic, comes from an incident of Clarissa's childhood:

> She had gone up into the tower alone and left them blackberrying in the sun. The door had shut, and there among the dust of fallen plaster and the litter of birds' nests how distant the view had looked, and the sounds came thin and chill (once on Leith Hill, she remembered) (pp. 38–39).

The passage is one of great emotional subtlety: Woolf does not intervene with narrative explanations, but leaves the memory itself to resonate for us, with its echoes of fairy-tale princesses locked in towers, as well as with the more symbolic nuances of a Yeatsian winding tower of age, and of human isolation and loneliness. For the attentive reader, these memories or dreams can deepen our understanding and compassion for Woolf's characters in the way an Edwardian omniscient narration might not achieve. Even the domineering, obtuse Lady Bruton becomes more human when we enter her dreams, in which she is eternally a bedraggled little tomboy jumping the brooks in Devonshire on her pony, completely the equal of her brothers.

Woolf's psychological notation also reflected the thinking of modernist philosophers. In *Time and Free Will* (1888), for example, Henri Bergson had dealt with the difference between historical time, which is external, linear, and measured in terms of the spatial distance travelled by a pendulum or the hands of a clock; and psychological time, which is internal, subjective, and measured by the relative emotional intensity of a moment. Bergson had also given guidance to writers seeking to capture the effects of emotional relativity, for he had suggested that a thought or feeling could be measured in terms of the number of perceptions, memories, and associations attached to it. For Woolf, the external event is significant primarily for the way it triggers and releases the inner life. While an exterior incident or perception may be only a brief flash of chronological time, its impact upon the individual consciousness may have a much greater duration and meaning. Like other modernist writers experimenting with the representation of consciousness, Woolf was interested in capturing the flux of random associations. In addition, she wanted to understand how half-buried memories and interpretations created mood.

Another major concern which Woolf shared with modernist thinkers and artists was the importance of perspective. Even concrete objects, the Cubists demonstrated, could only be partially represented from a single fixed perspective in the vocabulary of a realistic, mimetic painting. A Cubist painting attempted to render the object simultaneously from several points of view, and at several moments in time, combining these multiple perspectives in a kind of collage on the two-dimensional canvas plane. In the novel too, Proust had noted, there could be not only a two-dimensional 'plane psychology,' but also a depth 'psychology in space and time.' People are the product of their past as well as their present, the sum of multiple perspectives upon them, the ways that a variety of others perceive them. Thus it can be said that in trying to show us her characters from a variety of embedded viewpoints rather than from the fixed perspective of the omniscient narrator, Woolf 'breaks up the narrative plane . . . as the Cubists broke up the visual plane.'[15]

In addition, the narrative technique of *Mrs. Dalloway* is very cinematic. Woolf makes use of such devices as montage, close-ups, flashbacks, tracking shots, and rapid cuts in constructing a three-dimensional story.[16] Such transitional devices would have been familiar to her readers, who were flocking to the new cinema houses and seeing the latest American silent films. In *Mrs. Dalloway*, the cinema is one of the post-war developments that has altered the relation between the classes, and acted as a leveller. Everyone goes to the cinema, whereas the traditional entertainments of the music hall and the opera drew very different groups. At the party, the young socialites Lord Gayton and Nancy Blow are talking about the movies, but Peter Walsh also thinks how the young city workers will have 'two hours at the pictures' before it gets dark.

Surprisingly, there are only a few scattered references to the movies in all Woolf's vast correspondence and journals. In the index to volume three of her letters, for example, spanning the years 1923 to 1928, under the entry for 'recreations and habits' we find opera, concerts, theatre, woolwork, embroidery, stencilling, marionettes, polo, cricket, gardening, car-driving, walking, and cooking; but no movies. Nonetheless, in 1926, just after publishing *Mrs. Dalloway*, Woolf wrote a brief but brilliant essay on 'The cinema' which suggests how significant an impact this new medium was having on her work. She referred specifically to *Anna Karenina* and *The Cabinet of Dr. Caligari* as well as to newsreels and documentaries which poignantly recalled life before the war:

> We are beholding a world which has gone beneath the waves . . .
> The war sprung its chasm at the feet of all this innocence and ignorance but it was thus that we danced and pirouetted, toiled and desired, thus that the sun shone and the clouds scudded up to the very end.

These metaphors of a lost Atlantis echoed images of the war she had used in *Mrs. Dalloway*. Woolf was also struck by the narrative possibilities the camera offered in adaptations of novels. 'The past,' she observed, 'could be unrolled, distances annihilated, and the gulfs which dislocate novels (when, for instance, Tolstoy has to pass from Levin to Anna and in doing so jars his story and wrenches and arrests our sympathies) could by the sameness of the background, by the repetition of some scene, be smoothed away.'[17] Yet the cinema had not yet, in her opinion, begun to make the most of its 'picturemaking power,' its potential for symbolization and 'visual emotion.'

The historically meaningful and symbolically apt transitional devices of *Mrs. Dalloway* show how effectively Woolf used the lessons she had learned from the cinematic medium. Urban life, she believed, was made for cinematic representation: 'We get intimations only in the chaos of the streets, perhaps, when some momentary assembly of colour, sound, movement suggests that here is a scene waiting a new art to be transfixed.'[18] In the opening pages of the novel, an elegant closed motor car going up Bond Street provides a visual object upon which many people project their fantasies, allowing Woolf to pan from mind to mind with great economy and directness, and to capture the chaos in an image.

One of the most cinematic linking devices in *Mrs. Dalloway* is the sky-writing plane which is seen by the crowd around Buckingham Palace, and also by Septimus and Rezia in Regent's Park. Clarissa hears its 'strange high singing' right after she leaves her house when she crosses Victoria Street, but never sees it; when she returns home, she asks the maid what people are looking at.

> The sound of an aeroplane bored ominously into the ears of the crowd. There it was coming over the trees, letting out white smoke from behind, which curled and twisted, actually writing something! making letters in the sky! Every one looked up (p. 15).

The plane is advertising something mysterious and modern, Glaxo or Kreemo, or possibly toffee. To Septimus, however, the 'smoke words languishing and melting in the sky' (p. 17) are signs to him from the gods, apocalyptic messages that call on him to be the messiah. In its final arc, the plane is compared to Shelley's skylark, 'curving up and up, straight up, like something mounting in ecstasy, in pure delight,' while 'out from behind poured white smoke looping, writing a T, an O, an F.'

Gillian Beer has wittily described this passage as an erotic and playful one in which 'toffs and toffee are lexically indistinguishable, farts in the wake of lark, of sexual rapture.'[19] Virtually as soon as the aeroplane was invented it entered people's dreams as a symbol of sexual excitement, according to Freud. Moreover, skywriting was a brand-new phenomenon when Woolf was composing her novel. Invented by a British aviator, Major Jack Savage, 'aerial sign-writing' made its debut in London in August 1922. On 18 August, the London *Times* headlined:

SKY WRITING BY AIRCRAFT

WIDE SCOPE IN WAR AND PEACE

SIMPLE MEANS OF NEWS BROADCASTING

'If not in every part of the country,' *The Times* reported, 'at least for a hundred miles around London the writing of advertisements in the sky by aircraft has been seen by millions of people.' In New York that November, crowds watched in awe as the 'flying smoke writer,' Captain Cyril Turner, demonstrated the new invention by writing 'Hello, USA!' in the sky over Manhattan.

By 1923, sky-writing was an important advertising device for the
Daily Mail, and in the evenings city workers could see its name
written in the sky 'in giant letters of orange and silver.'[20]

Planes, cars and movies are among the most conspicuous
signs of modernity, and such references, along with Woolf's ex-
plicit repudiation of her Edwardian predecessors, encouraged
many critics to read *Mrs. Dalloway* as a textbook of modernism, 'a work conceived in response to the state of the novel, a
consciously "modern" novel.'[21] In an introduction to an American edition of *Mrs. Dalloway* in 1928, Woolf herself noted the
way it had been seen as an illustration of her theories of fiction:
'The author, it was said, was dissatisfied with the form of fiction
then in vogue, was determined to beg, borrow, steal, or even
create another of her own.'[22]

But great novels are not written from theoretical blueprints.
Woolf herself firmly denied that the book had its genesis in a
theory of literature, or that it was 'the deliberate offspring of
a method.' Instead, she explained,

> . . . the idea started as the oyster starts or the snail to secrete a
> house for itself. And this it did without any conscious direction.
> The little note book in which an attempt was made to forecast a
> plan was soon abandoned, and the book grew day by day, week
> by week, without any plan at all; except that which was dictated
> each morning in the act of writing . . . it was necessary to write
> the book first and to invent a theory afterwards.[23]

We know a great deal about the beginnings and the gradual
textual evolution of *Mrs. Dalloway*. Woolf's working notes are
preserved at the Berg Collection of the New York Public Library,
and her draft in the British Museum.[24] There is also a typescript
of a discarded chapter, 'The Prime Minister', and the seven short
stories published as *Mrs. Dalloway's Party*.[25] Moreover, Woolf
commented extensively on the progress of her novel in her journal, and discussed it in letters to friends. By reconstructing her
writing process, we can see her hard slow labour to find a language and form for her vision.

Clarissa Dalloway and her husband Richard are characters who originally appeared in Woolf's first novel, *The Voyage Out* (1915). There they are slightly comic figures. Clarissa is 'a tall slight woman, her body wrapped in furs, her face in veils', with artistic tastes and inclinations, but no brain whatsoever.[26] Richard Dalloway is a Conservative MP with the most conventional opinions on women's rights, literature, and politics. He vows at one point that he will be in his grave before a woman is ever allowed to vote in England.

In August 1922, Woolf wrote the short story 'Mrs. Dalloway in Bond Street,' with the idea that it might serve as the first chapter of a novel. By the end of the month, she was considering a sequel: 'Shall I write the next chapter of Mrs. D. – if she is to have a next chapter; & shall it be The Prime Minister?'[27] In a letter to Lady Ottoline Morrell, whose country house, Garsington, had been a literary salon during the war, Woolf joked about the book as her 'Garsington novel' of society high life.[28]

In this early phase, the novel emphasized the ironic social and political contrasts between Clarissa Dalloway, the society hostess in her 'prime', and the Prime Minister, who is driving through London, and will be a guest at the party. Each is empowered by an institution, whether the House or the Home; each has found an identity through a 'party'. The novel was to play with the public and the private, the feminine and the masculine, in broad, almost allegorical terms. A Mrs. Dalloway, buying gloves in Bond Street, is the epitome of the leisured lady of the ruling class for whom the Empire exists. The Prime Minister is the target of all the feelings of resentment and hopelessness felt by the excluded and deprived man in the street.

Woolf first imagined the book as a series of vignettes. At the beginning of October 1922, her working title was 'At Home' or 'The Party,' and she envisioned 'a short book consisting of six or seven chapters each complete separately.'[29] Woolf actually blocked out in her notebook the outline for eight chapters: '1. Mrs. Dalloway in Bond Street/ 2. The Prime Minister/ 3. Ancestors/ 4. A dialogue/ 5. The old ladies/ 6. Country House?/ 7. Cut flowers/ 8. The Party.'[30] Yet, as she could see, the separate

stories needed to be connected, perhaps by a climactic event:
'There must be some sort of fusion. And all must converge upon
the party at the end.'[31]

Gradually, throughout the month of October 1922, Woolf became dissatisfied with this plan; the idea of tightly contained
chapters seemed to be the opposite of her vision of a web or or-
ganism of relations. As she wrote to T. S. Eliot, the novel became
'too interwoven for a chapter broken off to be intelligible.'[32] By
14 October Woolf realized that 'Mrs Dalloway has branched
into a book; & I adumbrate here a study of insanity & suicide:
the world seen by the sane & the insane side by side – something
like that. Septimus Smith? – is that a good name?'[33] Over the next
few days, Woolf played with the idea of Clarissa and Septimus
as doubles. On 16 October, she writes in her notebook:

> Suppose it to be connected in this way: Sanity and insanity.
> Mrs. D. seeing the truth, SS seeing the insane truth. The pace to
> be given by the gradual increase of S's insanity on the one side;
> by the approach of the party on the other.[34]

The novel took shape very slowly, with Woolf making discoveries about its technique a step at a time. By 7 November, she
had hit on the idea of the aeroplane as a linking device. 'I shall
try to sketch out Mrs. D. & consult L. & write the aeroplane
chapter now'.[35] Perspective was a continual problem, and we can
trace her discoveries about it through steady entries over time.
On 9 November, 1922, she writes:

> Septimus (?) must be seen by someone. His wife? She to be
> bounded in S? Simple, instinctive, childless . . . She is to be a *real*
> character. He only real in so far as she sees him. Otherwise to
> exist in his view of things: which is always to be contrasting with
> Mrs. Dalloway.[36]

In May she took on the problem of representing Clarissa's
personality. At first she had planned that 'Septimus and Mrs.
Dalloway should be entirely dependent on each other.'[37] But as

the book developed, Woolf realized that she could not simply present Clarissa and Septimus in stark contrast to each other, or even in a triangular relation to the allegorical Prime Minister. Clarissa too 'must be seen by other people,' she writes on 26 February, 1923.[38] Rather, she needed to fill out and deepen their lives. Thus in May she came up with the idea of including an old suitor for Clarissa, Peter Walsh:

> There shd. now be a long talk between Mrs. D & some old buck. Hurry over. His view of her. Her substratums of feeling about dead youth the past: with her anxiety about Dick threading it together. Story to be provided by Elizabeth. Must all be kept in upstir; in extreme of feeling.[39]

The main problem Woolf faced in the novel was that of making her characters four-dimensional: getting the element of time into the book through the characters' memories. This preoccupied her through the summer of 1923, as she wrote about the period in which the novel itself is set. 'Too thin and unreal somehow,' she writes on 18 June.[40] After much struggle, a breakthrough came at the end of August:

> My discovery: how I dig out beautiful caves behind my charac-ters; I think that gives exactly what I want; humanity, humour, depth. The idea is that the caves shall connect, & each comes to daylight at the present moment.[41]

Yet the insight did not translate automatically into structure and language. In October, about one hundred pages into the novel, Woolf consoled herself for the slowness of the process – perhaps fifty words a morning – by recalling that it had taken 'a year's groping to discover what I call my tunnelling process, by which I tell the past by instalments, as I have need of it.[42]

Nonetheless, there were to be many more false starts and dead ends. Her notebooks show that she was trying to work towards the scene of the party, and its contrast with the death of Septimus: 'All must bear finally upon the party at the end;

which expresses life in every variety & full of antic[ipa]tion;
while S. dies.' The ways in which this movement was to be given
shape and structure evaded her, and she had in mind the models
of the Greek dramatists, whose plays she was reading. Should
she eliminate chapters and have an 'observer in the street' acting
as a connecting Chorus? Should she divide the text, 'like acts of
a play into five, say, or six scenes'?[43]

Through the spring and summer of 1924, as the book reached
its final pages, Woolf was still testing out various approaches
and ideas, realizing that she had underestimated the amount of
time and delicacy involved in writing certain linking scenes,
such as Peter Walsh eating dinner. Even as she came to the 'last
lap,' with the party, she sketched out various possibilities, and
noted, 'I don't want to tie myself down to that yet.'[44] Finally, the
whole novel had to be pulled together with images and allusions.
Cubist paintings, strange as they looked to the uninitiated eye,
had a unity on the canvas that came from the use of colour, and
from the boundary of the frame. In *Mrs. Dalloway*, the striking
of Big Ben acts as a temporal grid to organize the narrative.

Woolf's working title during most of the time she was writing
had been 'The Hours,' and the insistent chiming of clocks keeps
us aware of the passage of time and the measuring out of human
lives and seasons. A major motif of the book is the analogy between the hours and the female life cycle, what we would now
call the biological clock. Woolf gives us a full range of portraits
spanning the seven ages of woman. Elizabeth Dalloway is almost eighteen, just beginning her adult life. Rezia Smith is in her
twenties. Milly Brush and Doris Kilman are past forty. Clarissa
and Sally Seton are in their fifties. Millicent Bruton is sixty-two,
but dreams of being a little girl in Devon, playing with her
brothers in the clover. Miss Helena Parry, past eighty, lives in
her memories of India, and the glorious triumph of her book
about the orchids of Burma. Finally, there is the nameless old
woman Clarissa sees from her window, alone, putting out her
light, and going to bed.

Throughout the day Clarissa is haunted by the dirge from
Cymbeline:

> Fear no more the heat o' the sun
> Nor the furious winter's rages.

The heat of the sun stands for sexuality, for a kind of feminine blossoming and ripening which peaks in the heat waves of the June day and of the reproductive cycle, and ends in the furious winter of old age. Elizabeth is a 'hyacinth which has had no sun.' That is, she is a virginal flower, like a lily, as Sally Seton remarks. Clarissa's own sexuality has always been muted and moonlit; her one memory of erotic bliss has the delicate intensity of 'a match burning in a crocus' (p. 26).

The parallels between the sexual and the natural cycles are reinforced by the colour of women's attire, almost always green as if it were a kind of leafing or natural exfoliation of the female body. For the young girls this identification seems innate and spontaneous. Elizabeth is 'like a hyacinth, sheathed in glossy green'; at the party, the debutante Nancy Blow, though she is 'dressed at great expense by the greatest artists in Paris' looks as if 'her body had merely put forth, of its own accord, a green frill' (p. 151). Septimus is entranced by the memory of Miss Isabel Pole in a green dress walking in a square, and sees his wife Rezia as a 'flowering tree'. Clarissa too admires 'lovely old sea-green brooches' at the jewellers, and her favourite dress is 'a silver-green mermaid's dress.' Even Miss Kilman wears a green mackintosh coat.

In another sense, Clarissa's retrospect of her sexual history has to do with her time of life. Woolf's original intention was to show Mrs. Dalloway as a woman going through menopause. This theme is clearly, if euphemistically, alluded to in 'Mrs. Dalloway in Bond Street,' when Clarissa compares herself with the ailing Milly Whitbread, come up to London to see doctors for a vague woman's ailment:

> Of course, she thought, walking on, Milly is about my age – fifty, fifty-two. So it is probably *that*. Hugh's manner had said so, said it perfectly – dear old Hugh, thought Mrs. Dalloway, remembering with amusement, with gratitude, with emotion; how shy, like

a brother – one would rather die than speak to one's brother – Hugh had always been, when he was at Oxford; and came over; and perhaps one of them (drat the thing!) couldn't ride. How then could women sit in Parliament? How could they do things with men?

Although this passage was revised in the novel, and the references to menstruation and menopause edited out, Clarissa's time of life ('T. of L.', as Woolf would later call it in her diary)[45] has much to do with her sense of ageing, mortality, and loss. The illness or influenza which has turned her hair white and left her a kind of nun is a metaphor for the loss of fertility, for the unnamable 'women's ailments' of her generation. The passage is particularly ironic in the contrast between Clarissa's adolescent internalization of menstruation as a crippling obstacle to women's participation in public life, and the change which took place after the war, when for the first time, there were indeed eight women sitting in Parliament.

Menopause is sometimes called the 'little death' of women. As we see in the story, menopause not only could not be discussed in polite company, but was implicitly linked with illness. In the 1920s it fascinated and even obsessed Woolf. Although she was in her early forties when she wrote *Mrs. Dalloway*, Woolf was troubled by the decision imposed upon her by her doctors that she should not have children, a decision reflected in the portrait of Sir William Bradshaw, the man who 'forbade childbirth'. Menopause was the symbol of the irrevocable end of childbearing which, in her forties, she recognized as a practical if not a biological fact. The novel is preoccupied with these questions on many levels – in Septimus's mad horror of the body and reproduction, in Rezia's longing for a baby, and in Clarissa's coming to terms with the finality of a central aspect of her identity.

Moreover, according to the medical opinion of Woolf's day, menopause was a condition to be dreaded and feared as much as insanity, and indeed closely allied with it. The attitudes towards the menopausal woman which form an elegiac background to the novel were representative of Woolf's own generation. She had inherited a dismal mythology about the 'change of life' that made it a subject of deep interest and anxiety in her middle years. From the mid-nineteenth century on, menopause had been increasingly medicalized, and linked with depression, madness, and even suicide. Doctors warned that a menopausal woman's melancholia could lead her to kill herself. In a particularly grim description published in 1924, Helene Deutsch described menopause as a hopeless process of decline: 'Everything she acquired in puberty is now lost piece by piece; with the lapse of the reproductive service, her beauty vanishes, and usually the warm, vital flow of feminine emotional life as well.'[46]

Clarissa has internalized these views. She feels that her body, now that there is 'no more marrying, no more having of children' (p. 7) has become invisible, almost ceased to exist. Her fear of insubstantiality and social invisibility is triggered by the discovery that she has been excluded from Millicent Bruton's lunch party, a moment that leaves her feeling 'shrivelled, aged, breastless' (p. 25), and that introduces an extraordinary lyric meditation:

> There was an emptiness about the heart of life; an attic room. Women must put off their rich apparel. At midday they must disrobe . . . Narrower and narrower would her bed be.' (p. 25)

The passage hauntingly echoes the Fool's last speech in *King Lear*: 'And I'll go to bed at noon' (III. vi. 85). In her attic room, with its candle half-burnt down, Clarissa pauses 'at midday' to consider the midpoint of her life. For women, Woolf suggests, the prime years are solitary, and empty as the womb; the female body sheds its 'rich apparel' as the ageing woman must divest herself psychologically of her sexuality in a preparation for death. The narrow bed, with its tight white sheets, where she 'sleeps undisturbed,' is a figure for the grave. This decline is Clarissa's equivalent of the wintry retreat from Moscow she reads about alone at night.

But menopause involves reintegration as well as loss, and can lead to growth if a woman confronts both consciously and unconsciously issues regarding femininity, sexuality, and identity. Indeed, Clarissa works through some of these feelings during the course of her day, and does come to feel at peace with 'having done with the triumphs of youth'.

One major aspect of this process is Clarissa's confrontation with her sexual feelings for Sally Seton, and her effort to apply these insights to her own daughter's infatuation with the lesbian Miss Kilman. In her attic room, Clarissa remembers her girlhood fascination with Sally Seton, for whom she felt 'what men felt' (p. 25). With Sally there had been excitement, ecstasy, and a kiss: 'the most exquisite moment of her whole life' (p. 29). This remembered love between women seems much freer and richer than any of her feelings for men. Even with her beloved husband, Clarissa has been unable to overcome the inhibitions and timidity of her upbringing. Like many sensitive characters in Woolf's fiction, she understands her own capacities for bisexuality and sympathizes with them in others.

Yet these musings about the nature of her sexuality seem less an expression of Clarissa's lesbianism than an effort to understand a sexual dimension in her life that she feels is now irrevocably lost. She and Richard are no longer sharing a bedroom; sexual relations between them have ceased, and she can no longer expect that erotic pleasure will come to her. Richard is as repressed as she is, but a loving and tender partner who has accepted and perhaps not even missed this aspect of their marriage.

In part, Clarissa's concern about her lack of sexual responsiveness – after thirty years of a happy marriage – reflects the changes in attitude after the war. As the historian Susan Kent argues, 'British society sought in the establishment of harmonious marital relationships a resolution to the anxieties and political turmoil caused by the First World War.[47] The standards for sexual harmony within marriage were changing. Thus:

> discourses about female sexuality which before the war had emphasized women's lack of sexual impulse, and even distaste for

sexual intercourse, underwent modification to accommodate the
political, social, and economic requirements of the post-war period. The new accent on motherhood was accompanied by a
growing emphasis on the importance of sexual activity, sexual
pleasure, sexual compatibility, between husband and wife.[48]

When we think of Clarissa as a menopausal woman, the connections between her crisis and Septimus's become more clear
and sharp. Initially, Woolf had intended the book to end with
Clarissa's death: 'Mrs. Dalloway was originally to kill herself,
or perhaps merely to die at the end of the party.'[49] We may sur-
mise that in this plan, Woolf was thinking of Clarissa as a deeply
depressed woman, someone so sensitive to the suffering behind
the masquerade of gaiety around her that she becomes a scapegoat.

Instead, however, it is Septimus Smith who kills himself, and
who serves as Clarissa's double. He is linked to Clarissa through
his anxieties about sexuality and marriage; his anguish about
mortality and immortality; and his acute sensitivities to his sur-
roundings, which have gone over the line into madness. When
she first imagined the character of Septimus in October 1922,
Woolf saw him as a madman who believed himself to be Christ
and planned to assassinate the Prime Minister and become a
political martyr: 'As I am going to die I will kill the Prime
Minister . . . I shall be immortal, he thought, my name will be
on all the placards.'[50] Several themes muted in the final draft of
the book – the fascination with crime and assassination, the
sense of messianic martyrdom, and the post-war obsession with
publicity – appear in this early formulation. Although she did
not develop them fully, Woolf anticipated many of this century's
concerns with the psychology of the assassin and the serial killer.

In revision, however, Septimus became a figure specifically
connected with the war. At Clarissa's party, Sir William Bradshaw discusses a bill to deal with 'the deferred effects of shell
shock' (p. 156), and Septimus is a symbolic 'shell shock' case.
This term, alluding to the shell explosions military doctors

initially blamed for the epidemic of psychological disturbances among soldiers in World War I, actually described various forms of male hysteria in which the terror, anguish, and immobility of combat led to a variety of physical and emotional conversion symptoms: limps, contractions, paralysis, stammering, loss of voice, sexual impotence, blindness, deafness, heart palpitations, insomnia, nightmares, dizziness, or acute depression.

A widespread early military reaction to shell shock was to condemn it as a form of cowardice or malingering. At the War Office Committee of Enquiry into 'shell-shock' which met from 1920 to 1922, E. MacPather testified that cowardice was 'action under the influence of fear, and the ordinary kind of shell-shock, to my mind, was chronic and persisting fear.'[51] The unluckiest soldiers were threatened with court martial if they did not give up their disabling symptoms; others were subjected to punitive treatments involving electric shocks. Only a small percentage of officers received more enlightened care based on psychoanalytic concepts of repression and release.

As the historian Eric Leed explains in his book about World War I, the extraordinary range of hysterical symptoms that afflicted fighting men was 'a psychic effect not of war in general but of industrialized war in particular.'[52] The forced immobility and passivity of soldiers in the trenches facing long-range artillery, air bombardment, and a faceless enemy created anxieties that could not be dissipated in action or controlled through expression.

The psychoanalytic explanation of shell shock traced it to a web of emotional contradictions.

> The soldier was encouraged to kill at the expense of unleashing infantile sadistic impulses that had previously been successfully repressed. He was encouraged to form close emotional bonds with other men and yet homosexuality was forbidden. Moreover the whole lopsidedly masculine scenario . . . was reinforced by wartime ideology and propaganda – and by a recruitment drive that amongst other things promised the fulfilment of masculinity in the battlefield.[53]

Some Freudians argued that unconscious homosexual impulses contributed to the development of shell shock, a view that both scandalized conservative doctors and confirmed their view that only the unmanly and the effeminate could succumb to war neurosis.

In 1921, Freud had declared that 'most of the neurotic diseases which had been brought about by the war disappeared with the cessation of the war conditions.'[54] But he was wrong. Not only did shell shock not disappear with the Armistice, but also the worst outbreaks of neurosis came after the war. In the years immediately after the war, so many thousands of veterans sought medical treatment for nervous disorders that over a hundred special treatment centres had to be set up by 1922.[55] In 1922 Lord Southborough, addressing the House of Lords about a committee to investigate shell shock, insisted that it could not be forgotten or swept under the table:

'The subject of shell-shock cannot be referred to with any pleasure. All would desire to forget it – to forget . . . the roll of insanity, suicide, and death; to bury our recollections of the horrible disorder, and to keep on the surface nothing but the cherished memory of those who were the victims of this malignity.'[56]

Emotions that had to be repressed during combat came to the surface with renewed ferocity after the war, including the anxiety of survivors' guilt.

Although many Bloomsbury intellectuals in Woolf's circle had been pacifists during the war, she also had many friends, including Siegfried Sassoon, who had been in the trenches and who had experienced shell shock. Many elements of Septimus's experience suggest deferred war neurosis. During the war, Woolf writes ironically, he has developed manliness, which is to say that he has learned how to repress his feelings. When his best friend Evans is killed, 'Septimus, far from showing any emotion or recognising that here was the end of a friendship, congratulated himself upon feeling very little and very reasonably' (p. 73). Yet after the war, everything in his life has changed. He can no longer appreciate literature; he does not love his wife; he cannot bear the thought of having a child. The world seems a vicious and desperate place in which 'human beings have neither kindness, nor faith, nor charity beyond what serves to increase the pleasure of the moment' (p. 75). He suffers from 'headaches, sleeplessness, fears, dreams' (p. 77). In particular he is haunted by the spectre of Evans.

Some critics have argued that Septimus is a repressed homosexual whose madness is caused by sexual guilt. But this reading neglects the fact that his most intense romantic feelings are for Miss Isabel Pole, the upper-class woman who introduced him to literature at Morley College. He is tortured with guilt over his sexual fantasies about Miss Pole, whom consciously he had only wished to respect, venerate, and idolize. Unable to reconcile his unconscious desires with his strong feelings of propriety and even class superiority, Septimus sees all sexual desire as evil and sordid. Overall, he is a tragic figure of the class system, completely displaced by the war. His romantic and vocational dreams cannot be met in the England of 1923.

Moreover, shell shock cannot account for all of Septimus's symptoms. He is far more acutely disturbed than shell-shock patients. His visual and auditory hallucinations, his delusions of omnipotence, and his accompanying sense of guilt and martyrdom suggest schizophrenia. A voice constantly communicates with him, telling him that he is the messiah 'come to renew society' (p. 20). The natural world speaks to him in a series of codes and signals. The letters of the skywriting plane are 'smoke words . . . signalling their intention to provide him . . . with beauty, more beauty!' (p. 17) He feels so light that he might fly or fall into the flames except for his wife's hand on his knee holding him down; he believes that his voice 'in certain atmospheric conditions' (p. 17) can make trees come alive. The random noises in the street he takes as premeditated harmonies calling for 'the birth of a new religion' (p. 18); he thinks he can hear people's evil thoughts, 'making up lies as they passed in the street'. Sitting in the park, he notes down 'revelations', hears the birds singing messages to him in Greek, and sees the dead watching him from behind the railings.

In his delusional system, everything is conspiring to tell him that he has been chosen to learn the secret truths of life, and to convey them to the Prime Minister and the Cabinet. These truths are not judgements on the war, as in Sassoon's poems; rather, they are abstractions about universal love, and, alarmingly, the view that there is no crime. The other side of these delusions of grandeur is the delusion of terrible guilt: that he has 'committed an appalling crime and been condemned to death by human nature' (p. 81). The voices call upon him to destroy himself in the interests of mankind.

Woolf gives a finely detailed account of Septimus's desperate effort to distinguish between reality and hallucination. He dimly knows that what he takes as a musical crescendo is only an old man playing a penny whistle by the pub, or that the roses which seem to grow through his body are the figure on the boarding-house wallpaper. But he cannot keep these perceptions stable. It is characteristic of Septimus's deranged state of mind that he searches constantly for 'scientific' rationalizations to explain his ability to read minds, know the future, or see dogs turn into men: 'It was the heat wave presumably, operating upon a brain made sensitive by eons of evolution' (p. 57).

In short, Septimus is not just a sensitive man who has been traumatized by the war; he is in the grip of a very serious mental illness. The description of his sickness was difficult for Woolf to write, since it drew on her own memories of breakdowns. 'The mad part tries me so much, makes my mind squint so badly that I can hardly face spending the next weeks at it', she writes in June 1923.[57] Woolf's indignant representation of the kind of therapeutic advice Septimus receives from Doctors Holmes and Bradshaw also incorporates her own unhappy experience with doctors. She had been treated with the 'rest cure', a therapy designed for nervous women by the American physician Silas Weir Mitchell and imported to England in the 1880s. The rest cure involved isolation, complete bed rest for up to six weeks, a

rich diet and enforced weight gain, and the absence of all intellectual activity. It was a difficult and even maddening therapy
for Woolf, who deeply resented the infantilization of the experience. During the war, moreover, military doctors argued that
the rest cure was too feminizing a therapy to be useful in the
treatment of shell-shock patients, who needed meaningful activity to restore their self-esteem and equilibrium.

Woolf reserves her harshest satire for the doctors. The bluff
middle-class Holmes tries to deal with Septimus's anguish by
forcing him into the rigid mould of middle-class English masculine conduct, including doses of porridge and cricket. The upper-
class Bradshaw recognizes the severity of the case, but his cold
and arrogant manner, the style of someone accustomed to give
orders, is the one least likely to succeed in the light of Septimus's
delusions of persecution. As readers, we identify so closely with
Septimus's suffering, and with the pathos of Rezia's effort to
protect him, that we tend to be swept away by Woolf's anger
and to see Septimus as the victim of medical power, whose suicide is, as Clarissa says, a heroic act of defiance. But this view
cannot be sustained by a careful reading. Septimus has not only
threatened to kill himself, but wants his wife to die as well.
'Now we will kill ourselves', he tells her as they stand by the
river, with a look in his eyes 'when a train went by, or an omnibus' (p. 55). Rezia is brave and loving to stand by him, but he is
dangerous. Although they are tactless, snobbish, patronizing,
and obtuse, the doctors of Mrs. Dalloway are probably right in
recommending rest and seclusion for Septimus. Indeed, much as
she despised it, the rest cure was therapeutic to Woolf, and before the days of drugs, the best care available.

Yet in the contexts of the novel, the very extremity of Septimus's illness reflects the conditions of his society, one in which
the after-effects of the war have been evaded, where Proportion
is worshipped, and feelings have been numbed and anaesthe-
tized. The war seems to have left the 'governing classes' curiously untouched. They continue in their routines of civilized
luncheons, letters to The Times, well-meaning causes, Academy
paintings of sunsets and cows, and elegant parties. None of the

major upper-class characters in the novel has suffered a personal loss, or given a father, husband, or son to the bloodshed. The Dalloways have only a daughter; although Sally Seton is fifty-five, none of her five sons appears to be old enough to have fought. Even the circle of servants around the wealthy characters are either women or very old men. The Tomb of the Unknown Soldier, newly installed in Westminster Abbey, could almost stand for the anonymity of the dead for Clarissa's circle.

Historically, of course, this was not the case at all. Casualties among young officers were enormous. But Woolf wants us to see the emotional repression of English polite society. Alex Zwerdling notes that 'solidity, rigidity, stasis, the inability to communicate feelings' point to something in the nature of these characters that 'makes them incapable of reacting appropriately to the critical events of their time or of their own lives.' The governing class has reacted with stoic denial even to the trage-dies of the war, although like 'little Mr. Bowley,' they have be-come 'sealed with wax over the deeper sources of life.' Thus, Zwerdling persuasively argues, 'Woolf gives us a picture of a class impervious to change in a society that desperately needs or demands it, a class that worships tradition and settled order, but cannot accommodate the new and disturbing.'[58]

In this context, Septimus is a scapegoat, whose visionary emotional turbulence and lack of psychic defences has to be seen in contrast to the fatuousness, insensitivity, impassivity, and self-protective caution of the dominant codes. Septimus feels so much because others feel so little. He has wished to be a poet and an artist, not a clerk; and his disordered perceptions are also creative and powerful. In the forms of ballet, film, modernist poetry, and surrealist art, they were also to shape the new post-war culture whose greatness Woolf had predicted.

In life, Septimus would never be invited to the Dalloway party which his death symbolically interrupts. 'All must converge upon the party at the end', Woolf wrote in her notes. Indeed all that is snobbish and artificial about London society converges at the party. Here are gathered the pompous, the frivolous, the narrow-minded and the moribund. People arrive to be announced by the hired butler like ghosts of the past. The Prime Minister in his gold lace is an emblem of the hollowness of the occasion. As Zwerdling observes, 'The party at the end of the novel, for all its brilliance, is a kind of wake. It reveals the form of power without its substance.'[59] Clarissa's anxieties about the success or failure of this occasion seem trivial in view of what lies beyond the fairy-lights of her garden, and a reading which celebrates her as a great artist whose medium is parties does not seem justified.

Yet the party also is a communal event, and a comic pageant in which life itself is the cause of celebration. As Woolf takes us into the minds of the various guests, we see that their façades of festivity and good breeding conceal a terror of ageing and death. Coming together is a way for them to affirm continuity. For Sally and Peter it is an opportunity to remind themselves that they are still people of passion, that they feel deeply despite appearances. For old Mrs. Hilbery, the laughter is simply a way for her to forget that 'it is certain we must die'.

This society will not undergo radical change. Elizabeth, who has vague dreams of a life different from her mother's, will prob-ably repeat it. She too adores her dog more than her suitors, and is already being watched by admirers like Willie Titcomb. Yet although Richard Dalloway is too shy to tell his wife that he loves her, he does tell his daughter that she is lovely. For Clar-issa, the thought of Septimus's death is a reminder of the inten-sity and joy of a life, even if beyond the triumphs of youth. If her identification with Septimus is perhaps sentimental, nonetheless it is part of her realization of her own limits and possibilities. 'For there she was,' the novel ends, insisting that as readers too we must take Clarissa on her own terms. Despite its fascination with death, *Mrs. Dalloway* ends, as it begins, with a tribute to endurance, survival, and joy.

ELAINE SHOWALTER

NOTES

1. There are now several studies of *Mrs. Dalloway* alone. See Harold Bloom, ed., *Virginia Woolf's 'Mrs. Dalloway'* (Chelsea House, 1988); David Dowling, *Mrs. Dalloway: Mapping Streams of Consciousness* (Twayne, 1991); and Jeremy Hawthorn, *Virginia Woolf's 'Mrs. Dalloway': A Study in Alienation* (Sussex University Press, 1975). A. E. Fernald ed., *Mrs. Dalloway* (Cambridge, UK: Oxford University Press, 2021), including manuscript variants, will be the standard scholarly edition.

2. Margaret Drabble, 'Introduction,' *Pride and Prejudice* (Virago, 1989), p. xiii.

3. *Diary*, II, 15 October 1923, p. 272.

4. Jacqueline Rose, *The Haunting of Sylvia Plath* (Virago, 1991), p. 112.

5. Paul Bailey, 'Into the waves,' *Times Literary Supplement*, 13 May 1973.

6. Sandra M. Gilbert and Susan Gubar, *No Man's Land: The Place of the Woman Writer in the Twentieth Century*, vol. 2, *Sexchanges* (Yale University Press, 1989), pp. 317–18.

7. See Harvena Richter, 'The *Ulysses* Connection: Clarissa Dalloway's Bloomsday,' *Studies in the Novel* 21 (Fall 1989); pp. 305–19.

8. *Diary*, II: 19 June 1923, p. 248.

9. Alex Zwerdling, *Virginia Woolf and the Real World* (University of California Press, 1986), pp. 120–43.

10. *Diary*, II, 18 February 1922, p. 168.

11. *Diary*, II, 26 July 1922, p. 186.

12. *Mr. Bennett and Mrs. Brown* (1924): (retitled 'Character in Fiction'), *Essays*, III, pp. 420–36.

13. *The Tunnel* (1919), *Essays*, III, pp. 10–12.

14. For an excellent discussion of the evolution of Woolf's feminist modernism, see Makiko Minow-Pinkney, *Virginia Woolf and the Problem of the Subject: Feminine Writings in the Major Novels* (Harvester Wheatsheaf, 1987), pp. 1–23.

15. Herbert Marder, 'Split Perspectives: Types of Incongruity in *Mrs. Dalloway*,' *Papers in Language and Literature* 22 (Winter 1986): p. 59.

16. Winifred Holtby, an early critic of Woolf, was the first to note the major influence that the cinema had on her writing. See Holtby, *Virginia Woolf* (Wishart & Co., 1932), pp. 116–36.

17. 'The cinema,' in *CE*, II, p. 272.

18. Ibid., p. 272.

19. Gillian Beer, 'The island and the aeroplane: The case of Virginia Woolf,' in *Nation and Narration*, ed. Homi K. Bhabha (Routledge, 1990), p. 276.

20. Noreen Bronson, *Britain in the Nineteen-Twenties* (Weidenfeld & Nicolson, 1975), pp. 97–98.
21. Maureen Howard, introduction to *Mrs. Dalloway* (Harcourt Brace Jovanovich, 1981), p. viii.
22. Virginia Woolf, introduction to Modern Library edition of *Mrs. Dalloway* (Random House, 1928).
23. Ibid.
24. Woolf's working notes quoted here are taken from two notebooks in the Berg Collection: the earlier is the third notebook used for her previous novel, *Jacob's Room*, the entries for which begin on 12 March 1922. This is followed by a notebook whose entries run from 9 November 1922 to 2 August 1923 (the entries cited occur within the first nine pages). The holograph manuscript for most of the novel is contained in three notebooks in the British Library, Add. MSS 51044, 51045 and 51046. Elaine Showalter's introduction to the novel, with pictures of the British Library manuscripts, is on the British Library website: Elaine Showalter, "*Mrs. Dalloway*: Exploring Consciousness and the Modern World," Discovering Literature: 20th Century, British Library, 25 May 2016, www.bl.uk/20th-century-literature/articles /exploring-consciousness-and-the-modern-an-introduction-to -mrs-dalloway. There is also a video of Elaine Showalter talking about the novel and looking at the British Library manuscripts on YouTube, https://youtu.be/QM-fyF7xFtk.
25. The typescript of 'The Prime Minister' is in the Berg Collection, and a manuscript version occurs in *Jacob's Room* notebook 3. For the short stories, see *Mrs. Dalloway's Party*, ed. Stella McNichol (Hogarth Press, 1973). For the best account of the revisions of the novel, see Charles G. Hoffmann, 'From Short Story to Novel: The Manuscript Revisions of Virginia Woolf's *Mrs. Dalloway*,' *Modern Fiction Studies* 14 (Summer 1968), pp. 171–86.
26. *The Voyage Out* (1915, Penguin Books, 1992), p. 32.
27. *Diary*, II, 28 August 1922, p. 196.
28. Letter to Ottoline Morrell, 10? August 1922, *Letters*, II, p. 543.
29. Berg Collection, *Jacob's Room* notebook 3, 6 October 1922, p. 131.
30. Ibid.
31. Ibid.
32. Letter to T. S. Eliot, 5 May 1924, *Letters*, III, p. 106.
33. *Diary*, II, 14 October 1922, p. 207.
34. Berg Collection, *Jacob's Room*, notebook 3, p. 153.
35. *Diary*, II, 7 November 1922, p. 211.
36. Berg Collection, holograph notebook, 9 November 1922–2 August 1923.
37. Letter to Gerald Brenan, 14 June 1925, *Letters*, III, p. 189.

38. Berg Collection, holograph notebook, 9 November 1922–2 August 1923.
39. 7 May 1923, in Berg Collection, holograph notebook, 9 November 1922–2 August 1923.
40. 18 June 1923, in Berg Collection, holograph notebook, 9 November 1922–2 August 1923.
41. *Diary*, II, 30 August 1923, p. 263.
42. *Diary*, II, 15 October 1923, p. 272.
43. 26 February 1923, Berg Collection, holograph notebook, 9 November 1922–2 August 1923.
44. *Diary*, II, 7 September 1924, p. 312.
45. *Diary*, V, pp. 35, 63, 64.
46. Helene Deutsch, *The Psychology of Women* (1924).
47. Susan Kingsley Kent, 'Gender Reconstruction After the First World War,' in *British Feminism in the Twentieth Century*, ed. Harold L. Smith (Edward Elgar Publishing Ltd., 1990), p. 71.
48. Ibid., pp. 72–73.
49. Virginia Woolf's introduction to Modern Library edition of *Mrs. Dalloway*.
50. Berg Collection, holograph notebook, 12 March 1922, p. 139.
51. Eric Leed, *No Man's Land* (Cambridge University Press, 1979), p. 171.
52. Ibid., p. 164.
53. Martin Stone, 'Shell-shock and the Psychologists,' in *The Anatomy of Madness*, vol. 2, ed. W. F. Bynum, R. Porter, and M. Shepherd (Tavistock, 1985), p. 263.
54. Leed, *op. cit.* p. 187.
55. Stone, *op. cit.* p. 246.
56. Ted Bogacz, 'War Neurosis and Cultural Change,' *Journal of Contemporary History* 24 (1989), p. 227.
57. *Diary*, II, 19 June 1923, p. 249. In *A Writer's Diary*, Leonard Woolf misread 'squint' as 'squirt,' a particularly vivid physical image which makes readers wince.
58. Zwerdling, *op. cit.* p. 124.
59. Ibid., pp. 121–22.

Suggestions for Further Reading

WOOLF'S LIFE AND WRITINGS

The Letters of Virginia Woolf, ed. Nigel Nicolson and Joanne Trautmann (6 vols., Hogarth Press, 1975–80), particularly vol. III.

The Diary of Virginia Woolf, ed. Anne Olivier Bell (5 vols., Hogarth Press, 1977–84), particularly vols. II, III.

A Passionate Apprentice: The Early Journals 1897–1909, ed. Mitchell A. Leaska (Hogarth Press, 1990).

Moments of Being: Unpublished Autobiographical Writings, ed. Jeanne Schulkind (1976, rev. Hogarth Press, 1985).

The Essays of Virginia Woolf, ed. Andrew McNeillie (6 vols., Hogarth Press, 1986–2011), esp. 'Mr. Bennett and Mrs. Brown', retitled 'Character in Fiction', III, pp. 420–36.

Collected Essays, ed. Leonard Woolf (4 vols., Hogarth Press, 1966–67), esp. 'The Cinema', II, pp. 268–72.

The Complete Shorter Fiction, ed. Susan Dick (Hogarth Press, 1985), esp. 'Mrs. Dalloway in Bond Street' and the eight stories set at Mrs. Dalloway's party: 'The New Dress', 'Happiness', 'Ancestors', 'The Introduction', 'Together and Apart', 'The Man Who Loved His Kind', 'A Simple Melody', and 'A Summing Up'.

Quentin Bell, *Virginia Woolf, a Biography* (2 vols., Hogarth Press, 1972).

Hermione Lee, *Virginia Woolf* (New York: Knopf, 1997).

Phyllis Rose, *Woman of Letters: A Life of Virginia Woolf* (Oxford University Press, 1978).

CRITICAL DISCUSSIONS

Beer, Gillian, 'The island and the aeroplane: The case of Virginia Woolf' in *Nation and Narration*, ed. Homi K. Bhabha (Routledge, 1990), pp. 265–90.

Bloom, Harold, ed., *Virginia Woolf's 'Mrs. Dalloway'* (Chelsea House, 1988).

Bowlby, Rachel, *Virginia Woolf: Feminist Destinations* (Basil Black-well, 1988).

Clements, Patricia and Isobel Grundy, eds. *Virginia Woolf: New Critical Essays* (Barnes and Noble, 1983).

DiBattista, Maria, *Virginia Woolf's Major Novels: The Fables of Anon* (Yale University Press, 1980).

Dowling, David, *Mrs. Dalloway: Mapping Streams of Consciousness* (Twayne, 1991).

Hawthorn, Jeremy, *Virginia Woolf's 'Mrs. Dalloway': A Study in Alienation* (Sussex University Press, 1975).

Henke, Suzette A., 'Virginia Woolf's Septimus Smith: An Analysis of "Paraphernalia" and the Schizophrenic Use of Language', *Literature and Psychology* 31 (1981), pp. 13–23.

Hoffman, Charles G., 'From Short Story to Novel: The Manuscript Revisions of Virginia Woolf's *Mrs. Dalloway*', *Modern Fiction Studies* 14 (Summer 1968), pp. 171–86.

Holtby, Winifred, *Virginia Woolf* (Wishart, 1932).

Latham, Monica, *A Poetics of Postmodernism and Neomodernism: Rewriting Mrs. Dalloway* (London: Palgrave Macmillan, 2015).

Leaska, Mitchell, *The Novels of Virginia Woolf: From Beginning to End* (John Jay, 1977).

Lee, Hermione, *The Novels of Virginia Woolf* (Methuen, 1977).

Marcus, Jane, ed. *New Feminist Essays on Virginia Woolf* (University of Nebraska Press, 1981).

Marcus, Jane, ed. *Virginia Woolf: A Feminist Slant* (University of Nebraska Press, 1983).

Marder, Herbert, 'Split Perspectives: Types of Incongruity in *Mrs. Dalloway*', *Papers in Language and Literature* 22 (Winter 1986), pp. 51–69.

Miller, J. Hillis, *Fiction and Repetition: Seven English Novels* (Basil Blackwells, 1982).

Minow-Pinkney, Makiko, *Virginia Woolf and the Problem of the Subject: Feminine Writings in the Major Novels* (Harvester Wheatsheaf, 1987).

Richter, Harvena, 'The *Ulysses* Connection: Clarissa Dalloway's Bloomsday', *Studies in the Novel* 21 (Fall 1989), pp. 305–19.

Squier, Susan, *Virginia Woolf and London* (University of North Carolina Press, 1985).

Tambling, Jeremy, 'Repression in Mrs. Dalloway's London', *Essays in Criticism* 39 (April 1989), pp. 137–55.

Wyatt, Jean, 'Avoiding Self-definition: In defense of women's right to merge', *Women's Studies*, 13 (1986), pp. 115–26.

Zwerdling, Alex, *Virginia Woolf and the Real World* (University of California Press, 1986).

A Note on the Text

The text of this edition of *Mrs. Dalloway* is based on the original British edition published by Leonard and Virginia Woolf at The Hogarth Press, London, on 14 May 1925; the novel was reissued in September 1925 with a few textual changes. The first American edition was published by Harcourt, Brace & Company, New York, on 14 May 1925.

The typescript which Virginia Woolf sent to her printers, R. & R. Clark, Edinburgh, is not extant. Using it as copy, they sent her at least three sets of proofs. The set which she returned to them, and from which the first British edition was printed, is not extant. A second set, which she sent to her American publishers for the first American edition, is extant, and so is a third, which she sent to her friend Jacques Raverat, who was fatally ill (he died on 7 March 1925), so that he could see her novel before its publication. These two sets of proofs both contain corrections made by Virginia Woolf, corrections which do not always correspond with each other nor with the text of the first British edition. They have been fully collated by G. Patton Wright, along with the eight British editions and the three American ones, for his edition (*Mrs. Dalloway*. The Definitive Collected Edition of the Novels of Virginia Woolf. The Hogarth Press, London, 1990); the present editor is deeply indebted to his valuable labours, the results of which can be seen in the three appendices to his book.

Virginia Woolf's method of work was to write her novels by hand in notebooks, typing up each day's composition more or less without revision on the same day or the following one. If she then felt that further revision than could be made on the typescript was necessary, she returned to the notebook and composed the passage afresh. The holograph drafts of *Mrs. Dalloway* show much revision of this kind. They are mostly continuously written, but short passages of revision also crop up in a notebook devoted mainly to book reviews. Some of this holograph material is in the New York Public Library (Henry W. and Albert A. Berg Collection), the other and larger part of it in the British Library, London. It remains unpublished, but was transcribed in full, from photocopies kindly supplied by the libraries in question, by the present editor some years ago. Though it belongs to an earlier stage in composition than the lost typescript and the revised proofs, its readings can throw light on some passages in *Mrs. Dalloway* where the author's intentions are in doubt.

The Appendix to the present edition lists all the substantive emendations to the text of the first British edition which have been adopted in this edition. It also records such conjectural substantive emendations as the present editor thinks worthy of consideration. Very few emendations of a non-substantive kind have been made, Virginia Woolf's characteristically light punctuation being usually retained; it has not been thought necessary to offer the reader a list of these minor emendations.

The question of substantive emendation is bound up with that of inaccuracy and discrepancy. From the first item in the Appendix it will be seen that Virginia Woolf promptly changed 'Brooks's' to 'White's' when she recognized that she had given the bow window to the wrong building in St. James's Street. Yet a reference to Elizabeth, at the party, 'in red', when it is more than once stated that her dress is pink, remained unchanged till the edition of 1947 (published six years after her death), an edition which also for the first time corrected the one misspelling of Mr. Wilkins's name as Wilkin. The fact that his name once appears as Wilkin in the author's holograph (not in the same place as in the novel) shows how easily such a mistake could arise, and the editions printed before 1947 show how easily it could be overlooked or tolerated. Clearly it should be emended.

But is the reference to Elizabeth 'in red' a mistake of the same order? Or the two earlier references to Rezia's 'sisters', when later references make it clear that she is the younger of two sisters? Or the discrepancies between the ages of Peter and Hugh, and of Peter and Clarissa? How far should an editor go in rectifying the inconsistencies of an author who revised her work heavily and saw it through the press herself? Rather than adopt an inflexible rule, the present editor has tried to determine each particular case on its merits, discussing the details in the textual notes of the Appendix.

STELLA McNICHOL

MRS. DALLOWAY

MRS. DALLOWAY.

Mrs. Dalloway said she would buy the flowers herself.

For Lucy had her work cut out for her. The doors would be taken off their hinges; Rumpelmayer's men were coming. And then, thought Clarissa Dalloway, what a morning – fresh as if issued to children on a beach.

What a lark! What a plunge! For so it had always seemed to her when, with a little squeak of the hinges, which she could hear now, she had burst open the French windows and plunged at Bourton¹ into the open air. How fresh, how calm, stiller than this of course, the air was in the early morning; like the flap of a wave; the kiss of a wave; chill and sharp and yet (for a girl of eighteen as she then was) solemn, feeling as she did, standing there at the open window, that something awful was about to happen; looking at the flowers, at the trees with the smoke winding off them and the rooks rising, falling; standing and looking until Peter Walsh said, 'Musing among the vegetables?' – was that it? – 'I prefer men to cauliflowers' – was that it? He must have said it at breakfast one morning when she had gone out on to the terrace – Peter Walsh. He would be back from India one of these days, June or July, she forgot which, for his letters were awfully dull; it was his sayings one remembered; his eyes, his pocket-knife, his smile, his grumpiness and, when millions of things had utterly vanished – how strange it was! – a few sayings like this about cabbages.

She stiffened a little on the kerb, waiting for Durtnall's van to pass. A charming woman, Scrope Purvis thought her (knowing

her as one does know people who live next door to one in Westminster); a touch of the bird about her, of the jay, blue-green,
light, vivacious, though she was over fifty, and grown very white
since her illness.[2] There she perched, never seeing him, waiting
to cross, very upright. *In London*

For having lived in Westminster – how many years now? over
twenty, – one feels even in the midst of the traffic, or waking at
night, Clarissa was positive, a particular hush, or solemnity; an
indescribable pause; a suspense (but that might be her heart,
affected, they said, by influenza) before Big Ben strikes. There!
Out it boomed. First a warning, musical; then the hour, irrevocable. The leaden circles dissolved in the air. Such fools we are,
she thought, crossing Victoria Street. For Heaven only knows
why one loves it so, how one sees it so, making it up, building it
round one, tumbling it, creating it every moment afresh; but the
veriest frumps, the most dejected of miseries sitting on doorsteps
(drink their downfall) do the same; can't be dealt with, she felt
positive, by Acts of Parliament for that very reason: they love
life. In people's eyes, in the swing, tramp, and trudge; in the
bellow and the uproar; the carriages, motor cars, omnibuses,
vans, sandwich men shuffling and swinging; brass bands; barrel
organs; in the triumph and the jingle and the strange high singing of some aeroplane overhead was what she loved; life; London; this moment of June.

For it was the middle of June. The War was over, except for
some one like Mrs. Foxcroft at the Embassy last night eating her
heart out because that nice boy was killed and now the old
Manor House must go to a cousin; or Lady Bexborough who
opened a bazaar, they said, with the telegram in her hand, John,
her favourite, killed; but it was over; thank Heaven – over. It was
June. The King and Queen were at the Palace. And everywhere,
though it was still so early, there was a beating, a stirring of
galloping ponies, tapping of cricket bats; Lords, Ascot, Ranelagh[3]
and all the rest of it; wrapped in the soft mesh of the grey-blue
morning air, which, as the day wore on, would unwind them,
and set down on their lawns and pitches the bouncing ponies,
whose forefeet just struck the ground and up they sprung, the

describing London (margin note)

post-war? (margin note)

whirling young men, and laughing girls in their transparent
muslins who, even now, after dancing all night, were taking
their absurd woolly dogs for a run; and even now, at this hour,
discreet old dowagers were shooting out in their motor cars on
errands of mystery; and the shopkeepers were fidgeting in their
windows with their paste and diamonds, their lovely old sea-green
brooches in eighteenth-century settings to tempt Americans (but
one must economise, not buy things rashly for Elizabeth), and
she, too, loving it as she did with an absurd and faithful passion,
being part of it, since her people were courtiers once in the time
of the Georges, she, too, was going that very night to kindle and
illuminate; to give her party. But how strange, on entering the
Park, the silence; the mist; the hum; the slow-swimming happy
ducks; the pouched birds waddling; and who should be coming
along with his back against the Government buildings, most
appropriately, carrying a despatch box stamped with the Royal
Arms, who but Hugh Whitbread; her old friend Hugh – the
admirable Hugh!

'Good-morning to you, Clarissa!' said Hugh, rather extravagantly, for they had known each other as children. 'Where are
you off to?'

'I love walking in London,' said Mrs. Dalloway. 'Really, it's
better than walking in the country.'

They had just come up – unfortunately – to see doctors. Other
people came to see pictures; go to the opera; take their daughters
out; the Whitbreads came 'to see doctors'. Times without number Clarissa had visited Evelyn Whitbread in a nursing home.
Was Evelyn ill again? Evelyn was a good deal out of sorts, said
Hugh, intimating by a kind of pout or swell of his very well-
covered, manly, extremely handsome, perfectly upholstered
body (he was almost too well dressed always, but presumably
had to be, with his little job at Court) that his wife had some
internal ailment, nothing serious, which, as an old friend, Clarissa Dalloway would quite understand without requiring him
to specify. Ah yes, she did of course; what a nuisance; and felt
very sisterly and oddly conscious at the same time of her hat.
Not the right hat for the early morning, was that it? For Hugh

*the doorways
are having
a party
tonight*

always made her feel, as he bustled on, raising his hat rather extravagantly and assuring her that she might be a girl of eighteen, and of course he was coming to her party to-night, Evelyn absolutely insisted, only a little late he might be after the party at the Palace to which he had to take one of Jim's boys, – she always felt a little skimpy beside Hugh; schoolgirlish; but attached to him, partly from having known him always, but she did think him a good sort in his own way, though Richard was nearly driven mad by him, and as for Peter Walsh, he had never to this day forgiven her for liking him.

She could remember scene after scene at Bourton – Peter furious; Hugh not, of course, his match in any way, but still not a positive imbecile as Peter made out; not a mere barber's block. When his old mother wanted him to give up shooting or to take her to Bath he did it, without a word; he was really unselfish, and as for saying, as Peter did, that he had no heart, no brain, nothing but the manners and breeding of an English gentleman, that was only her dear Peter at his worst; and he could be intolerable; he could be impossible; but adorable to walk with on a morning like this.

(June had drawn out every leaf on the trees. The mothers of Pimlico gave suck to their young. Messages were passing from the Fleet to the Admiralty.⁴ Arlington Street and Piccadilly seemed to chafe the very air in the Park and lift its leaves hotly, brilliantly, on waves of that divine vitality which Clarissa loved. To dance, to ride, she had adored all that.)

For they might be parted for hundreds of years, she and Peter; she never wrote a letter and his were dry sticks; but suddenly it would come over her, If he were with me now what would he say? – some days, some sights bringing him back to her calmly, without the old bitterness; which perhaps was the reward of having cared for people; they came back in the middle of St. James's Park on a fine morning – indeed they did. But Peter – however beautiful the day might be, and the trees and the grass, and the little girl in pink – Peter never saw a thing of all that. He would put on his spectacles, if she told him to; he would look. It was *he wanted to marry her*

the state of the world that interested him; Wagner, Pope's
poetry,⁵ people's characters eternally, and the defects of her own
soul. How he scolded her! How they argued! She would marry
a Prime Minister and stand at the top of a staircase; the perfect
hostess he called her (she had cried over it in her bedroom), she
had the makings of the perfect hostess, he said.

So she would still find herself arguing in St. James's Park, still
making out that she had been right – and she had too – not to
marry him. For in marriage a little licence, a little independence
there must be between people living together day in day out in the
same house; which Richard gave her, and she him. (Where was
he this morning, for instance? Some committee, she never asked
what.) But with Peter everything had to be shared; everything
gone into. And it was intolerable, and when it came to that scene
in the little garden by the fountain, she had to break with him or
they would have been destroyed, both of them ruined, she was
convinced; though she had borne about with her for years like an
arrow sticking in her heart the grief, the anguish; and then the
horror of the moment when some one told her at a concert that
he had married a woman met on the boat going to India! Never
should she forget all that! Cold, heartless, a prude, he called her.
Never could she understand how he cared. But those Indian
women did presumably – silly, pretty, flimsy nincompoops. And
she wasted her pity. For he was quite happy, he assured her –
perfectly happy, though he had never done a thing that they talked
of; his whole life had been a failure. It made her angry still.

She had reached the Park gates. She stood for a moment, looking at the omnibuses in Piccadilly. *I've been there*

She would not say of any one in the world now that they were
this or were that. She felt very young; at the same time unspeakably aged. She sliced like a knife through everything; at the same
time was outside, looking on. She had a perpetual sense, as she
watched the taxi cabs, of being out, out, far out to sea and alone;
she always had the feeling that it was very, very dangerous to
live even one day. Not that she thought herself clever, or much
out of the ordinary. How she had got through life on the few

twigs of knowledge Fräulein Daniels gave them she could not think. She knew nothing; no language, no history; she scarcely read a book now, except memoirs in bed; and yet to her it was absolutely absorbing; all this; the cabs passing; and she would not say of Peter, she would not say of herself, I am this, I am that.

Her only gift was knowing people almost by instinct, she thought, walking on. If you put her in a room with some one, up went her back like a cat's; or she purred. Devonshire House, Bath House,[6] the house with the china cockatoo, she had seen them all lit up once; and remembered Sylvia, Fred, Sally Seton – such hosts of people; and dancing all night; and the waggons plodding past to market; and driving home across the Park. She remembered once throwing a shilling into the Serpentine.[7] But every one remembered; what she loved was this, here, now, in front of her; the fat lady in the cab. Did it matter then, she asked herself, walking towards Bond Street, did it matter that she must inevitably cease completely; all this must go on without her; did she resent it; or did it not become consoling to believe that death ended absolutely? but that somehow in the streets of London, on the ebb and flow of things, here, there, she survived, Peter survived, lived in each other, she being part, she was positive, of the trees at home; of the house there, ugly, rambling all to bits and pieces as it was; part of people she had never met; being laid out like a mist between the people she knew best, who lifted her on their branches as she had seen the trees lift the mist, but it spread ever so far, her life, herself. But what was she dreaming as she looked into Hatchards' shop window?[8] What was she trying to recover? What image of white dawn in the country, as she read in the book spread open:

> Fear no more the heat o' the sun
> Nor the furious winter's rages.

This late age of the world's experience had bred in them all, all men and women, a well of tears. Tears and sorrows; courage and endurance, a perfectly upright and stoical bearing. Think, for

So Clarissa (!) is visiting Evelyn her nursing home in London.

example, of the woman she admired most, Lady Bexborough, opening the bazaar.

There were Jorrocks' *Jaunts and Jollities*; there were *Soapy Sponge* and Mrs. Asquith's *Memoirs* and *Big Game Shooting in Nigeria*,[9] all spread open. Ever so many books there were; but none that seemed exactly right to take to Evelyn Whitbread in her nursing home. Nothing that would serve to amuse her and make that indescribably dried-up little woman look, as Clarissa came in, just for a moment cordial; before they settled down for the usual interminable talk of women's ailments. How much she wanted it – that people should look pleased as she came in, Clarissa thought and turned and walked back towards Bond Street, annoyed, because it was silly to have other reasons for doing things. Much rather would she have been one of those people like Richard who did things for themselves, whereas, she thought, waiting to cross, half the time she did things not simply, not for themselves; but to make people think this or that; perfect idiocy she knew (and now the policeman held up his hand) for no one was ever for a second taken in. Oh if she could have had her life over again! she thought, stepping on to the pavement, could have looked even differently!

She would have been, in the first place, dark like Lady Bexborough, with a skin of crumpled leather and beautiful eyes. She would have been, like Lady Bexborough, slow and stately; rather large; interested in politics like a man; with a country house; very dignified, very sincere. Instead of which she had a narrow pea-stick figure; a ridiculous little face, beaked like a bird's. That she held herself well was true; and had nice hands and feet; and dressed well, considering that she spent little. But often now this body she wore (she stopped to look at a Dutch picture), this body, with all its capacities, seemed nothing – nothing at all. She had the oddest sense of being herself invisible; unseen; unknown; there being no more marrying, no more having of children now, but only this astonishing and rather solemn progress with the rest of them, up Bond Street, this being Mrs. Dalloway; not even Clarissa any more; this being Mrs. Richard Dalloway.

Bond Street fascinated her; Bond Street early in the morning

in the season; its flags flying; its shops; no splash; no glitter, one
roll of tweed in the shop where her father had bought his suits
for fifty years; a few pearls; salmon on an iceblock.

'That is all,' she said, looking at the fishmonger's. 'That is all,'
she repeated, pausing for a moment at the window of a glove
shop where, before the War, you could buy almost perfect
gloves. And her old Uncle William used to say a lady is known
by her shoes and her gloves. He had turned on his bed one morning in the middle of the War. He had said, 'I have had enough.'
Gloves and shoes; she had a passion for gloves; but her own
daughter, her Elizabeth, cared not a straw for either of them.

Not a straw, she thought, going on up Bond Street to a shop
where they kept flowers for her when she gave a party. Elizabeth
really cared for her dog most of all. The whole house this morning smelt of tar. Still, better poor Grizzle[10] than Miss Kilman;
better distemper and tar and all the rest of it than sitting mewed
in a stuffy bedroom with a prayer book! Better anything, she
was inclined to say. But it might be only a phase, as Richard
said, such as all girls go through. It might be falling in love. But
why with Miss Kilman? who had been badly treated of course;
one must make allowances for that, and Richard said she was
very able, had a really historical mind. Anyhow they were in-
separable, and Elizabeth, her own daughter, went to Commu-
nion; and how she dressed, how she treated people who came to
lunch she did not care a bit, it being her experience that the religious ecstasy made people callous (so did causes); dulled their
feelings, for Miss Kilman would do anything for the Russians,
starved herself for the Austrians, but in private inflicted positive
torture, so insensitive was she, dressed in a green mackintosh
coat. Year in year out she wore that coat; she perspired; she was
never in the room five minutes without making you feel her superiority, your inferiority; how poor she was; how rich you were;
how she lived in a slum without a cushion or a bed or a rug or
whatever it might be, all her soul rusted with that grievance
sticking in it, her dismissal from school during the War – poor
embittered unfortunate creature! For it was not her one hated
but the idea of her, which undoubtedly had gathered in to itself

a great deal that was not Miss Kilman; had become one of those spectres with which one battles in the night; one of those spectres who stand astride us and suck up half our life-blood, dominators and tyrants; for no doubt with another throw of the dice, had the black been uppermost and not the white, she would have loved Miss Kilman! But not in this world. No.

It rasped her, though, to have stirring about in her this brutal monster! to hear twigs cracking and feel hooves planted down in the depths of that leaf-encumbered forest, the soul; never to be content quite, or quite secure, for at any moment the brute would be stirring, this hatred, which, especially since her illness, had power to make her feel scraped, hurt in her spine; gave her physical pain, and made all pleasure in beauty, in friendship, in being well, in being loved and making her home delightful rock, quiver, and bend as if indeed there were a monster grubbing at the roots, as if the whole panoply of content were nothing but self love! this hatred!

Nonsense, nonsense! she cried to herself, pushing through the swing doors of Mulberry's the florists.

She advanced, light, tall, very upright, to be greeted at once by button-faced Miss Pym, whose hands were always bright red, as if they had been stood in cold water with the flowers.

There were flowers: delphiniums, sweet peas, bunches of lilac; and carnations, masses of carnations. There were roses; there were irises. Ah yes – so she breathed in the earthy garden sweet smell as she stood talking to Miss Pym who owed her help, and thought her kind, for kind she had been years ago; very kind, but she looked older, this year, turning her head from side to side among the irises and roses and nodding tufts of lilac with her eyes half closed, snuffing in, after the street uproar, the delicious scent, the exquisite coolness. And then, opening her eyes, how fresh, like frilled linen clean from a laundry laid in wicker trays, the roses looked; and dark and prim the red carnations, holding their heads up; and all the sweet peas spreading in their bowls, tinged violet, snow white, pale – as if it were the evening and girls in muslin frocks came out to pick sweet peas and roses after the superb summer's day, with its almost blue-black sky, its

delphiniums, its carnations, its arum lilies was over; and it was
the moment between six and seven when every flower – roses,
carnations, irises, lilac – glows; white, violet, red, deep orange;
every flower seems to burn by itself, softly, purely in the misty
beds; and how she loved the grey white moths spinning in and
out, over the cherry pie, over the evening primroses!

And as she began to go with Miss Pym from jar to jar, choosing, nonsense, nonsense, she said to herself, more and more
gently, as if this beauty, this scent, this colour, and Miss Pym liking her, trusting her, were a wave which she let flow over her and
surmount that hatred, that monster, surmount it all; and it lifted
her up and up when – oh! a pistol shot in the street outside![11]

'Dear, those motor cars,' said Miss Pym, going to the window
to look, and coming back and smiling apologetically with her
hands full of sweet peas, as if those motor cars, those tyres of
motor cars, were all *her* fault.

The violent explosion which made Mrs. Dalloway jump and
Miss Pym go to the window and apologise came from a motor
car which had drawn to the side of the pavement precisely opposite Mulberry's shop window. Passers-by who, of course,
stopped and stared, had just time to see a face of the very greatest importance against the dove-grey upholstery, before a male
hand drew the blind and there was nothing to be seen except a
square of dove grey.

Yet rumours were at once in circulation from the middle of
Bond Street to Oxford Street on one side, to Atkinson's scent
shop on the other, passing invisibly, inaudibly, like a cloud,
swift, veil-like upon hills, falling indeed with something of a
cloud's sudden sobriety and stillness upon faces which a second
before had been utterly disorderly. But now mystery had brushed
them with her wing; they had heard the voice of authority; the
spirit of religion was abroad with her eyes bandaged tight and
her lips gaping wide. But nobody knew whose face had been
seen. Was it the Prince of Wales's, the Queen's, the Prime Minister's?[12] Whose face was it? Nobody knew.

Edgar J. Watkiss, with his roll of lead piping round his arm, said audibly, humorously of course: 'The Proime Minister's kyar.'

Septimus Warren Smith, who found himself unable to pass, heard him.

Septimus Warren Smith, aged about thirty, pale-faced, beak-nosed, wearing brown shoes and a shabby overcoat, with hazel eyes which had that look of apprehension in them which makes complete strangers apprehensive too. The world has raised its whip; where will it descend?

Everything had come to a standstill. The throb of the motor engines sounded like a pulse irregularly drumming through an entire body. The sun became extraordinarily hot because the motor car had stopped outside Mulberry's shop window; old ladies on the tops of omnibuses spread their black parasols; here a green, here a red parasol opened with a little pop. Mrs. Dalloway, coming to the window with her arms full of sweet peas, looked out with her little pink face pursed in enquiry. Every one looked at the motor car. Septimus looked. Boys on bicycles sprang off. Traffic accumulated. And there the motor car stood, with drawn blinds, and upon them a curious pattern like a tree, Septimus thought, and this gradual drawing together of everything to one centre before his eyes, as if some horror had come almost to the surface and was about to burst into flames, terrified him. The world wavered and quivered and threatened to burst into flames. It is I who am blocking the way, he thought. Was he not being looked at and pointed at; was he not weighted there, rooted to the pavement, for a purpose? But for what purpose?

'Let us go on, Septimus,' said his wife, a little woman, with large eyes in a sallow pointed face; an Italian girl.

But Lucrezia herself could not help looking at the motor car and the tree pattern on the blinds. Was it the Queen in there – the Queen going shopping?

The chauffeur, who had been opening something, turning something, shutting something, got on to the box.

'Come on,' said Lucrezia.

But her husband, for they had been married four, five years

now, jumped, started, and said, 'All right!' angrily, as if she had
interrupted him.

People must notice; people must see. People, she thought,
looking at the crowd staring at the motor car; the English people, with their children and their horses and their clothes, which
she admired in a way; but they were 'people' now, because Septimus had said, 'I will kill myself'; an awful thing to say. Suppose they had heard him? She looked at the crowd. Help, help!
she wanted to cry out to butchers' boys and women. Help! Only
last autumn she and Septimus had stood on the Embankment
wrapped in the same cloak and, Septimus reading a paper instead of talking, she had snatched it from him and laughed in
the old man's face who saw them! But failure one conceals. She
must take him away into some park.

'Now we will cross,' she said.

She had a right to his arm, though it was without feeling. He
would give her, who was so simple, so impulsive, only twenty-
four, without friends in England, who had left Italy for his sake,
a piece of bone.

The motor car with its blinds drawn and an air of inscrutable
reserve proceeded towards Piccadilly, still gazed at, still ruffling
the faces on both sides of the street with the same dark breath
of veneration whether for Queen, Prince, or Prime Minister nobody knew. The face itself had been seen only once by three
people for a few seconds. Even the sex was now in dispute. But
there could be no doubt that greatness was seated within; greatness was passing, hidden, down Bond Street, removed only by a
hand's-breadth from ordinary people who might now, for the
first and last time, be within speaking distance of the majesty of
England, of the enduring symbol of the state which will be
known to curious antiquaries, sifting the ruins of time, when
London is a grass-grown path and all those hurrying along the
pavement this Wednesday morning are but bones with a few
wedding rings mixed up in their dust and the gold stoppings of
innumerable decayed teeth. The face in the motor car will then
be known.

It is probably the Queen, thought Mrs. Dalloway, coming out

of Mulberry's with her flowers; the Queen. And for a second she wore a look of extreme dignity standing by the flower shop in the sunlight while the car passed at a foot's pace, with its blinds drawn. The Queen going to some hospital; the Queen opening some bazaar, thought Clarissa.

The crush was terrific for the time of day. Lords, Ascot, Hurlingham,[13] what was it? she wondered, for the street was blocked. The British middle classes sitting sideways on the tops of omnibuses with parcels and umbrellas, yes, even furs on a day like this, were, she thought, more ridiculous, more unlike anything there has ever been than one could conceive; and the Queen herself held up; the Queen herself unable to pass. Clarissa was suspended on one side of Brook Street; Sir John Buckhurst, the old Judge on the other, with the car between them (Sir John had laid down the law for years and liked a well-dressed woman) when the chauffeur, leaning ever so slightly, said or showed something to the policeman, who saluted and raised his arm and jerked his head and moved the omnibus to the side and the car passed through. Slowly and very silently it took its way.

Clarissa guessed; Clarissa knew of course; she had seen something white, magical, circular, in the footman's hand, a disc inscribed with a name, – the Queen's, the Prince of Wales's, the Prime Minister's? – which, by force of its own lustre, burnt its way through (Clarissa saw the car diminishing, disappearing), to blaze among candelabras, glittering stars, breasts stiff with oak leaves,[14] Hugh Whitbread and all his colleagues, the gentlemen of England, that night in Buckingham Palace. And Clarissa, too, gave a party. She stiffened a little; so she would stand at the top of her stairs.

The car had gone, but it had left a slight ripple which flowed through glove shops and hat shops and tailors' shops on both sides of Bond Street. For thirty seconds all heads were inclined the same way – to the window. Choosing a pair of gloves – should they be to the elbow or above it, lemon or pale grey? – ladies stopped; when the sentence was finished something had happened. Something so trifling in single instances that no mathematical instrument, though capable of transmitting shocks in

China, could register the vibration; yet in its fulness rather formidable and in its common appeal emotional; for in all the hat
shops and tailors' shops strangers looked at each other and
thought of the dead; of the flag; of Empire. In a public house in
a back street a Colonial insulted the House of Windsor[15] which
led to words, broken beer glasses, and a general shindy, which
echoed strangely across the way in the ears of girls buying white
underlinen threaded with pure white ribbon for their weddings.
For the surface agitation of the passing car as it sunk grazed
something very profound.

Gliding across Piccadilly, the car turned down St. James's
Street. Tall men, men of robust physique, well-dressed men with
their tail-coats and their white slips and their hair raked back
who, for reasons difficult to discriminate, were standing in the
bow window of White's[16] with their hands behind the tails of
their coats, looking out, perceived instinctively that greatness
was passing, and the pale light of the immortal presence fell
upon them as it had fallen upon Clarissa Dalloway. At once they
stood even straighter, and removed their hands, and seemed
ready to attend their Sovereign, if need be, to the cannon's
mouth, as their ancestors had done before them. The white busts
and the little tables in the background covered with copies of the
Tatler[17] and syphons of soda water seemed to approve; seemed
to indicate the flowing corn and the manor houses of England;
and to return the frail hum of the motor wheels as the walls of
a whispering gallery return a single voice expanded and made
sonorous by the might of a whole cathedral. Shawled Moll Pratt
with her flowers on the pavement wished the dear boy well (it
was the Prince of Wales for certain) and would have tossed the
price of a pot of beer – a bunch of roses – into St. James's Street
out of sheer light-heartedness and contempt of poverty had
she not seen the constable's eye upon her, discouraging an old
Irishwoman's loyalty. The sentries at St. James's saluted; Queen
Alexandra's policeman approved.[18]

A small crowd meanwhile had gathered at the gates of Buckingham Palace. Listlessly, yet confidently, poor people all of
them, they waited; looked at the Palace itself with the flag flying;

at Victoria, billowing on her mound,[19] admired her shelves of running water, her geraniums; singled out from the motor cars in the Mall first this one, then that; bestowed emotion, vainly, upon commoners out for a drive; recalled their tribute to keep it unspent while this car passed and that; and all the time let rumour accumulate in their veins and thrill the nerves in their thighs at the thought of Royalty looking at them; the Queen bowing; the Prince saluting; at the thought of the heavenly life divinely bestowed upon Kings; of the equerries and deep curt-sies; of the Queen's old doll's house;[20] of Princess Mary married to an Englishman, and the Prince – ah! the Prince! who took wonderfully, they said, after old King Edward, but was ever so much slimmer. The Prince lived at St. James's; but he might come along in the morning to visit his mother.

So Sarah Bletchley said with her baby in her arms, tipping her foot up and down as though she were by her own fender in Pimlico, but keeping her eyes on the Mall, while Emily Coates ranged over the Palace windows and thought of the housemaids, the innumerable housemaids, the bedrooms, the innumerable bedrooms. Joined by an elderly gentleman with an Aberdeen terrier, by men without occupation, the crowd increased. Little Mr. Bowley, who had rooms in the Albany[21] and was sealed with wax over the deeper sources of life but could be unsealed sud-denly, inappropriately, sentimentally, by this sort of thing – poor women waiting to see the Queen go past – poor women, nice little children, orphans, widows, the War – tut-tut – actually had tears in his eyes. A breeze flaunting ever so warmly down the Mall through the thin trees, past the bronze heroes, lifted some flag flying in the British breast of Mr. Bowley and he raised his hat as the car turned into the Mall and held it high as the car approached; and let the poor mothers of Pimlico press close to him, and stood very upright. The car came on.

Suddenly Mrs. Coates looked up into the sky. The sound of an aeroplane bored ominously into the ears of the crowd. There it was coming over the trees, letting out white smoke from be-hind, which curled and twisted, actually writing something! making letters in the sky![22] Every one looked up.

Dropping dead down the aeroplane soared straight up, curved in a loop, raced, sank, rose, and whatever it did, wherever it went, out fluttered behind it a thick ruffled bar of white smoke which curled and wreathed upon the sky in letters. But what letters? A C was it? an E, then an L? Only for a moment did they lie still; then they moved and melted and were rubbed out up in the sky, and the aeroplane shot further away and again, in a fresh space of sky, began writing a K, an E, a Y perhaps?

'Glaxo,' said Mrs. Coates in a strained, awe-stricken voice, gazing straight up, and her baby, lying stiff and white in her arms, gazed straight up.

'Kreemo,' murmured Mrs. Bletchley, like a sleepwalker. With his hat held out perfectly still in his hand, Mr. Bowley gazed straight up. All down the Mall people were standing and looking up into the sky. As they looked the whole world became perfectly silent, and a flight of gulls crossed the sky, first one gull leading, then another, and in this extraordinary silence and peace, in this pallor, in this purity, bells struck eleven times, the sound fading up there among the gulls.

The aeroplane turned and raced and swooped exactly where it liked, swiftly, freely, like a skater –

'That's an E,' said Mrs. Bletchley –

or a dancer –

'It's toffee,' murmured Mr. Bowley –

(and the car went in at the gates and nobody looked at it), and shutting off the smoke, away and away it rushed, and the smoke faded and assembled itself round the broad white shapes of the clouds.

It had gone; it was behind the clouds. There was no sound. The clouds to which the letters E, G, or L had attached themselves moved freely, as if destined to cross from West to East on a mission of the greatest importance which would never be revealed, and yet certainly so it was – a mission of the greatest importance. Then suddenly, as a train comes out of a tunnel, the aeroplane rushed out of the clouds again, the sound boring into the ears of all people in the Mall, in the Green Park, in Piccadilly, in Regent Street, in Regent's Park, and the bar of smoke curved behind and it dropped down, and it soared up and wrote one letter after another – but what word was it writing?

Lucrezia Warren Smith, sitting by her husband's side on a seat in Regent's Park in the Broad Walk, looked up.

'Look, look, Septimus!' she cried. For Dr. Holmes had told her to make her husband (who had nothing whatever seriously the matter with him but was a little out of sorts) take an interest in things outside himself.

So, thought Septimus, looking up, they are signalling to me. Not indeed in actual words; that is, he could not read the language yet; but it was plain enough, this beauty, this exquisite beauty, and tears filled his eyes as he looked at the smoke words languishing and melting in the sky and bestowing upon him in their inexhaustible charity and laughing goodness one shape after another of unimaginable beauty and signalling their intention to provide him, for nothing, for ever, for looking merely, with beauty, more beauty! Tears ran down his cheeks.

It was toffee; they were advertising toffee, a nursemaid told Rezia. Together they began to spell t . . . o . . . f . . .

'K . . . R . . .' said the nursemaid, and Septimus heard her say 'Kay Arr' close to his ear, deeply, softly, like a mellow organ, but with a roughness in her voice like a grasshopper's, which rasped his spine deliciously and sent running up into his brain waves of sound which, concussing, broke. A marvellous discovery indeed – that the human voice in certain atmospheric conditions (for one must be scientific, above all scientific) can quicken trees into life! Happily Rezia put her hand with a tremendous weight on his knee so that he was weighted down, transfixed, or the excitement of the elm trees rising and falling, rising and falling with all their leaves alight and the colour thinning and thickening from blue to the green of a hollow wave, like plumes on horses' heads, feathers on ladies', so proudly they rose and fell, so superbly, would have sent him mad. But he would not go mad. He would shut his eyes; he would see no more.

But they beckoned; leaves were alive; trees were alive. And the leaves being connected by millions of fibres with his own body, there on the seat, fanned it up and down; when the branch stretched he, too, made that statement. The sparrows fluttering, rising, and falling in jagged fountains were part of the pattern; the white and blue, barred with black branches. Sounds made harmonies with premeditation; the spaces between them were as significant as the sounds. A child cried. Rightly far away a horn sounded. All taken together meant the birth of a new religion——

'Septimus!' said Rezia. He started violently. People must notice.

'I am going to walk to the fountain and back,' she said.

For she could stand it no longer. Dr. Holmes might say there was nothing the matter. Far rather would she that he were dead! She could not sit beside him when he stared so and did not see her and made everything terrible; sky and tree, children playing, dragging carts, blowing whistles, falling down; all were terrible. And he would not kill himself; and she could tell no one. 'Septimus has been working too hard' – that was all she could say, to her own mother. To love makes one solitary, she thought. She could tell nobody, not even Septimus now, and looking back, she saw him sitting in his shabby overcoat alone, on the seat, hunched up, staring. And it was cowardly for a man to say he would kill himself, but Septimus had fought; he was brave; he was not Septimus now. She put on her lace collar. She put on her new hat and he never noticed; and he was happy without her. Nothing could make her happy without him! Nothing! He was selfish. So men are. For he was not ill. Dr. Holmes said there was nothing the matter with him. She spread her hand before her. Look! Her wedding ring slipped – she had grown so thin. It was she who suffered – but she had nobody to tell.

Far was Italy and the white houses and the room where her sister sat making hats, and the streets crowded every evening with people walking, laughing out loud, not half alive like people here, huddled up in Bath chairs, looking at a few ugly flowers stuck in pots!

'For you should see the Milan gardens,' she said aloud. But to whom?

There was nobody. Her words faded. So a rocket fades. Its sparks, having grazed their way into the night, surrender to it, dark descends, pours over the outlines of houses and towers;

bleak hill-sides soften and fall in. But though they are gone, the
night is full of them; robbed of colour, blank of windows, they
exist more ponderously, give out what the frank daylight fails to
transmit – the trouble and suspense of things conglomerated
there in the darkness; huddled together in the darkness; reft of
the relief which dawn brings when, washing the walls white and
grey, spotting each window-pane, lifting the mist from the fields,
showing the red-brown cows peacefully grazing, all is once more
decked out to the eye; exists again. I am alone; I am alone! she
cried, by the fountain in Regent's Park (staring at the Indian and
his cross), as perhaps at midnight, when all boundaries are lost,
the country reverts to its ancient shape, as the Romans saw it,
lying cloudy, when they landed, and the hills had no names and
rivers wound they knew not where – such was her darkness;[23]
when suddenly, as if a shelf were shot forth and she stood on
it, she said how she was his wife, married years ago in Milan,
his wife, and would never, never tell that he was mad! Turning,
the shelf fell; down, down she dropped. For he was gone, she
thought – gone, as he threatened, to kill himself – to throw
himself under a cart! But no; there he was; still sitting alone on
the seat, in his shabby overcoat, his legs crossed, staring, talking
aloud.

Men must not cut down trees. There is a God. (He noted such
revelations on the backs of envelopes.) Change the world. No
one kills from hatred. Make it known (he wrote it down). He
waited. He listened. A sparrow perched on the railing opposite
chirped Septimus, Septimus, four or five times over and went
on, drawing its notes out, to sing freshly and piercingly in Greek
words how there is no crime and, joined by another sparrow,
they sang in voices prolonged and piercing in Greek words,[24]
from trees in the meadow of life beyond a river where the dead
walk, how there is no death.

There was his hand; there the dead. White things were assembling behind the railings opposite. But he dared not look.
Evans was behind the railings!

'What are you saying?' said Rezia suddenly, sitting down
by him.

Interrupted again! She was always interrupting.

Away from people – they must get away from people, he said (jumping up), right away over there, where there were chairs beneath a tree and the long slope of the park dipped like a length of green stuff with a ceiling cloth of blue and pink smoke high above, and there was a rampart of far irregular houses, hazed in smoke, the traffic hummed in a circle, and on the right, dun-coloured animals stretched long necks over the Zoo palings, barking, howling. There they sat down under a tree.

'Look,' she implored him, pointing at a little troop of boys carrying cricket stumps, and one shuffled, spun round on his heel and shuffled, as if he were acting a clown at the music hall.

'Look,' she implored him, for Dr. Holmes had told her to make him notice real things, go to a music hall, play cricket – that was the very game, Dr. Holmes said, a nice out-of-door game, the very game for her husband.

'Look,' she repeated.

Look the unseen bade him, the voice which now communicated with him who was the greatest of mankind, Septimus, lately taken from life to death, the Lord who had come to renew society, who lay like a coverlet, a snow blanket smitten only by the sun, for ever unwasted, suffering for ever, the scapegoat, the eternal sufferer, but he did not want it, he moaned, putting from him with a wave of his hand that eternal suffering, that eternal loneliness.

'Look,' she repeated, for he must not talk aloud to himself out of doors.

'Oh look,' she implored him. But what was there to look at? A few sheep. That was all.

The way to Regent's Park Tube Station – could they tell her the way to Regent's Park Tube Station – Maisie Johnson wanted to know. She was only up from Edinburgh two days ago.

'Not this way – over there!' Rezia exclaimed, waving her aside, lest she should see Septimus.

Both seemed queer, Maisie Johnson thought. Everything seemed very queer. In London for the first time, come to take up a post at her uncle's in Leadenhall Street, and now walking through Regent's Park in the morning, this couple on the chairs gave her quite a turn; the young woman seeming foreign, the man looking queer; so that should she be very old she would still remember and make it jangle again among her memories how she had walked through Regent's Park on a fine summer's morning fifty years ago. For she was only nineteen and had got her way at last, to come to London; and now how queer it was, this couple she had asked the way of, and the girl started and jerked her hand, and the man – he seemed awfully odd; quarrelling, perhaps; parting for ever, perhaps; something was up, she knew; and now all these people (for she returned to the Broad Walk), the stone basins, the prim flowers, the old men and women, invalids most of them in Bath chairs – all seemed, after Edinburgh, so queer. And Maisie Johnson, as she joined that gently trudging, vaguely gazing, breeze-kissed company – squirrels perching and preening, sparrow fountains fluttering for crumbs, dogs busy with the railings, busy with each other, while the soft warm air washed over them and lent to the fixed unsurprised gaze with which they received life something whimsical and mollified – Maisie Johnson positively felt she must cry Oh! (for that young man on the seat had given her quite a turn. Something was up, she knew).

Horror! horror! she wanted to cry. (She had left her people; they had warned her what would happen.)

Why hadn't she stayed at home? she cried, twisting the knob of the iron railing.

That girl, thought Mrs. Dempster (who saved crusts for the squirrels and often ate her lunch in Regent's Park), don't know a thing yet; and really it seemed to her better to be a little stout, a little slack, a little moderate in one's expectations. Percy drank. Well, better to have a son, thought Mrs. Dempster. She had had a hard time of it, and couldn't help smiling at a girl like that. You'll get married, for you're pretty enough, thought Mrs. Dempster. Get married, she thought, and then you'll know. Oh, the cooks, and so on. Every man has his ways. But whether I'd have chosen quite like that if I could have known, thought Mrs. Dempster, and could not help wishing to whisper a word to

Maisie Johnson; to feel on the creased pouch of her worn old
face the kiss of pity. For it's been a hard life, thought Mrs.
Dempster. What hadn't she given to it? Roses; figure; her feet
too. (She drew the knobbed lumps beneath her skirt.)

Roses, she thought sardonically. All trash, m'dear. For really,
what with eating, drinking, and mating, the bad days and good,
life had been no mere matter of roses, and what was more, let
me tell you, Carrie Dempster had no wish to change her lot with
any woman's in Kentish Town! But, she implored, pity. Pity, for
the loss of roses. Pity she asked of Maisie Johnson, standing by
the hyacinth beds.

Ah, but that aeroplane! Hadn't Mrs. Dempster always longed
to see foreign parts? She had a nephew, a missionary. It soared
and shot. She always went on the sea at Margate, not out o' sight
of land, but she had no patience with women who were afraid of
water. It swept and fell. Her stomach was in her mouth. Up again.
There's a fine young feller aboard of it, Mrs. Dempster wagered,
and away and away it went, fast and fading, away and away the
aeroplane shot; soaring over Greenwich and all the masts; over
the little island of grey churches, St. Paul's and the rest, till, on
either side of London, fields spread out and dark brown woods
where adventurous thrushes, hopping boldly, glancing quickly,
snatched the snail and tapped him on a stone, once, twice, thrice.

Away and away the aeroplane shot, till it was nothing but a
bright spark; an aspiration; a concentration; a symbol (so it
seemed to Mr. Bentley, vigorously rolling his strip of turf at
Greenwich) of man's soul; of his determination, thought Mr.
Bentley, sweeping round the cedar tree, to get outside his body,
beyond his house, by means of thought, Einstein, speculation,
mathematics, the Mendelian theory[25] – away the aeroplane shot.

Then, while a seedy-looking nondescript man carrying a
leather bag stood on the steps of St. Paul's Cathedral, and hesitated, for within was what balm, how great a welcome, how
many tombs with banners waving over them, tokens of victories
not over armies, but over, he thought, that plaguy spirit of truth
seeking which leaves me at present without a situation, and
more than that, the cathedral offers company, he thought, in-

vites you to membership of a society; great men belong to it; martyrs have died for it; why not enter in, he thought, put this leather bag stuffed with pamphlets before an altar, a cross, the symbol of something which has soared beyond seeking and questing and knocking of words together and has become all 'spirit, disembodied, ghostly – why not enter in? he thought and while he hesitated out flew the aeroplane over Ludgate Circus.

It was strange; it was still. Not a sound was to be heard above the traffic. Unguided it seemed; sped of its own free will. And now, curving up and up, straight up, like something mounting in ecstasy, in pure delight, out from behind poured white smoke looping, writing a T, an O, an F.

'What are they looking at?' said Clarissa Dalloway to the maid who opened her door.

The hall of the house was cool as a vault. Mrs. Dalloway raised her hand to her eyes, and, as the maid shut the door to, and she heard the swish of Lucy's skirts, she felt like a nun who has left the world and feels fold round her the familiar veils and the response to old devotions. The cook whistled in the kitchen. She heard the click of the typewriter. It was her life, and, bending her head over the hall table, she bowed beneath the influence, felt blessed and purified, saying to herself, as she took the pad with the telephone message on it, how moments like this are buds on the tree of life, flowers of darkness they are, she thought (as if some lovely rose had blossomed for her eyes only); not for a moment did she believe in God; but all the more, she thought, taking up the pad, must one repay in daily life to servants, yes, to dogs and canaries, above all to Richard her husband, who was the foundation of it – of the gay sounds, of the green lights, of the cook even whistling, for Mrs. Walker was Irish and whistled all day long – one must pay back from this secret deposit of exquisite moments, she thought, lifting the pad, while Lucy stood by her, trying to explain how

'Mr. Dalloway, ma'am'——

Clarissa read on the telephone pad, 'Lady Bruton wishes to know if Mr. Dalloway will lunch with her today.'

'Mr. Dalloway, ma'am, told me to tell you he would be lunching out.'

'Dear!' said Clarissa, and Lucy shared as she meant her to her
disappointment (but not the pang); felt the concord between
them; took the hint; thought how the gentry love; gilded her
own future with calm; and, taking Mrs. Dalloway's parasol,
handled it like a sacred weapon which a Goddess, having acquit-
ted herself honourably in the field of battle, sheds, and placed it
in the umbrella stand.

'Fear no more,' said Clarissa. Fear no more the heat o' the
sun; for the shock of Lady Bruton asking Richard to lunch without her made the moment in which she had stood shiver, as a
plant on the river-bed feels the shock of a passing oar and shivers: so she rocked: so she shivered.

Millicent Bruton, whose lunch parties were said to be extraordinarily amusing, had not asked her. No vulgar jealousy
could separate her from Richard. But she feared time itself, and
read on Lady Bruton's face, as if it had been a dial cut in impas-
sive stone, the dwindling of life; how year by year her share was
sliced; how little the margin that remained was capable any
longer of stretching, of absorbing, as in the youthful years, the
colours, salts, tones of existence, so that she filled the room she
entered, and felt often as she stood hesitating one moment on
the threshold of her drawing-room, an exquisite suspense, such
as might stay a diver before plunging while the sea darkens and
brightens beneath him, and the waves which threaten to break,
but only gently split their surface, roll and conceal and encrust
as they just turn over the weeds with pearl.

She put the pad on the hall table. She began to go slowly upstairs, with her hand on the banisters, as if she had left a party,
where now this friend now that had flashed back her face, her
voice; had shut the door and gone out and stood alone, a single
figure against the appalling night, or rather, to be accurate,
against the stare of this matter-of-fact June morning; soft with
the glow of rose petals for some, she knew, and felt it, as she
paused by the open staircase window which let in blinds flap-
ping, dogs barking, let in, she thought, feeling herself suddenly

shrivelled, aged, breastless, the grinding, blowing, flowering of
the day, out of doors, out of the window, out of her body and
brain which now failed, since Lady Bruton, whose lunch parties
were said to be extraordinarily amusing, had not asked her.

Like a nun withdrawing, or a child exploring a tower,[26] she
went, upstairs, paused at the window, came to the bathroom.
There was the green linoleum and a tap dripping. There was an
emptiness about the heart of life; an attic room. Women must
put off their rich apparel. At midday they must disrobe. She
pierced the pincushion and laid her feathered yellow hat on the
bed. The sheets were clean, tight stretched in a broad white band
from side to side. Narrower and narrower would her bed be. The
candle was half burnt down and she had read deep in Baron
Marbot's *Memoirs*.[27] She had read late at night of the retreat
from Moscow. For the House sat so long that Richard insisted,
after her illness, that she must sleep undisturbed. And really she
preferred to read of the retreat from Moscow. He knew it. So
the room was an attic; the bed narrow; and lying there reading,
for she slept badly, she could not dispel a virginity preserved
through childbirth which clung to her like a sheet. Lovely in
girlhood, suddenly there came a moment – for example on the
river beneath the woods at Cliveden – when, through some contraction of this cold spirit, she had failed him. And then at Constantinople, and again and again. She could see what she lacked.
It was not beauty; it was not mind. It was something central
which permeated; something warm which broke up surfaces and
rippled the cold contact of man and woman, or of women together. For *that* she could dimly perceive. She resented it, had a
scruple picked up Heaven knows where, or, as she felt, sent by
Nature (who is invariably wise); yet she could not resist sometimes yielding to the charm of a woman, not a girl, of a woman
confessing, as to her they often did, some scrape, some folly.
And whether it was pity, or their beauty, or that she was older,
or some accident – like a faint scent, or a violin next door (so
strange is the power of sounds at certain moments), she did
undoubtedly then feel what men felt. Only for a moment; but it
was enough. It was a sudden revelation, a tinge like a blush

which one tried to check and then, as it spread, one yielded to
its expansion, and rushed to the farthest verge and there quivered and felt the world come closer, swollen with some astonishing significance, some pressure of rapture, which split its thin
skin and gushed and poured with an extraordinary alleviation
over the cracks and sores! Then, for that moment, she had seen
an illumination; a match burning in a crocus; an inner meaning
almost expressed. But the close withdrew; the hard softened. It
was over – the moment. Against such moments (with women
too) there contrasted (as she laid her hat down) the bed and
Baron Marbot and the candle half-burnt. Lying awake, the floor
creaked; the lit house was suddenly darkened, and if she raised
her head she could just hear the click of the handle released as
gently as possible by Richard, who slipped upstairs in his socks
and then, as often as not, dropped his hot-water bottle and
swore! How she laughed!

But this question of love (she thought, putting her coat away),
this falling in love with women. Take Sally Seton; her relation in the old days with Sally Seton. Had not that, after all,
been love?

She sat on the floor – that was her first impression of Sally –
she sat on the floor with her arms round her knees, smoking a
cigarette. Where could it have been? The Mannings'? The
Kinloch-Joneses'? At some party (where, she could not be certain), for she had a distinct recollection of saying to the man she
was with, 'Who is *that*?' And he had told her, and said that
Sally's parents did not get on (how that shocked her – that
one's parents should quarrel!). But all that evening she could not
take her eyes off Sally. It was an extraordinary beauty of the
kind she most admired, dark, large-eyed, with that quality
which, since she hadn't got it herself, she always envied – a sort
of abandonment, as if she could say anything, do anything; a
quality much commoner in foreigners than in English-women.
Sally always said she had French blood in her veins, an ancestor
had been with Marie Antoinette, had his head cut off, left a ruby
ring. Perhaps that summer she came to stay at Bourton, walking
in quite unexpectedly without a penny in her pocket, one night

after dinner, and upsetting poor Aunt Helena to such an extent that she never forgave her. There had been some awful quarrel at home. She literally hadn't a penny that night when she came to them – had pawned a brooch to come down. She had rushed off in a passion. They sat up till all hours of the night talking. Sally it was who made her feel, for the first time, how sheltered the life at Bourton was. She knew nothing about sex – nothing about social problems. She had once seen an old man who had dropped dead in a field – she had seen cows just after their calves were born. But Aunt Helena never liked discussion of anything (when Sally gave her William Morris,[28] it had to be wrapped in brown paper). There they sat, hour after hour, talking in her bedroom at the top of the house, talking about life, how they were to reform the world. They meant to found a society to abolish private property, and actually had a letter written, though not sent out. The ideas were Sally's, of course – but very soon she was just as excited – read Plato in bed before breakfast; read Morris; read Shelley by the hour.

Sally's power was amazing, her gift, her personality. There was her way with flowers, for instance. At Bourton they always had stiff little vases all the way down the table. Sally went out, picked hollyhocks, dahlias – all sorts of flowers that had never been seen together – cut their heads off, and made them swim on the top of water in bowls.[29] The effect was extraordinary – coming in to dinner in the sunset. (Of course Aunt Helena thought it wicked to treat flowers like that.) Then she forgot her sponge, and ran along the passage naked. That grim old house-maid, Ellen Atkins, went about grumbling – 'Suppose any of the gentlemen had seen?' Indeed she did shock people. She was untidy, Papa said.

The strange thing, on looking back, was the purity, the integrity, of her feeling for Sally. It was not like one's feeling for a man. It was completely disinterested, and besides, it had a quality which could only exist between women, between women just grown up. It was protective, on her side; sprang from a sense of being in league together, a presentiment of something that was bound to part them (they spoke of marriage always as a catastrophe), which led to this chivalry, this protective feeling which was much more on her side than Sally's. For in those days she was completely reckless; did the most idiotic things out of bravado; bicycled round the parapet on the terrace; smoked cigars. Absurd, she was – very absurd. But the charm was overpowering, to her at least, so that she could remember standing in her bedroom at the top of the house holding the hot-water can in her hands and saying aloud, 'She is beneath this roof . . . She is beneath this roof!'[30]

No, the words meant absolutely nothing to her now. She could not even get an echo of her old emotion. But she could remember going cold with excitement, and doing her hair in a kind of ecstasy (now the old feeling began to come back to her, as she took out her hairpins, laid them on the dressing-table, began to do her hair), with the rooks flaunting up and down in the pink evening light, and dressing, and going downstairs, and feeling as she crossed the hall 'if it were now to die, 'twere now to be most happy'.[31] That was her feeling – Othello's feeling, and she felt it, she was convinced, as strongly as Shakespeare meant Othello to feel it, all because she was coming down to dinner in a white frock to meet Sally Seton!

She was wearing pink gauze – was that possible? She *seemed*, anyhow, all light, glowing, like some bird or air-ball that has flown in, attached itself for a moment to a bramble. But nothing is so strange when one is in love (and what was this except being in love?) as the complete indifference of other people. Aunt Helena just wandered off after dinner; Papa read the paper. Peter Walsh might have been there, and old Miss Cummings; Joseph Breitkopf certainly was, for he came every summer, poor old man, for weeks and weeks, and pretended to read German with her, but really played the piano and sang Brahms without any voice.

All this was only a background for Sally. She stood by the fireplace talking, in that beautiful voice which made everything she said sound like a caress, to Papa, who had begun to be attracted rather against his will (he never got over lending her one

of his books and finding it soaked on the terrace), when suddenly she said, 'What a shame to sit indoors!' and they all went
out on to the terrace and walked up and down. Peter Walsh and
Joseph Breitkopf went on about Wagner. She and Sally fell a
little behind. Then came the most exquisite moment of her whole
life passing a stone urn with flowers in it. Sally stopped; picked
a flower; kissed her on the lips. The whole world might have
turned upside down! The others disappeared; there she was
alone with Sally. And she felt that she had been given a present,
wrapped up, and told just to keep it, not to look at it – a diamond,
something infinitely precious, wrapped up, which, as they walked
(up and down, up and down), she uncovered, or the radiance
burnt through, the revelation, the religious feeling! – when old
Joseph and Peter faced them:

'Star-gazing?' said Peter.

It was like running one's face against a granite wall in the
darkness! It was shocking; it was horrible!

Not for herself. She felt only how Sally was being mauled
already, maltreated; she felt his hostility; his jealousy; his determination to break into their companionship. All this she saw as
one sees a landscape in a flash of lightning – and Sally (never
had she admired her so much!) gallantly taking her way unvan-
quished. She laughed. She made old Joseph tell her the names of
the stars, which he liked doing very seriously. She stood there:
she listened. She heard the names of the stars.

'Oh this horror!' she said to herself, as if she had known all
along that something would interrupt, would embitter her moment of happiness.

Yet, after all, how much she owed to him later. Always, when
she thought of him she thought of their quarrels for some
reason – because she wanted his good opinion so much, perhaps.
She owed him words: 'sentimental', 'civilised'; they started up
every day of her life as if he guarded her. A book was sentimental; an attitude to life sentimental. 'Sentimental', perhaps she
was to be thinking of the past. What would he think, she wondered, when he came back?

That she had grown older? Would he say that, or would she
see him thinking when he came back, that she had grown older?
It was true. Since her illness she had turned almost white.

Laying her brooch on the table, she had a sudden spasm, as
if, while she mused, the icy claws had had the chance to fix in
her. She was not old yet. She had just broken into her fifty-
second year. Months and months of it were still untouched.
June, July, August! Each still remained almost whole, and, as
if to catch the falling drop, Clarissa (crossing to the dressing-
table) plunged into the very heart of the moment, transfixed
it, there – the moment of this June morning on which was the
pressure of all the other mornings, seeing the glass, the dressing-
table, and all the bottles afresh, collecting the whole of her at
one point (as she looked into the glass), seeing the delicate pink
face of the woman who was that very night to give a party; of
Clarissa Dalloway; of herself.

How many million times she had seen her face, and always
with the same imperceptible contraction! She pursed her lips
when she looked in the glass. It was to give her face point. That
was her self – pointed; dartlike; definite. That was her self when
some effort, some call on her to be her self, drew the parts together, she alone knew how different, how incompatible and
composed so for the world only into one centre, one diamond,
one woman who sat in her drawing-room and made a meeting-
point, a radiancy no doubt in some dull lives, a refuge for the
lonely to come to, perhaps; she had helped young people, who
were grateful to her; had tried to be the same always, never
showing a sign of all the other sides of her – faults, jealousies,
vanities, suspicions, like this of Lady Bruton not asking her to
lunch; which, she thought (combing her hair finally), is utterly
base! Now, where was her dress?

Her evening dresses hung in the cupboard. Clarissa, plunging
her hand into the softness, gently detached the green dress and
carried it to the window. She had torn it. Some one had trod on
the skirt. She had felt it give at the Embassy party at the top
among the folds. By artificial light the green shone, but lost its
colour now in the sun. She would mend it. Her maids had too

much to do. She would wear it to-night. She would take her silks, her scissors, her – what was it? – her thimble, of course, down into the drawing-room, for she must also write, and see that things generally were more or less in order.

Strange, she thought, pausing on the landing, and assembling that diamond shape, that single person, strange how a mistress knows the very moment, the very temper of her house! Faint sounds rose in spirals up the well of the stairs; the swish of a mop; tapping; knocking; a loudness when the front door opened; a voice repeating a message in the basement; the chink of silver on a tray; clean silver for the party. All was for the party.

(And Lucy, coming into the drawing-room with her tray held out, put the giant candlesticks on the mantelpiece, the silver casket in the middle, turned the crystal dolphin towards the clock. They would come; they would stand; they would talk in the mincing tones which she could imitate, ladies and gentlemen. Of all, her mistress was loveliest – mistress of silver, of linen, of china, for the sun, the silver, doors off their hinges, Rumpelmayer's men, gave her a sense, as she laid the paper-knife on the inlaid table, of something achieved. Behold! Behold! she said, speaking to her old friends in the baker's shop, where she had first seen service at Caterham, prying into the glass. She was Lady Angela, attending Princess Mary, when in came Mrs. Dalloway.)

'Oh Lucy,' she said, 'the silver does look nice!'

'And how,' she said, turning the crystal dolphin to stand straight, 'how did you enjoy the play last night?' 'Oh, they had to go before the end!' she said. 'They had to be back at ten!' she said. 'So they don't know what happened,' she said. 'That does seem hard luck,' she said (for her servants stayed later, if they asked her). 'That does seem rather a shame,' she said, taking the old bald-looking cushion in the middle of the sofa and putting it in Lucy's arms, and giving her a little push, and crying:

'Take it away! Give it to Mrs. Walker with my compliments! Take it away!' she cried.

And Lucy stopped at the drawing-room door, holding the cushion, and said, very shyly, turning a little pink, Couldn't she help to mend that dress?

But, said Mrs. Dalloway, she had enough on her hands already, quite enough of her own to do without that.

'But, thank you, Lucy, oh, thank you,' said Mrs. Dalloway, and thank you, thank you, she went on saying (sitting down on the sofa with her dress over her knees, her scissors, her silks), thank you, thank you, she went on saying in gratitude to her servants generally for helping her to be like this, to be what she wanted, gentle, generous-hearted. Her servants liked her. And then this dress of hers – where was the tear? and now her needle to be threaded. This was a favourite dress, one of Sally Parker's, the last almost she ever made, alas, for Sally had now retired, lived at Ealing, and if ever I have a moment, thought Clarissa (but never would she have a moment any more), I shall go and see her at Ealing. For she was a character, thought Clarissa, a real artist. She thought of little out-of-the-way things; yet her dresses were never queer. You could wear them at Hatfield; at Buckingham Palace. She had worn them at Hatfield; at Buckingham Palace.

Quiet descended on her, calm, content, as her needle, drawing the silk smoothly to its gentle pause, collected the green folds together and attached them, very lightly, to the belt. So on a summer's day waves collect, overbalance, and fall; collect and fall; and the whole world seems to be saying 'that is all' more and more ponderously, until even the heart in the body which lies in the sun on the beach says too, That is all. Fear no more, says the heart. Fear no more, says the heart, committing its burden to some sea, which sighs collectively for all sorrows, and renews, begins, collects, lets fall. And the body alone listens to the passing bee; the wave breaking; the dog barking, far away barking and barking.

'Heavens, the front-door bell!' exclaimed Clarissa, staying her needle. Roused, she listened.

'Mrs. Dalloway will see me,' said the elderly man in the hall. 'Oh yes, she will see *me*,' he repeated, putting Lucy aside very benevolently, and running upstairs ever so quickly. 'Yes, yes, yes,' he muttered as he ran upstairs. 'She will see me. After five years in India, Clarissa will see me.'

'Who can – what can,' asked Mrs. Dalloway (thinking it was outrageous to be interrupted at eleven o'clock on the morning of the day she was giving a party), hearing a step on the stairs. She heard a hand upon the door. She made to hide her dress, like a virgin protecting chastity, respecting privacy. Now the brass knob slipped. Now the door opened, and in came – for a single second she could not remember what he was called! so surprised she was to see him, so glad, so shy, so utterly taken aback to have Peter Walsh come to her unexpectedly in the morning! (She had not read his letter.)

'And how are you?' said Peter Walsh, positively trembling; taking both her hands; kissing both her hands. She's grown older, he thought, sitting down. I shan't tell her anything about it, he thought, for she's grown older. She's looking at me, he thought, a sudden embarrassment coming over him, though he had kissed her hands. Putting his hand into his pocket, he took out a large pocket-knife and half opened the blade.

Exactly the same, thought Clarissa; the same queer look; the same check suit; a little out of the straight his face is, a little thinner, dryer, perhaps, but he looks awfully well, and just the same.

'How heavenly it is to see you again!' she exclaimed. He had his knife out. That's so like him, she thought.

He had only reached town last night, he said; would have to go down into the country at once; and how was everything, how was everybody – Richard? Elizabeth?

'And what's all this?' he said, tilting his pen-knife towards her green dress.

He's very well dressed, thought Clarissa; yet he always criticises *me*.

Here she is mending her dress; mending her dress as usual, he thought; here she's been sitting all the time I've been in India; mending her dress; playing about; going to parties; running to the House and back and all that, he thought, growing more and more irritated, more and more agitated, for there's nothing in the world so bad for some women as marriage, he thought; and politics; and having a Conservative husband, like the admirable

Richard. So it is, so it is, he thought, shutting his knife with a snap.

'Richard's very well. Richard's at a Committee,' said Clarissa. And she opened her scissors, and said, did he mind her just finishing what she was doing to her dress, for they had a party that night?

'Which I shan't ask you to,' she said. 'My dear Peter!' she said. But it was delicious to hear her say that – my dear Peter! Indeed, it was all so delicious – the silver, the chairs; all so delicious!

Why wouldn't she ask him to her party? he asked.

Now of course, thought Clarissa, he's enchanting! perfectly enchanting! Now I remember how impossible it was ever to make up my mind – and why did I make up my mind – not to marry him, she wondered, that awful summer?

'But it's so extraordinary that you should have come this morning!' she cried, putting her hands, one on top of another, down on her dress.

'Do you remember,' she said, 'how the blinds used to flap at Bourton?'

'They did,' he said; and he remembered breakfasting alone, very awkwardly, with her father; who had died; and he had not written to Clarissa. But he had never got on well with old Parry, that querulous, weak-kneed old man, Clarissa's father, Justin Parry.

'I often wish I'd got on better with your father,' he said.

'But he never liked any one who – our friends,' said Clarissa; and could have bitten her tongue for thus reminding Peter that he had wanted to marry her.

Of course I did, thought Peter; it almost broke my heart too, he thought; and was overcome with his own grief, which rose like a moon looked at from a terrace, ghastly beautiful with light from the sunken day. I was more unhappy than I've ever been since, he thought. And as if in truth he were sitting there on the terrace he edged a little towards Clarissa; put his hand out; raised it; let it fall. There above them it hung, that moon. She too seemed to be sitting with him on the terrace, in the moon-light.

'Herbert has it now,' she said. 'I never go there now,' she said.

Then, just as happens on a terrace in the moonlight, when one person begins to feel ashamed that he is already bored, and yet as the other sits silent, very quiet, sadly looking at the moon, does not like to speak, moves his foot, clears his throat, notices some iron scroll on a table leg, stirs a leaf, but says nothing – so Peter Walsh did now. For why go back like this to the past? he thought. Why make him think of it again? Why make him suf-fer, when she had tortured him so infernally? Why?

'Do you remember the lake?' she said, in an abrupt voice, under the pressure of an emotion which caught her heart, made the muscles of her throat stiff, and contracted her lips in a spasm as she said 'lake'. For she was a child, throwing bread to the ducks, between her parents, and at the same time a grown woman com-ing to her parents who stood by the lake, holding her life in her arms which, as she neared them, grew larger and larger in her arms, until it became a whole life, a complete life, which she put down by them and said, 'This is what I have made of it! This!' And what had she made of it? What, indeed? sitting there sewing this morning with Peter.

She looked at Peter Walsh; her look, passing through all that time and that emotion, reached him doubtfully; settled on him tearfully; and rose and fluttered away, as a bird touches a branch and rises and flutters away. Quite simply she wiped her eyes.

'Yes,' said Peter. 'Yes, yes, yes,' he said, as if she drew up to the surface something which positively hurt him as it rose. Stop! Stop! he wanted to cry. For he was not old; his life was not over; not by any means. He was only just past fifty. Shall I tell her, he thought, or not? He would like to make a clean breast of it all. But she is too cold, he thought; sewing, with her scissors; Daisy would look ordinary beside Clarissa. And she would think me a failure, which I am in their sense, he thought; in the Dallo-ways' sense. Oh yes, he had no doubt about that; he was a failure, compared with all this – the inlaid table, the mounted paper-knife, the dolphin and the candlesticks, the chair-covers and the old valuable English tinted prints – he was a failure! I detest the smugness of the whole affair, he thought; Richard's doing, not Clarissa's; save that she married him. (Here Lucy came into the room, carrying silver, more silver, but charming, slender, graceful she looked, he thought, as she stooped to put it down.) And this has been going on all the time! he thought; week after week; Clarissa's life; while I – he thought; and at once everything seemed to radiate from him; journeys; rides; quarrels; adventures; bridge parties; love affairs; work; work, work! and he took out his knife quite openly – his old hornhandled knife which Clarissa could swear he had had these thirty years – and clenched his fist upon it.

What an extraordinary habit that was, Clarissa thought; always playing with a knife. Always making one feel, too, frivolous; empty-minded; a mere silly chatterbox, as he used. But I too, she thought, and, taking up her needle, summoned, like a Queen whose guards have fallen asleep and left her unprotected (she had been quite taken aback by this visit – it had upset her) so that any one can stroll in and have a look at her where she lies with the brambles curving over her, summoned to her help the things she did; the things she liked; her husband; Elizabeth; her self, in short, which Peter hardly knew now, all to come about her and beat off the enemy.

'Well, and what's happened to you?' she said. So before a battle begins, the horses paw the ground; toss their heads; the light shines on their flanks; their necks curve. So Peter Walsh and Clarissa, sitting side by side on the blue sofa, challenged each other. His powers chafed and tossed in him. He assembled from different quarters all sorts of things; praise; his career at Oxford; his marriage, which she knew nothing whatever about; how he had loved; and altogether done his job.

'Millions of things!' he exclaimed, and, urged by the assembly of powers which were now charging this way and that and giving him the feeling at once frightening and extremely exhilarating of being rushed through the air on the shoulders of people he could no longer see, he raised his hands to his forehead.

Clarissa sat very upright; drew in her breath.

'I am in love,' he said, not to her however, but to some one raised up in the dark so that you could not touch her but must lay your garland down on the grass in the dark.

'In love,' he repeated, now speaking rather dryly to Clarissa Dalloway; 'in love with a girl in India.' He had deposited his garland. Clarissa could make what she would of it.

'In love!' she said. That he at his age should be sucked under in his little bow-tie by that monster! And there's no flesh on his neck; his hands are red; and he's six months older than I am! her eye flashed back to her; but in her heart she felt, all the same; he is in love. He has that, she felt; he is in love.

But the indomitable egotism which for ever rides down the hosts opposed to it, the river which says on, on, on; even though, it admits, there may be no goal for us whatever, still on, on; this indomitable egotism charged her cheeks with colour; made her look very young; very pink; very bright-eyed as she sat with her dress upon her knee, and her needle held to the end of green silk, trembling a little. He was in love! Not with her. With some younger woman, of course.

'And who is she?' she asked.

Now this statue must be brought from its height and set down between them.

'A married woman, unfortunately,' he said; 'the wife of a Major in the Indian Army.'

And with a curious ironical sweetness he smiled as he placed her in this ridiculous way before Clarissa.

(All the same, he is in love, thought Clarissa.)

'She has,' he continued, very reasonably, 'two small children; a boy and a girl; and I have come over to see my lawyers about the divorce.'

There they are! he thought. Do what you like with them, Clarissa! There they are! And second by second it seemed to him that the wife of the Major in the Indian Army (his Daisy) and her two small children became more and more lovely as Clarissa looked at them; as if he had set light to a grey pellet on a plate and there had risen up a lovely tree in the brisk sea-salted air of their intimacy (for in some ways no one understood him, felt with him, as Clarissa did) – their exquisite intimacy.

She flattered him; she fooled him, thought Clarissa; shaping the woman, the wife of the Major in the Indian Army, with three strokes of a knife. What a waste! What a folly! All his life long Peter had been fooled like that; first getting sent down from Oxford; next marrying the girl on the boat going out to India; now the wife of a Major – thank Heaven she had refused to marry him! Still, he was in love; her old friend, her dear Peter, he was in love.

'But what are you going to do?' she asked him. Oh the lawyers and solicitors, Messrs. Hooper and Grateley of Lincoln's Inn, they were going to do it, he said. And he actually pared his nails with his pocket-knife.

For Heaven's sake, leave your knife alone! she cried to herself in irrepressible irritation; it was his silly unconventionality, his weakness; his lack of the ghost of a notion what any one else was feeling that annoyed her, had always annoyed her; and now at his age, how silly!

I know all that, Peter thought; I know what I'm up against, he thought, running his finger along the blade of his knife, Clarissa and Dalloway and all the rest of them; but I'll show Clarissa – and then to his utter surprise, suddenly thrown by those uncontrollable forces, thrown through the air, he burst into tears; wept; wept without the least shame, sitting on the sofa, the tears running down his cheeks.

And Clarissa had leant forward, taken his hand, drawn him to her, kissed him, – actually had felt his face on hers before she could down the brandishing of silver-flashing plumes like pampas grass in a tropic gale in her breast, which, subsiding, left her holding his hand, patting his knee, and feeling as she sat back extraordinarily at her ease with him and light-hearted, all in a clap it came over her, If I had married him, this gaiety would have been mine all day!

It was all over for her. The sheet was stretched and the bed narrow. She had gone up into the tower alone and left them blackberrying in the sun. The door had shut, and there among the dust of fallen plaster and the litter of birds' nests how distant the view had looked, and the sounds came thin and chill (once on Leith Hill,[32] she remembered), and Richard, Richard! she cried, as a sleeper in the night starts and stretches a hand in the dark for help. Lunching with Lady Bruton, it came back to her. He has left me; I am alone for ever, she thought, folding her hands upon her knee.

Peter Walsh had got up and crossed to the window and stood with his back to her, flicking a bandanna handkerchief from side to side. Masterly and dry and desolate he looked, his thin shoulder-blades lifting his coat slightly; blowing his nose violently. Take me with you, Clarissa thought impulsively, as if he were starting directly upon some great voyage; and then, next moment, it was as if the five acts of a play that had been very exciting and moving were now over and she had lived a lifetime in them and had run away, had lived with Peter, and it was now over.

Now it was time to move, and, as a woman gathers her things together, her cloak, her gloves, her opera-glasses, and gets up to go out of the theatre into the street, she rose from the sofa and went to Peter.

And it was awfully strange, he thought, how she still had the power, as she came tinkling, rustling, still had the power as she came across the room, to make the moon, which he detested, rise at Bourton on the terrace in the summer sky.

'Tell me,' he said, seizing her by the shoulders. 'Are you happy, Clarissa? Does Richard——'

The door opened.

'Here is my Elizabeth,' said Clarissa, emotionally, histrionically, perhaps.

'How d'y do?' said Elizabeth coming forward.

The sound of Big Ben striking the half-hour struck out between them with extraordinary vigour, as if a young man, strong, indifferent, inconsiderate, were swinging dumb-bells this way and that.

'Hullo, Elizabeth!' cried Peter, stuffing his handkerchief into his pocket, going quickly to her, saying 'Good-bye Clarissa' without looking at her, leaving the room quickly, and running downstairs and opening the hall door.

'Peter! Peter!' cried Clarissa, following him out on to the landing. 'My party to-night! Remember my party to-night!' she cried, having to raise her voice against the roar of the open air, and, overwhelmed by the traffic and the sound of all the clocks striking, her voice crying 'Remember my party to-night!' sounded frail and thin and very far away as Peter Walsh shut the door.

Remember my party, remember my party, said Peter Walsh as he stepped down the street, speaking to himself rhythmically, in time with the flow of the sound, the direct downright sound of Big Ben striking the half-hour. (The leaden circles dissolved in the air.) Oh these parties, he thought; Clarissa's parties. Why does she give these parties, he thought. Not that he blamed her or this effigy of a man in a tail-coat with a carnation in his button-hole coming towards him. Only one person in the world could be as he was, in love. And there he was, this fortunate man, himself, reflected in the plate-glass window of a motor-car manufacturer in Victoria Street. All India lay behind him; plains, mountains; epidemics of cholera; a district twice as big as Ireland; decisions he had come to alone – he, Peter Walsh; who was now really for the first time in his life, in love. Clarissa had grown hard, he thought; and a trifle sentimental into the bargain, he suspected, looking at the great motor-cars capable of doing – how many miles on how many gallons? For he had a turn for mechanics; had invented a plough in his district, had ordered wheel-barrows from England, but the coolies wouldn't use them, all of which Clarissa knew nothing whatever about.

The way she said 'Here is my Elizabeth!' – that annoyed him. Why not 'Here's Elizabeth' simply? It was insincere. And Elizabeth didn't like it either. (Still the last tremors of the great booming voice shook the air round him; the half-hour; still early; only half-past eleven still.) For he understood young people; he liked them. There was always something cold in Clarissa, he thought. She had always, even as a girl, a sort of timidity, which in middle age becomes conventionality, and then it's all up, it's all up, he thought, looking rather drearily into the glassy depths, and wondering whether by calling at that hour he had annoyed her; overcome with shame suddenly at having been a fool; wept; been emotional; told her everything, as usual, as usual.

As a cloud crosses the sun, silence falls on London; and falls on the mind. Effort ceases. Time flaps on the mast. There we stop; there we stand. Rigid, the skeleton of habit alone upholds the human frame. Where there is nothing, Peter Walsh said to himself; feeling hollowed out, utterly empty within. Clarissa refused me, he thought. He stood there thinking, Clarissa refused me.

Ah, said St. Margaret's[33] like a hostess who comes into her drawing-room on the very stroke of the hour and finds her guests there already, I am not late. No, it is precisely half-past eleven, she says. Yet, though she is perfectly right, her voice, being the voice of the hostess, is reluctant to inflict its individuality. Some grief for the past holds it back; some concern for the present. It is half-past eleven, she says, and the sound of St. Margaret's glides into the recesses of the heart and buries itself in ring after ring of sound, like something alive which wants to confide itself, to disperse itself, to be, with a tremor of delight, at rest – like Clarissa herself, thought Peter Walsh, coming downstairs on the stroke of the hour in white. It is Clarissa herself, he thought, with a deep emotion, and an extraordinarily clear, yet puzzling, recollection of her, as if this bell had come into the room years ago, where they sat at some moment of great intimacy, and had gone from one to the other and had left, like a bee with honey, laden with the moment. But what room? What moment? And why had he been so profoundly happy when the clock was striking? Then, as the sound of St. Margaret's languished, he thought, She has been ill, and the sound expressed languor and suffering. It was her heart, he remembered; and the sudden loudness of the final stroke tolled for death that surprised in the midst of life, Clarissa falling where she stood, in her drawing-room. No! No! he cried. She is not dead! I am not old, he cried, and marched up Whitehall, as if there rolled down to him, vigorous, unending, his future.

He was not old, or set, or dried in the least. As for caring what they said of him – the Dalloways, the Whitbreads, and their set, he cared not a straw – not a straw (though it was true he would have, some time or other, to see whether Richard couldn't help him to some job). Striding, staring, he glared at the statue of the Duke of Cambridge.[34] He had been sent down from Oxford – true. He had been a Socialist, in some sense a failure – true. Still the future of civilisation lies, he thought, in the hands of young men like that; of young men such as he was, thirty years ago; with their love of abstract principles; getting books sent out to them all the way from London to a peak in the Himalayas; reading science; reading philosophy. The future lies in the hands of young men like that, he thought.

A patter like the patter of leaves in a wood came from behind, and with it a rustling, regular thudding sound, which as it overtook him drummed his thoughts, strict in step, up Whitehall, without his doing. Boys in uniform, carrying guns, marched with their eyes ahead of them, marched, their arms stiff, and on their faces an expression like the letters of a legend written round the base of a statue praising duty, gratitude, fidelity, love of England.

It is, thought Peter Walsh, beginning to keep step with them, a very fine training. But they did not look robust. They were weedy for the most part, boys of sixteen, who might, to-morrow, stand behind bowls of rice, cakes of soap on counters. Now they wore on them unmixed with sensual pleasure or daily preoccupations the solemnity of the wreath which they had fetched from Finsbury Pavement to the empty tomb.[35] They had taken their vow. The traffic respected it; vans were stopped.

I can't keep up with them, Peter Walsh thought, as they marched up Whitehall, and sure enough, on they marched, past him, past every one, in their steady way, as if one will worked legs and arms uniformly, and life, with its varieties, its irreticences, had been laid under a pavement of monuments and wreaths and drugged into a stiff yet staring corpse by discipline. One had to respect it; one might laugh; but one had to respect it, he thought. There they go, thought Peter Walsh, pausing at the edge of the pavement; and all the exalted statues, Nelson, Gordon, Havelock,[36] the black, the spectacular images of great soldiers stood looking ahead of them, as if they too had made the same renunciation (Peter Walsh felt he, too, had made it, the great renunciation), trampled under the same temptations, and achieved at length a marble stare. But the stare Peter Walsh did not want for himself in the least; though he could respect it in others. He could respect it in boys. They don't know the troubles of the flesh yet, he thought, as the marching boys disappeared in the direction of the Strand – all that I've been through, he thought, crossing the road, and standing under Gordon's statue, Gordon whom as a boy he had worshipped; Gordon standing lonely with one leg raised and his arms crossed, – poor Gordon, he thought.

And just because nobody yet knew he was in London, except Clarissa, and the earth, after the voyage, still seemed an island to him, the strangeness of standing alone, alive, unknown, at half-past eleven in Trafalgar Square overcame him. What is it? Where am I? And why, after all, does one do it? he thought, the divorce seeming all moonshine. And down his mind went flat as a marsh, and three great emotions bowled over him; understanding; a vast philanthropy; and finally, as if the result of the others, an irrepressible, exquisite delight; as if inside his brain by another hand strings were pulled, shutters moved, and he, having nothing to do with it, yet stood at the opening of endless avenues, down which if he chose he might wander. He had not felt so young for years.

He had escaped! was utterly free – as happens in the downfall of habit when the mind, like an unguarded flame, bows and bends and seems about to blow from its holding. I haven't felt so young for years! thought Peter, escaping (only of course for an hour or so) from being precisely what he was, and feeling like a child who runs out of doors, and sees, as he runs, his old nurse waving at the wrong window. But she's extraordinarily attractive, he thought, as, walking across Trafalgar Square in the direction of the Haymarket, came a young woman who, as she passed Gordon's statue, seemed, Peter Walsh thought (susceptible as he

was), to shed veil after veil, until she became the very woman he
had always had in mind; young, but stately; merry, but discreet;
black, but enchanting.

Straightening himself and stealthily fingering his pocket-knife
he started after her to follow this woman, this excitement, which
seemed even with its back turned to shed on him a light which
connected them, which singled him out, as if the random uproar
of the traffic had whispered through hollowed hands his name,
not Peter, but his private name which he called himself in his
own thoughts. 'You,' she said, only 'you', saying it with her
white gloves and her shoulders. Then the thin long cloak which
the wind stirred as she walked past Dent's shop in Cockspur
Street blew out with an enveloping kindness, a mournful tenderness, as of arms that would open and take the tired——

But she's not married; she's young; quite young, thought
Peter, the red carnation he had seen her wear as she came across
Trafalgar Square burning again in his eyes and making her lips
red. But she waited at the kerbstone. There was a dignity about
her. She was not worldly, like Clarissa; not rich, like Clarissa.
Was she, he wondered as she moved, respectable? Witty, with a
lizard's flickering tongue, he thought (for one must invent, must
allow oneself a little diversion), a cool waiting wit, a darting wit;
not noisy.

She moved; she crossed; he followed her. To embarrass her
was the last thing he wished. Still if she stopped he would say
'Come and have an ice,' he would say, and she would answer,
perfectly simply, 'Oh yes.'

But other people got between them in the street, obstruct-
ing him, blotting her out. He pursued; she changed. There was
colour in her cheeks; mockery in her eyes; he was an adventurer,
reckless, he thought, swift, daring, indeed (landed as he was last
night from India) a romantic buccaneer, careless of all these
damned proprieties, yellow dressing-gowns, pipes, fishing-rods,
in the shop windows; and respectability and evening parties and
spruce old men wearing white slips beneath their waistcoats. He
was a buccaneer. On and on she went, across Piccadilly, and up
Regent Street, ahead of him, her cloak, her gloves, her shoulders

combining with the fringes and the laces and the feather boas in the windows to make the spirit of finery and whimsy which dwindled out of the shops on to the pavement, as the light of a lamp goes wavering at night over hedges in the darkness.

Laughing and delightful, she had crossed Oxford Street and Great Portland Street and turned down one of the little streets, and now, and now, the great moment was approaching, for now she slackened, opened her bag, and with one look in his direction, but not at him, one look that bade farewell, summed up the whole situation and dismissed it triumphantly, for ever, had fitted her key, opened the door, and gone! Clarissa's voice saying, Remember my party, Remember my party, sang in his ears. The house was one of those flat red houses with hanging flower-baskets of vague impropriety. It was over.

Well, I've had my fun; I've had it, he thought, looking up at the swinging baskets of pale geraniums. And it was smashed to atoms – his fun, for it was half made up, as he knew very well; invented, this escapade with the girl; made up, as one makes up the better part of life, he thought – making oneself up; making her up; creating an exquisite amusement, and something more. But odd it was, and quite true; all this one could never share – it smashed to atoms.

He turned; went up the street, thinking to find somewhere to sit, till it was time for Lincoln's Inn – for Messrs. Hooper and Grateley. Where should he go? No matter. Up the street, then, towards Regent's Park. His boots on the pavement struck out 'no matter'; for it was early, still very early.

It was a splendid morning too. Like the pulse of a perfect heart, life struck straight through the streets. There was no fumbling – no hesitation. Sweeping and swerving, accurately, punctually, noiselessly, there, precisely at the right instant, the motor-car stopped at the door. The girl, silk-stockinged, feathered, evanescent, but not to him particularly attractive (for he had had his fling), alighted. Admirable butlers, tawny chow dogs, halls laid in black and white lozenges with white blinds blowing, Peter saw through the opened door and approved of. A splendid achievement in its own way, after all, London; the season; civilisation. Coming as he did from a respectable Anglo-Indian family which for at least three generations had administered the affairs of a continent (it's strange, he thought, what a sentiment I have about that, disliking India, and empire, and army as he did), there were moments when civilisation, even of this sort, seemed dear to him as a personal possession; moments of pride in England; in butlers; chow dogs; girls in their security. Ridiculous enough, still there it is, he thought. And the doctors and men of business and capable women all going about their business, punctual, alert, robust, seemed to him wholly admirable, good fellows, to whom one would entrust one's life, companions in the art of living, who would see one through. What with one thing and another, the show was really very tolerable; and he would sit down in the shade and smoke.

There was Regent's Park. Yes. As a child he had walked in Regent's Park – odd, he thought, how the thought of childhood keeps coming back to me – the result of seeing Clarissa, perhaps; for women live much more in the past than we do, he thought. They attach themselves to places; and their fathers – a woman's always proud of her father. Bourton was a nice place, a very nice place, but I could never get on with the old man, he thought. There was quite a scene one night – an argument about something or other, what, he could not remember. Politics presumably.

Yes, he remembered Regent's Park; the long straight walk; the little house where one bought air-balls[37] to the left; an absurd statue with an inscription somewhere or other. He looked for an empty seat. He did not want to be bothered (feeling a little drowsy as he did) by people asking him the time. An elderly grey nurse, with a baby asleep in its perambulator – that was the best he could do for himself; sit down at the far end of the seat by that nurse.

She's a queer-looking girl, he thought, suddenly remembering Elizabeth as she came into the room and stood by her mother. Grown big; quite grown-up, not exactly pretty; handsome rather; and she can't be more than eighteen. Probably she doesn't get on with Clarissa. 'Here's my Elizabeth' – that sort of thing – why not 'Here's Elizabeth' simply? – trying to make out, like most mothers, that things are what they're not. She trusts to her charm too much, he thought. She overdoes it.

The rich benignant cigar smoke eddied coolly down his throat; he puffed it out again in rings which breasted the air bravely for a moment; blue, circular – I shall try and get a word alone with Elizabeth to-night, he thought – then began to wobble into hour-glass shapes and taper away; odd shapes they take, he thought. Suddenly he closed his eyes, raised his hand with an effort, and threw away the heavy end of his cigar. A great brush swept smooth across his mind, sweeping across it moving branches, children's voices, the shuffle of feet, and people passing, and humming traffic, rising and falling traffic. Down, down he sank into the plumes and feathers of sleep, sank, and was muffled over.

The grey nurse resumed her knitting as Peter Walsh, on the hot seat beside her, began snoring. In her grey dress, moving her hands indefatigably yet quietly, she seemed like the champion of the rights of sleepers, like one of those spectral presences which rise in twilight in woods made of sky and branches. The solitary traveller, haunter of lanes, disturber of ferns, and devastator of great hemlock plants, looking up suddenly, sees the giant figure at the end of the ride.

By conviction an atheist perhaps, he is taken by surprise with moments of extraordinary exaltation. Nothing exists outside us except a state of mind, he thinks; a desire for solace, for relief, for something outside these miserable pigmies, these feeble, these ugly, these craven men and women. But if he can conceive of her, then in some sort she exists, he thinks, and advancing down the path with his eyes upon sky and branches he rapidly endows them with womanhood; sees with amazement how grave they become; how majestically, as the breeze stirs them, they dispense with a dark flutter of the leaves charity, comprehension, absolution, and then, flinging themselves suddenly aloft, confound the piety of their aspect with a wild carouse.

Such are the visions which proffer great cornucopias full of fruit to the solitary traveller, or murmur in his ear like sirens lolloping away on the green sea waves, or are dashed in his face like bunches of roses, or rise to the surface like pale faces which fishermen flounder through floods to embrace.

Such are the visions which ceaselessly float up, pace beside, put their faces in front of, the actual thing; often overpowering the solitary traveller and taking away from him the sense of the earth, the wish to return, and giving him for substitute a general peace, as if (so he thinks as he advances down the forest ride) all this fever of living were simplicity itself; and myriads of things merged in one thing; and this figure, made of sky and branches as it is, had risen from the troubled sea (he is elderly, past fifty now) as a shape might be sucked up out of the waves to shower down from her magnificent hands compassion, comprehension, absolution. So, he thinks, may I never go back to the lamplight; to the sitting-room; never finish my book; never knock out my pipe; never ring for Mrs. Turner to clear away; rather let me walk straight on to this great figure, who will, with a toss of her head, mount me on her streamers and let me blow to nothingness with the rest.

Such are the visions. The solitary traveller is soon beyond the wood; and there, coming to the door with shaded eyes, possibly to look for his return, with hands raised, with white apron blowing, is an elderly woman who seems (so powerful is this infirmity) to seek, over the desert, a lost son; to search for a rider destroyed; to be the figure of the mother whose sons have been killed in the battles of the world. So, as the solitary traveller advances down the village street where the women stand knitting and the men dig in the garden, the evening seems ominous; the figures still; as if some august fate, known to them, awaited without fear, were about to sweep them into complete annihilation.

Indoors among ordinary things, the cupboard, the table, the window-sill with its geraniums, suddenly the outline of the land-lady, bending to remove the cloth, becomes soft with light, an adorable emblem which only the recollection of cold human contacts forbids us to embrace. She takes the marmalade; she shuts it in the cupboard.

'There is nothing more to-night, sir?'
But to whom does the solitary traveller make reply?

So the elderly nurse knitted over the sleeping baby in Regent's Park. So Peter Walsh snored.

He woke with extreme suddenness, saying to himself, 'The death of the soul.'

'Lord, Lord!' he said to himself out loud, stretching and opening his eyes. 'The death of the soul.' The words attached themselves to some scene, to some room, to some past he had been dreaming of. It became clearer; the scene, the room, the past he had been dreaming of.

It was at Bourton that summer, early in the 'nineties, when he was so passionately in love with Clarissa. There were a great many people there, laughing and talking, sitting round a table after tea, and the room was bathed in yellow light and full of cigarette smoke. They were talking about a man who had married his housemaid, one of the neighbouring squires, he had forgotten his name. He had married his housemaid, and she had been brought to Bourton to call – an awful visit it had been. She was absurdly overdressed, 'like a cockatoo,' Clarissa had said, imitating her, and she never stopped talking. On and on she went, on and on. Clarissa imitated her. Then somebody said – Sally Seton it was – did it make any real difference to one's feelings to know that before they'd married she had had a baby? (In those days, in mixed company, it was a bold thing to say.) He could see Clarissa now, turning bright pink; somehow contracting; and saying, 'Oh, I shall never be able to speak to her again!' Whereupon the whole party sitting round the tea-table seemed to wobble. It was very uncomfortable.

He hadn't blamed her for minding the fact, since in those days a girl brought up as she was, knew nothing, but it was her manner that annoyed him; timid; hard; arrogant; prudish. 'The death of the soul.' He had said that instinctively, ticketing the moment as he used to do – the death of her soul.

Every one wobbled; every one seemed to bow, as she spoke, and then to stand up different. He could see Sally Seton, like a child who has been in mischief, leaning forward, rather flushed, wanting to talk, but afraid, and Clarissa did frighten people. (She was Clarissa's greatest friend, always about the place, an attractive creature, handsome, dark, with the reputation in those days of great daring, and he used to give her cigars, which she smoked in her bedroom, and she had either been engaged to somebody or quarrelled with her family, and old Parry disliked them both equally, which was a great bond.) Then Clarissa, still with an air of being offended with them all, got up, made some excuse, and went off, alone. As she opened the door, in came that great shaggy dog which ran after sheep. She flung herself upon him, went into raptures. It was as if she said to Peter – it was all aimed at him, he knew – 'I know you thought me absurd about that woman just now; but see how extraordinarily sympathetic I am; see how I love my Rob!'

They had always this queer power of communicating without words. She knew directly he criticised her. Then she would do something quite obvious to defend herself, like this fuss with the dog – but it never took him in, he always saw through Clarissa. Not that he said anything, of course; just sat looking glum. It was that way their quarrels often began.

She shut the door. At once he became extremely depressed. It all seemed useless – going on being in love; going on quarrelling; going on making it up, and he wandered off alone, among out-houses, stables, looking at the horses. (The place was quite a humble one; the Parrys were never very well off; but there were always grooms and stable-boys about – Clarissa loved riding – and an old coachman – what was his name? – an old nurse, old Moody, old Goody, some such name they called her,[38] whom one was taken to visit in a little room with lots of photographs, lots of bird-cages.)

It was an awful evening! He grew more and more gloomy, not about that only; about everything. And he couldn't see her; couldn't explain to her; couldn't have it out. There were always people about – she'd go on as if nothing had happened. That was the devilish part of her – this coldness, this woodenness, something very profound in her, which he had felt again this morning talking to her; an impenetrability. Yet Heaven knows he loved her. She had some queer power of fiddling on one's nerves, turning one's nerves to fiddle-strings, yes.

He had gone in to dinner rather late, from some idiotic idea of making himself felt, and had sat down by old Miss Parry – Aunt Helena – Mr. Parry's sister, who was supposed to preside. There she sat in her white Cashmere shawl, with her head against the window – a formidable old lady, but kind to him, for he had found her some rare flower, and she was a great botanist, marching off in thick boots with a black tin collecting box slung between her shoulders. He sat down beside her, and couldn't speak. Everything seemed to race past him; he just sat there, eating. And then half-way through dinner he made himself look across at Clarissa for the first time. She was talking to a young man on her right. He had a sudden revelation. 'She will marry that man,' he said to himself. He didn't even know his name.

For of course it was that afternoon, that very afternoon, that Dalloway had come over; and Clarissa called him 'Wickham'; that was the beginning of it all. Somebody had brought him over; and Clarissa got his name wrong. She introduced him to everybody as Wickham.[39] At last he said 'My name is Dalloway!' – that was his first view of Richard – a fair young man, rather awkward, sitting on a deck-chair, and blurting out 'My name is Dalloway!' Sally got hold of it; always after that she called him 'My name is Dalloway!'

He was a prey to revelations at that time. This one – that she would marry Dalloway – was blinding – overwhelming at the moment. There was a sort of – how could he put it? – a sort of ease in her manner to him; something maternal; something gentle. They were talking about politics. All through dinner he tried to hear what they were saying.

Afterwards he could remember standing by old Miss Parry's chair in the drawing-room. Clarissa came up, with her perfect manners, like a real hostess, and wanted to introduce him to some one – spoke as if they had never met before, which enraged him. Yet even then he admired her for it. He admired her courage; her social instinct; he admired her power of carrying things through. 'The perfect hostess,' he said to her, whereupon she winced all over. But he meant her to feel it. He would have done anything to hurt her, after seeing her with Dalloway. So she left him. And he had a feeling that they were all gathered together in a conspiracy against him – laughing and talking – behind his back. There he stood by Miss Parry's chair as though he had been cut out of wood, talking about wild flowers. Never, never had he suffered so infernally! He must have forgotten even to pretend to listen; at last he woke up; he saw Miss Parry looking rather disturbed, rather indignant, with her prominent eyes fixed. He almost cried out that he couldn't attend because he was in Hell! People began going out of the room. He heard them talking about fetching cloaks; about its being cold on the water, and so on. They were going boating on the lake by moonlight – one of Sally's mad ideas. He could hear her describing the moon. And they all went out. He was left quite alone.

'Don't you want to go with them?' said Aunt Helena poor old lady! – she had guessed. And he turned round and there was Clarissa again. She had come back to fetch him. He was overcome by her generosity – her goodness.

'Come along,' she said. 'They're waiting.'

He had never felt so happy in the whole of his life! Without a word they made it up. They walked down to the lake. He had twenty minutes of perfect happiness. Her voice, her laugh, her dress (something floating, white, crimson), her spirit, her adventurousness; she made them all disembark and explore the island; she startled a hen; she laughed; she sang. And all the time, he knew perfectly well, Dalloway was falling in love with her; she was falling in love with Dalloway; but it didn't seem to matter. Nothing mattered. They sat on the ground and talked – he and Clarissa. They went in and out of each other's minds without any effort. And then in a second it was over. He said to himself as they were getting into the boat, 'She will marry that man,' dully, without any resentment; but it was an obvious thing. Dalloway would marry Clarissa.

Dalloway rowed them in. He said nothing. But somehow as they watched him start, jumping on to his bicycle to ride twenty

miles through the woods, wobbling off down the drive, waving
his hand and disappearing, he obviously did feel, instinctively,
tremendously, strongly, all that; the night; the romance; Clarissa. He deserved to have her.

For himself, he was absurd. His demands upon Clarissa (he
could see it now) were absurd. He asked impossible things. He
made terrible scenes. She would have accepted him still, perhaps, if he had been less absurd. Sally thought so. She wrote him
all that summer long letters; how they had talked of him; how
she had praised him, how Clarissa burst into tears! It was an
extraordinary summer – all letters, scenes, telegrams – arriving
at Bourton early in the morning, hanging about till the servants
were up; appalling *tête-à-têtes* with old Mr. Parry at breakfast;
Aunt Helena formidable but kind; Sally sweeping him off for
talks in the vegetable garden; Clarissa in bed with headaches.

The final scene, the terrible scene which he believed had mattered more than anything in the whole of his life (it might be an
exaggeration – but still, so it did seem now), happened at three
o'clock in the afternoon of a very hot day. It was a trifle that led
up to it – Sally at lunch saying something about Dalloway, and
calling him 'My name is Dalloway'; whereupon Clarissa suddenly stiffened, coloured, in a way she had, and rapped out
sharply, 'We've had enough of that feeble joke.' That was all; but
for him it was as if she had said, 'I'm only amusing myself with
you; I've an understanding with Richard Dalloway.' So he took
it. He had not slept for nights. 'It's got to be finished one way or
the other,' he said to himself. He sent a note to her by Sally asking her to meet him by the fountain at three. 'Something very
important has happened,' he scribbled at the end of it.

The fountain was in the middle of a little shrubbery, far from
the house, with shrubs and trees all round it. There she came,
even before the time, and they stood with the fountain between
them, the spout (it was broken) dribbling water incessantly. How
sights fix themselves upon the mind! For example, the vivid
green moss.

She did not move. 'Tell me the truth, tell me the truth,' he kept
on saying. He felt as if his forehead would burst. She seemed

contracted, petrified. She did not move. 'Tell me the truth,' he repeated, when suddenly that old man Breitkopf popped his head in carrying the *Times*; stared at them; gaped; and went away. They neither of them moved. 'Tell me the truth,' he repeated. He felt that he was grinding against something physically hard; she was unyielding. She was like iron, like flint, rigid up the backbone. And when she said, 'It's no use. It's no use. This is the end' – after he had spoken for hours, it seemed, with the tears running down his cheeks – it was as if she had hit him in the face. She turned, she left him, she went away.

'Clarissa!' he cried. 'Clarissa!' But she never came back. It was over. He went away that night. He never saw her again.

It was awful, he cried, awful, awful!

Still, the sun was hot. Still, one got over things. Still, life had a way of adding day to day. Still, he thought, yawning and beginning to take notice – Regent's Park had changed very little since he was a boy, except for the squirrels – still, presumably there were compensations – when little Elise Mitchell, who had been picking up pebbles to add to the pebble collection which she and her brother were making on the nursery mantelpiece, plumped her handful down on the nurse's knee and scudded off again full tilt into a lady's legs. Peter Walsh laughed out.

But Lucrezia Warren Smith was saying to herself, It's wicked; why should I suffer? she was asking, as she walked down the broad path. No; I can't stand it any longer, she was saying, having left Septimus, who wasn't Septimus any longer, to say hard, cruel, wicked things, to talk to himself, to talk to a dead man, on the seat over there; when the child ran full tilt into her, fell flat, and burst out crying.

That was comforting rather. She stood her upright, dusted her frock, kissed her.

But for herself she had done nothing wrong; she had loved Septimus; she had been happy; she had had a beautiful home, and there her sister lived still, making hats. Why should *she* suffer?

The child ran straight back to its nurse, and Rezia saw her

scolded, comforted, taken up by the nurse who put down her
knitting, and the kind-looking man gave her his watch to blow
open to comfort her – but why should *she* be exposed? Why not
left in Milan? Why tortured? Why?

Slightly waved by tears the broad path, the nurse, the man in
grey, the perambulator, rose and fell before her eyes. To be
rocked by this malignant torturer was her lot. But why? She was
like a bird sheltering under the thin hollow of a leaf, who blinks
at the sun when the leaf moves; starts at the crack of a dry twig.
She was exposed; she was surrounded by the enormous trees,
vast clouds of an indifferent world, exposed; tortured; and why
should she suffer? Why?

She frowned; she stamped her foot. She must go back again
to Septimus since it was almost time for them to be going to Sir
William Bradshaw. She must go back and tell him, go back to
him sitting there on the green chair under the tree, talking to
himself, or to that dead man Evans, whom she had only seen
once for a moment in the shop. He had seemed a nice quiet man;
a great friend of Septimus's, and he had been killed in the War.
But such things happen to every one. Every one has friends who
were killed in the War. Every one gives up something when they
marry. She had given up her home. She had come to live here, in
this awful city. But Septimus let himself think about horrible
things, as she could too, if she tried. He had grown stranger and
stranger. He said people were talking behind the bedroom walls.
Mrs. Filmer thought it odd. He saw things too – he had seen an
old woman's head in the middle of a fern. Yet he could be happy
when he chose. They went to Hampton Court on top of a bus,
and they were perfectly happy. All the little red and yellow flowers were out on the grass, like floating lamps he said, and talked
and chattered and laughed, making up stories. Suddenly he said,
'Now we will kill ourselves,' when they were standing by the
river, and he looked at it with a look which she had seen in his
eyes when a train went by, or an omnibus – a look as if something fascinated him; and she felt he was going from her and she
caught him by the arm. But going home he was perfectly quiet –
perfectly reasonable. He would argue with her about killing

themselves; and explain how wicked people were; how he could see them making up lies as they passed in the street. He knew all their thoughts, he said; he knew everything. He knew the meaning of the world, he said.

Then when they got back he could hardly walk. He lay on the sofa and made her hold his hand to prevent him from falling down, down, he cried, into the flames! and saw faces laughing at him, calling him horrible disgusting names, from the walls, and hands pointing round the screen. Yet they were quite alone. But he began to talk aloud, answering people, arguing, laughing, crying, getting very excited and making her write things down. Perfect nonsense it was; about death; about Miss Isabel Pole. She could stand it no longer. She would go back.

She was close to him now, could see him staring at the sky, muttering, clasping his hands. Yet Dr. Holmes said there was nothing the matter with him. What, then, had happened – why had he gone, then, why, when she sat by him, did he start, frown at her, move away, and point at her hand, take her hand, look at it terrified?

Was it that she had taken off her wedding ring? 'My hand has grown so thin,' she said; 'I have put it in my purse,' she told him.

He dropped her hand. Their marriage was over, he thought, with agony, with relief. The rope was cut; he mounted; he was free, as it was decreed that he, Septimus, the lord of men, should be free; alone (since his wife had thrown away her wedding ring; since she had left him), he, Septimus, was alone, called forth in advance of the mass of men to hear the truth, to learn the meaning, which now at last, after all the toils of civilisation – Greeks, Romans, Shakespeare, Darwin, and now himself – was to be given whole to . . . 'To whom?' he asked aloud, 'To the Prime Minister,' the voices which rustled above his head replied. The supreme secret must be told to the Cabinet; first, that trees are alive; next, there is no crime; next, love, universal love, he muttered, gasping, trembling, painfully drawing out these profound truths which needed, so deep were they, so difficult, an immense effort to speak out, but the world was entirely changed by them for ever.

No crime; love; he repeated, fumbling for his card and pencil, when a Skye terrier snuffed his trousers and he started in an agony of fear. It was turning into a man! He could not watch it happen! It was horrible, terrible to see a dog become a man! At once the dog trotted away.

Heaven was divinely merciful, infinitely benignant. It spared him, pardoned his weakness. But what was the scientific explanation (for one must be scientific above all things)? Why could he see through bodies, see into the future, when dogs will become men? It was the heat wave presumably, operating upon a brain made sensitive by eons of evolution. Scientifically speaking, the flesh was melted off the world. His body was macerated until only the nerve fibres were left. It was spread like a veil upon a rock.

He lay back in his chair, exhausted but upheld. He lay resting, waiting, before he again interpreted, with effort, with agony, to mankind. He lay very high, on the back of the world. The earth thrilled beneath him. Red flowers grew through his flesh; their stiff leaves rustled by his head. Music began clanging against the rocks up here. It is a motor horn down in the street, he muttered; but up here it cannoned from rock to rock, divided, met in shocks of sound which rose in smooth columns (that music should be visible was a discovery) and became an anthem, an anthem twined round now by a shepherd boy's piping (That's an old man playing a penny whistle by the public-house, he muttered) which, as the boy stood still, came bubbling from his pipe, and then, as he climbed higher, made its exquisite plaint while the traffic passed beneath. This boy's elegy is played among the traffic, thought Septimus. Now he withdraws up into the snows, and roses hang about him – the thick red roses which grow on my bedroom wall, he reminded himself. The music stopped. He has his penny, he reasoned it out, and has gone on to the next public-house.

But he himself remained high on his rock, like a drowned sailor on a rock. I leant over the edge of the boat and fell down, he thought. I went under the sea. I have been dead, and yet am now alive, but let me rest still, he begged (he was talking to

himself again – it was awful, awful!); and as, before waking, the
voices of birds and the sound of wheels chime and chatter in a
queer harmony, grow louder and louder, and the sleeper feels
himself drawing to the shores of life, so he felt himself drawing
towards life, the sun growing hotter, cries sounding louder,
something tremendous about to happen.

He had only to open his eyes; but a weight was on them; a
fear. He strained; he pushed; he looked; he saw Regent's Park
before him. Long streamers of sunlight fawned at his feet. The
trees waved, brandished. We welcome, the world seemed to say;
we accept; we create. Beauty, the world seemed to say. And as if
to prove it (scientifically) wherever he looked, at the houses, at
the railings, at the antelopes stretching over the palings, beauty
sprang instantly. To watch a leaf quivering in the rush of air was
an exquisite joy. Up in the sky swallows swooping, swerving,
flinging themselves in and out, round and round, yet always
with perfect control as if elastics held them; and the flies rising
and falling; and the sun spotting now this leaf, now that, in
mockery, dazzling it with soft gold in pure good temper; and
now and again some chime (it might be a motor horn) tinkling
divinely on the grass stalks – all of this, calm and reasonable as
it was, made out of ordinary things as it was, was the truth now;
beauty, that was the truth now. Beauty was everywhere.

'It is time,' said Rezia.

The word 'time' split its husk; poured its riches over him; and
from his lips fell like shells, like shavings from a plane, without
his making them, hard, white, imperishable, words, and flew to
attach themselves to their places in an ode to Time; an immortal
ode to Time. He sang. Evans answered from behind the tree.
The dead were in Thessaly, Evans sang, among the orchids.
There they waited till the War was over, and now the dead, now
Evans himself –

'For God's sake don't come!' Septimus cried out. For he could
not look upon the dead.

But the branches parted. A man in grey was actually walking towards them. It was Evans! But no mud was on him; no
wounds; he was not changed. I must tell the whole world, Sep-

timus cried, raising his hand (as the dead man in the grey suit came nearer), raising his hand like some colossal figure who has lamented the fate of man for ages in the desert alone with his hands pressed to his forehead, furrows of despair on his cheeks, and now sees light on the desert's edge which broadens and strikes the iron-black figure (and Septimus half rose from his chair), and with legions of men prostrate behind him he, the giant mourner, receives for one moment on his face the whole –

'But I am so unhappy, Septimus,' said Rezia, trying to make him sit down.

The millions lamented; for ages they had sorrowed. He would turn round, he would tell them in a few moments, only a few moments more, of this relief, of this joy, of this astonishing revelation –

'The time, Septimus,' Rezia repeated. 'What is the time?'

He was talking, he was starting, this man must notice him. He was looking at them.

'I will tell you the time,' said Septimus, very slowly, very drowsily, smiling mysteriously at the dead man in the grey suit. As he sat smiling, the quarter struck – the quarter to twelve.

And that is being young, Peter Walsh thought as he passed them. To be having an awful scene – the poor girl looked absolutely desperate – in the middle of the morning. But what was it about, he wondered; what had the young man in the overcoat been saying to her to make her look like that; what awful fix had they got themselves into, both to look so desperate as that on a fine summer morning? The amusing thing about coming back to England, after five years, was the way it made, anyhow the first days, things stand out as if one had never seen them before; lovers squabbling under a tree; the domestic family life of the parks. Never had he seen London look so enchanting – the softness of the distances; the richness; the greenness; the civilisation, after India, he thought, strolling across the grass.

This susceptibility to impressions had been his undoing, no doubt. Still at his age he had, like a boy or a girl even, these alternations of mood; good days, bad days, for no reason whatever, happiness from a pretty face, downright misery at the sight of a frump. After India of course one fell in love with every woman one met. There was a freshness about them; even the poorest dressed better than five years ago surely; and to his eye the fashions had never been so becoming; the long black cloaks; the slimness; the elegance; and then the delicious and apparently universal habit of paint. Every woman, even the most respectable, had roses blooming under glass; lips cut with a knife; curls of Indian ink; there was design, art, everywhere; a change of some sort had undoubtedly taken place. What did the young people think about? Peter Walsh asked himself.

Those five years – 1918 to 1923 – had been, he suspected, somehow very important. People looked different. Newspapers seemed different. Now, for instance, there was a man writing quite openly in one of the respectable weeklies about water-closets. That you couldn't have done ten years ago – written quite openly about water-closets in a respectable weekly. And then this taking out a stick of rouge, or a powder-puff, and making up in public. On board ship coming home there were lots of young men and girls – Betty and Bertie he remembered in particular – carrying on quite openly; the old mother sitting and watching them with her knitting, cool as a cucumber. The girl would stand still and powder her nose in front of every one. And they weren't engaged; just having a good time; no feelings hurt on either side. As hard as nails she was – Betty Whatshername – but a thorough good sort. She would make a very good wife at thirty – she would marry when it suited her to marry; marry some rich man and live in a large house near Manchester.

Who was it now who had done that? Peter Walsh asked himself, turning into the Broad Walk – married a rich man and lived in a large house near Manchester? Somebody who had written him a long, gushing letter quite lately about 'blue hydrangeas'. It was seeing blue hydrangeas that made her think of him and the old days – Sally Seton, of course! It was Sally Seton – the last person in the world one would have expected to marry a rich man and live in a large house near Manchester, the wild, the daring, the romantic Sally!

But of all that ancient lot, Clarissa's friends – Whitbreads,

Kindersleys, Cunninghams, Kinloch-Joneses – Sally was probably the best. She tried to get hold of things by the right end
anyhow. She saw through Hugh Whitbread anyhow – the admirable Hugh – when Clarissa and the rest were at his feet.

'The Whitbreads?' he could hear her saying. 'Who are the
Whitbreads? Coal merchants. Respectable tradespeople.'

Hugh she detested for some reason. He thought of nothing
but his own appearance, she said. He ought to have been a
Duke. He would be certain to marry one of the Royal Princesses. And of course Hugh had the most extraordinary, the
most natural, the most sublime respect for the British aristoc-
racy of any human being he had ever come across. Even Clarissa
had to own that. Oh, but he was such a dear, so unselfish, gave
up shooting to please his old mother – remembered his aunts'
birthdays, and so on.

Sally, to do her justice, saw through all that. One of the things
he remembered best was an argument one Sunday morning at
Bourton about women's rights (that antediluvian topic),⁴⁰ when
Sally suddenly lost her temper, flared up, and told Hugh that he
represented all that was most detestable in British middle-class
life. She told him that she considered him responsible for the
state of 'those poor girls in Piccadilly' – Hugh, the perfect gentleman, poor Hugh! – never did a man look more horrified! She
did it on purpose, she said afterwards (for they used to get together in the vegetable garden and compare notes). 'He's read
nothing, thought nothing, felt nothing,' he could hear her saying in that very emphatic voice which carried so much farther
than she knew. The stable boys had more life in them than
Hugh, she said. He was a perfect specimen of the public school
type, she said. No country but England could have produced
him. She was really spiteful, for some reason; had some grudge
against him. Something had happened – he forgot what – in the
smoking-room. He had insulted her – kissed her? Incredible!
Nobody believed a word against Hugh, of course. Who could?
Kissing Sally in the smoking-room! If it had been some Honourable Edith or Lady Violet, perhaps; but not that ragamuffin
Sally without a penny to her name, and a father or a mother

gambling at Monte Carlo. For of all the people he had ever met Hugh was the greatest snob – the most obsequious – no, he didn't cringe exactly. He was too much of a prig for that. A first-rate valet was the obvious comparison – somebody who walked behind carrying suit cases; could be trusted to send telegrams – indispensable to hostesses. And he'd found his job – married his Honourable Evelyn; got some little post at Court, looked after the King's cellars, polished the Imperial shoe-buckles, went about in knee-breeches and lace ruffles. How remorseless life is! A little job at Court!

He had married this lady, the Honourable Evelyn, and they lived hereabouts, so he thought (looking at the pompous houses overlooking the Park), for he had lunched there once in a house which had, like all Hugh's possessions, something that no other house could possibly have – linen cupboards it might have been. You had to go and look at them – you had to spend a great deal of time always admiring whatever it was – linen cupboards, pillow-cases, old oak furniture, pictures, which Hugh had picked up for an old song. But Mrs. Hugh sometimes gave the show away. She was one of those obscure mouse-like little women who admire big men. She was almost negligible. Then suddenly she would say something quite unexpected – something sharp. She had the relics of the grand manner, perhaps. The steam coal was a little too strong for her – it made the atmosphere thick. And so there they lived, with their linen cupboards and their old masters and their pillow-cases fringed with real lace, at the rate of five or ten thousand a year presumably, while he, who was two years older than Hugh, cadged for a job.

At fifty-three he had to come and ask them to put him into some secretary's office, to find him some usher's job teaching little boys Latin, at the beck and call of some mandarin in an office, something that brought in five hundred a year; for if he married Daisy, even with his pension, they could never do on less. Whitbread could do it presumably; or Dalloway. He didn't mind what he asked Dalloway. He was a thorough good sort; a bit limited; a bit thick in the head; yes; but a thorough good sort. Whatever he took up he did in the same matter-of-fact sensible way; without a touch of imagination, without a spark of brilliancy, but with the inexplicable niceness of his type. He ought to have been a country gentleman – he was wasted on politics. He was at his best out of doors, with horses and dogs – how good he was, for instance, when that great shaggy dog of Clarissa's got caught in a trap and had its paw half torn off, and Clarissa turned faint and Dalloway did the whole thing; bandaged, made splints; told Clarissa not to be a fool. That was what she liked him for, perhaps – that was what she needed. 'Now, my dear, don't be a fool. Hold this – fetch that,' all the time talking to the dog as if it were a human being.

But how could she swallow all that stuff about poetry? How could she let him hold forth about Shakespeare? Seriously and solemnly Richard Dalloway got on his hind legs and said that no decent man ought to read Shakespeare's sonnets because it was like listening at keyholes (besides, the relationship was not one that he approved). No decent man ought to let his wife visit a deceased wife's sister. Incredible! The only thing to do was to pelt him with sugared almonds – it was at dinner. But Clarissa sucked it all in; thought it so honest of him; so independent of him; Heaven knows if she didn't think him the most original mind she'd ever met!

That was one of the bonds between Sally and himself. There was a garden where they used to walk, a walled-in place, with rose-bushes and giant cauliflowers – he could remember Sally tearing off a rose, stopping to exclaim at the beauty of the cabbage leaves in the moonlight (it was extraordinary how vividly it all came back to him, things he hadn't thought of for years), while she implored him, half laughing of course, to carry off Clarissa, to save her from the Hughs and the Dalloways and all the other 'perfect gentlemen' who would 'stifle her soul' (she wrote reams of poetry in those days), make a mere hostess of her, encourage her worldliness. But one must do Clarissa justice. She wasn't going to marry Hugh anyhow. She had a perfectly clear notion of what she wanted. Her emotions were all on the surface. Beneath, she was very shrewd – a far better judge of character than Sally, for instance, and with it all, purely feminine; with

that extraordinary gift, that woman's gift, of making a world of
her own wherever she happened to be. She came into a room; she
stood, as he had often seen her, in a doorway with lots of people
round her. But it was Clarissa one remembered. Not that she was
striking; not beautiful at all; there was nothing picturesque
about her; she never said anything specially clever; there she was,
however; there she was.

No, no, no! He was not in love with her any more! He only
felt, after seeing her that morning, among her scissors and silks,
making ready for the party, unable to get away from the thought
of her; she kept coming back and back like a sleeper jolting
against him in a railway carriage; which was not being in love,
of course; it was thinking of her, criticising her, starting again,
after thirty years, trying to explain her. The obvious thing to say
of her was that she was worldly; cared too much for rank and
society and getting on in the world – which was true in a sense;
she had admitted it to him. (You could always get her to own up
if you took the trouble; she was honest.) What she would say
was that she hated frumps, fogies, failures, like himself presumably; thought people had no right to slouch about with their
hands in their pockets; must do something, be something; and
these great swells, these Duchesses, these hoary old Countesses
one met in her drawing-room, unspeakably remote as he felt
them to be from anything that mattered a straw, stood for something real to her. Lady Bexborough, she said once, held herself
upright (so did Clarissa herself; she never lounged in any sense
of the word; she was straight as a dart, a little rigid in fact). She
said they had a kind of courage which the older she grew the
more she respected. In all this there was a great deal of Dalloway, of course; a great deal of the public-spirited, British Empire, tariff-reform,[41] governing-class spirit, which had grown on
her, as it tends to do. With twice his wits, she had to see things
through his eyes – one of the tragedies of married life. With a
mind of her own, she must always be quoting Richard – as if
one couldn't know to a tittle what Richard thought by reading
the *Morning Post*[42] of a morning! These parties, for example,
were all for him, or for her idea of him (to do Richard justice he

would have been happier farming in Norfolk). She made her drawing-room a sort of meeting-place; she had a genius for it. Over and over again he had seen her take some raw youth, twist him, turn him, wake him up; set him going. Infinite numbers of dull people conglomerated round her, of course. But odd unexpected people turned up; an artist sometimes; sometimes a writer; queer fish in that atmosphere. And behind it all was that network of visiting, leaving cards, being kind to people; running about with bunches of flowers, little presents; So-and-so was going to France – must have an air-cushion; a real drain on her strength; all that interminable traffic that women of her sort keep up; but she did it genuinely, from a natural instinct.

Oddly enough, she was one of the most thoroughgoing sceptics he had ever met, and possibly (this was a theory he used to make up to account for her, so transparent in some ways, so inscrutable in others), possibly she said to herself, As we are a doomed race, chained to a sinking ship (her favourite reading as a girl was Huxley and Tyndall,[43] and they were fond of these nautical metaphors), as the whole thing is a bad joke, let us, at any rate, do our part; mitigate the sufferings of our fellow-prisoners (Huxley again); decorate the dungeon with flowers and air-cushions; be as decent as we possibly can. Those ruffians, the Gods, shan't have it all their own way – her notion being that the Gods, who never lost a chance of hurting, thwarting and spoiling human lives, were seriously put out if, all the same, you behaved like a lady. That phase came directly after Sylvia's death – that horrible affair. To see your own sister killed by a falling tree (all Justin Parry's fault – all his carelessness) before your very eyes, a girl too on the verge of life, the most gifted of them, Clarissa always said, was enough to turn one bitter. Later she wasn't so positive, perhaps; she thought there were no Gods; no one was to blame; and so she evolved this atheist's religion of doing good for the sake of goodness.

And of course she enjoyed life immensely. It was her nature to enjoy (though, goodness only knows, she had her reserves; it was a mere sketch, he often felt, that even he, after all these years, could make of Clarissa). Anyhow there was no bitterness in her; none of that sense of moral virtue which is so repulsive in good women. She enjoyed practically everything. If you walked with her in Hyde Park now it was a bed of tulips, now a child in a perambulator, now some absurd little drama she made up on the spur of the moment. (Very likely she would have talked to those lovers, if she had thought them unhappy.) She had a sense of comedy that was really exquisite, but she needed people, always people, to bring it out, with the inevitable result that she frittered her time away, lunching, dining, giving these incessant parties of hers, talking nonsense, saying things she didn't mean, blunting the edge of her mind, losing her discrimination. There she would sit at the head of the table taking infinite pains with some old buffer who might be useful to Dalloway – they knew the most appalling bores in Europe – or in came Elizabeth and every thing must give way to *her*. She was at a High School, at the inarticulate stage last time he was over, a round-eyed, pale-faced girl, with nothing of her mother in her, a silent stolid creature, who took it all as a matter of course, let her mother make a fuss of her, and then said 'May I go now?' like a child of four; going off, Clarissa explained, with that mixture of amusement and pride which Dalloway himself seemed to rouse in her, to play hockey. And now Elizabeth was 'out', presumably; thought him an old fogy, laughed at her mother's friends. Ah well, so be it. The compensation of growing old, Peter Walsh thought, coming out of Regent's Park, and holding his hat in hand, was simply this; that the passions remain as strong as ever, but one has gained – at last! – the power which adds the supreme flavour to existence – the power of taking hold of experience, of turning it round, slowly, in the light.

A terrible confession it was (he put his hat on again), but now, at the age of fifty-three, one scarcely needed people any more. Life itself, every moment of it, every drop of it, here, this instant, now, in the sun, in Regent's Park, was enough. Too much, indeed. A whole lifetime was too short to bring out, now that one had acquired the power, the full flavour; to extract every ounce of pleasure, every shade of meaning; which both were so much more solid than they used to be, so much less personal. It was impossible that he should ever suffer again as Clarissa had made him suffer. For hours at a time (pray God that one might say these things without being overheard!), for hours and days he never thought of Daisy.

Could it be that he was in love with her, then, remembering the misery, the torture, the extraordinary passion of those days? It was a different thing altogether – a much pleasanter thing – the truth being, of course, that now *she* was in love with *him*. And that perhaps was the reason why, when the ship actually sailed, he felt an extraordinary relief, wanted nothing so much as to be alone; was annoyed to find all her little attentions – cigars, notes, a rug for the voyage – in his cabin. Every one if they were honest would say the same; one doesn't want people after fifty; one doesn't want to go on telling women they are pretty; that's what most men of fifty would say, Peter Walsh thought, if they were honest.

But then these astonishing accesses of emotion – bursting into tears this morning, what was all that about? What could Clarissa have thought of him? thought him a fool presumably, not for the first time. It was jealousy that was at the bottom of it – jealousy which survives every other passion of mankind, Peter Walsh thought, holding his pocket-knife at arm's length. She had been meeting Major Orde, Daisy said in her last letter; said it on purpose, he knew; said it to make him jealous; he could see her wrinkling her forehead as she wrote, wondering what she could say to hurt him; and yet it made no difference; he was furious! All this pother of coming to England and seeing lawyers wasn't to marry her, but to prevent her from marrying anybody else. That was what tortured him, that was what came over him when he saw Clarissa so calm, so cold, so intent on her dress or whatever it was; realising what she might have spared him, what she had reduced him to – a whimpering, snivelling old ass. But women, he thought, shutting his pocket-knife, don't know what passion is. They don't know the meaning of it to men. Clarissa was as cold as an icicle. There she would sit on the sofa by his side, let him take her hand, give him one kiss on the cheek – Here he was at the crossing.

A sound interrupted him;[44] a frail quivering sound, a voice
bubbling up without direction, vigour, beginning or end, running weakly and shrilly and with an absence of all human meaning into

> ee um fah um so
> foo swee too eem oo –

the voice of no age or sex, the voice of an ancient spring spouting
from the earth; which issued, just opposite Regent's Park Tube
Station, from a tall quivering shape, like a funnel, like a rusty
pump, like a wind-beaten tree for ever barren of leaves which
lets the wind run up and down its branches singing

> ee um fah um so
> foo swee too eem oo,

and rocks and creaks and moans in the eternal breeze.

Through all ages – when the pavement was grass, when it was
swamp, through the age of tusk and mammoth, through the age
of silent sunrise – the battered woman – for she wore a skirt –
with her right hand exposed, her left clutching at her side, stood
singing of love[45] – love which has lasted a million years, she sang,
love which prevails, and millions of years ago, her lover, who had
been dead these centuries, had walked, she crooned, with her in
May; but in the course of ages, long as summer days, and flam-
ing, she remembered, with nothing but red asters, he had gone;
death's enormous sickle had swept those tremendous hills, and
when at last she laid her hoary and immensely aged head on the
earth, now become a mere cinder of ice, she implored the Gods
to lay by her side a bunch of purple heather, there on her high
burial place which the last rays of the last sun caressed; for then
the pageant of the universe would be over.

As the ancient song bubbled up opposite Regent's Park Tube
Station, still the earth seemed green and flowery; still, though it
issued from so rude a mouth, a mere hole in the earth, muddy
too, matted with root fibres and tangled grasses, still the old

bubbling burbling song, soaking through the knotted roots of infinite ages, and skeletons and treasure, streamed away in rivulets over the pavement and all along the Marylebone Road, and down towards Euston, fertilising, leaving a damp stain.

Still remembering how once in some primeval May she had walked with her lover, this rusty pump, this battered old woman with one hand exposed for coppers, the other clutching her side, would still be there in ten million years, remembering how once she had walked in May, where the sea flows now, with whom it did not matter – he was a man, oh yes, a man who had loved her. But the passage of ages had blurred the clarity of that ancient May day; the bright petalled flowers were hoar and silver frosted; and she no longer saw, when she implored him (as she did now quite clearly) 'look in my eyes with thy sweet eyes intently,' she no longer saw brown eyes, black whiskers or sunburnt face, but only a looming shape, a shadow shape, to which, with the bird-like freshness of the very aged, she still twittered 'give me your hand and let me press it gently' (Peter Walsh couldn't help giving the poor creature a coin as he stepped into his taxi), 'and if some one should see, what matter they?' she demanded; and her fist clutched at her side, and she smiled, pocketing her shilling, and all peering inquisitive eyes seemed blotted out, and the passing generations – the pavement was crowded with bustling middle-class people – vanished, like leaves, to be trodden under, to be soaked and steeped and made mould of by that eternal spring –

> ee um fah um so
> foo swee too eem oo.

'Poor old woman,' said Rezia Warren Smith.

Oh poor old wretch! she said, waiting to cross.

Suppose it was a wet night? Suppose one's father, or somebody who had known one in better days had happened to pass, and saw one standing there in the gutter? And where did she sleep at night?

Cheerfully, almost gaily, the invincible thread of sound wound up into the air like the smoke from a cottage chimney, winding up clean beech trees and issuing in a tuft of blue smoke among the topmost leaves. 'And if some one should see, what matter they?'

Since she was so unhappy, for weeks and weeks now, Rezia had given meanings to things that happened, almost felt sometimes that she must stop people in the street, if they looked good, kind people, just to say to them 'I am unhappy'; and this old woman singing in the street 'if some one should see, what matter they?' made her suddenly quite sure that everything was going to be right. They were going to Sir William Bradshaw; she thought his name sounded nice; he would cure Septimus at once. And then there was a brewer's cart, and the grey horses had upright bristles of straw in their tails; there were newspaper placards. It was a silly, silly dream, being unhappy.

So they crossed, Mr. and Mrs. Septimus Warren Smith, and was there, after all, anything to draw attention to them, anything to make a passer-by suspect here is a young man who carries in him the greatest message in the world, and is, moreover, the happiest man in the world, and the most miserable? Perhaps they walked more slowly than other people, and there was something hesitating, trailing, in the man's walk, but what more natural for a clerk, who has not been in the West End on a week-day at this hour for years, than to keep looking at the sky, looking at this, that and the other, as if Portland Place were a room he had come into when the family are away, the chandeliers being hung in holland bags, and the caretaker, as she lets in long shafts of dusty light upon deserted, queer-looking armchairs, lifting one corner of the long blinds, explains to the visitors what a wonderful place it is; how wonderful, but at the same time, he thinks, how strange.

To look at, he might have been a clerk, but of the better sort; for he wore brown boots; his hands were educated; so, too, his profile – his angular, big-nosed, intelligent, sensitive profile; but not his lips altogether, for they were loose; and his eyes (as eyes tend to be), eyes merely; hazel, large; so that he was, on the whole, a border case, neither one thing nor the other; might end with a house at Purley and a motor car, or continue renting apartments in back streets all his life; one of those half-educated, self-educated men whose education is all learnt from books borrowed from public libraries, read in the evening after the day's work, on the advice of well-known authors consulted by letter.

As for the other experiences, the solitary ones, which people go through alone, in their bedrooms, in their offices, walking the fields and the streets of London, he had them; had left home, a mere boy, because of his mother; she lied; because he came down to tea for the fiftieth time with his hands unwashed; because he could see no future for a poet in Stroud; and so, making a confidant of his little sister, had gone to London leaving an absurd note behind him, such as great men have written, and the world has read later when the story of their struggles has become famous.

London has swallowed up many millions of young men called Smith; thought nothing of fantastic Christian names like Septimus with which their parents have thought to distinguish them. Lodging off the Euston Road, there were experiences, again experiences, such as change a face in two years from a pink innocent oval to a face lean, contracted, hostile. But of all this what could the most observant of friends have said except what a gardener says when he opens the conservatory door in the morning and finds a new blossom on his plant: – It has flowered; flowered from vanity, ambition, idealism, passion, loneliness, courage, laziness, the usual seeds, which all muddled up (in a room off the Euston Road), made him shy, and stammering, made him anxious to improve himself, made him fall in love with Miss Isabel Pole, lecturing in the Waterloo Road[46] upon Shakespeare.

Was he not like Keats? she asked; and reflected how she might give him a taste of *Antony and Cleopatra* and the rest; lent him books; wrote him scraps of letters; and lit in him such a fire as burns only once in a lifetime, without heat, flickering a red gold flame infinitely ethereal and insubstantial over Miss Pole; *Antony and Cleopatra*; and the Waterloo Road. He thought her beautiful, believed her impeccably wise; dreamed of her, wrote poems to her, which, ignoring the subject, she corrected in red ink; he saw her, one summer evening, walking in a green dress in a square. 'It has flowered,' the gardener might have said, had he opened the door; had he come in, that is to say, any night about this time, and found him writing; found him tearing up his writing; found him finishing a masterpiece at three o'clock in the morning and running out to pace the streets, and visiting churches, and fasting one day, drinking another, devouring Shakespeare, Darwin, *The History of Civilisation*, and Bernard Shaw.[47]

Something was up, Mr. Brewer knew; Mr. Brewer, managing clerk at Sibleys and Arrowsmiths, auctioneers, valuers, land and estate agents; something was up, he thought, and, being paternal with his young men, and thinking very highly of Smith's abilities, and prophesying that he would, in ten or fifteen years, succeed to the leather arm-chair in the inner room under the skylight with the deed-boxes round him, 'if he keeps his health,' said Mr. Brewer, and that was the danger – he looked weakly; advised football, invited him to supper and was seeing his way to consider recommending a rise of salary, when something happened which threw out many of Mr. Brewer's calculations, took away his ablest young fellows, and eventually, so prying and insidious were the fingers of the European War, smashed a plaster cast of Ceres, ploughed a hole in the geranium beds, and utterly ruined the cook's nerves at Mr. Brewer's establishment at Muswell Hill.

Septimus was one of the first to volunteer. He went to France to save an England which consisted almost entirely of Shakespeare's plays and Miss Isabel Pole in a green dress walking in a square. There in the trenches the change which Mr. Brewer desired when he advised football was produced instantly; he developed manliness; he was promoted; he drew the attention, indeed the affection of his officer, Evans by name. It was a case of two dogs playing on a hearth-rug; one worrying a paper screw, snarling, snapping, giving a pinch, now and then, at the old dog's ear; the other lying somnolent, blinking at the fire, raising a paw, turning and growling good-temperedly. They had to be together, share with each other, fight with each other, quarrel with each other. But when Evans (Rezia, who had only seen him once, called him 'a quiet man', a sturdy red-haired man, undemonstrative in the company of women), when Evans was killed, just before the Armistice, in Italy, Septimus, far from showing any emotion or recognising that here was the end of a friendship, congratulated himself upon feeling very little and very reasonably. The War had taught him. It was sublime. He had gone through the whole show, friendship, European War, death, had won promotion, was still under thirty and was bound to survive. He was right there. The last shells missed him. He watched them explode with indifference. When peace came he was in Milan, billeted in the house of an innkeeper with a court-yard, flowers in tubs, little tables in the open, daughters making hats, and to Lucrezia, the younger daughter, he became engaged one evening when the panic was on him – that he could not feel.

For now that it was all over, truce signed, and the dead buried, he had, especially in the evening, these sudden thunder-claps of fear. He could not feel. As he opened the door of the room where the Italian girls sat making hats, he could see them; could hear them; they were rubbing wires among coloured beads in saucers; they were turning buckram shapes this way and that; the table was all strewn with feathers, spangles, silks, ribbons; scissors were rapping on the table; but something failed him; he could not feel. Still, scissors rapping, girls laughing, hats being made protected him; he was assured of safety; he had a refuge. But he could not sit there all night. There were moments of waking in the early morning. The bed was falling; he was falling. Oh for the scissors and the lamplight and the buckram shapes! He asked Lucrezia to marry him, the younger of the two, the gay, the frivolous, with those little artist's fingers that she would hold up and say 'It is all in them.' Silk, feathers, what not were alive to them.

'It is the hat that matters most,' she would say, when they walked out together. Every hat that passed, she would examine; and the cloak and the dress and the way the woman held herself. Ill-dressing, over-dressing she stigmatised, not savagely, rather with impatient movements of the hands, like those of a painter who puts from him some obvious well-meant glaring imposture; and then, generously, but always critically, she would welcome a shop-girl who had turned her little bit of stuff gallantly, or praise, wholly, with enthusiastic and professional understanding, a French lady descending from her carriage, in chinchilla, robes, pearls.

'Beautiful!' she would murmur, nudging Septimus, that he might see. But beauty was behind a pane of glass. Even taste (Rezia liked ices, chocolates, sweet things) had no relish to him. He put down his cup on the little marble table. He looked at people outside; happy they seemed, collecting in the middle of the street, shouting, laughing, squabbling over nothing. But he could not taste, he could not feel. In the tea-shop among the tables and the chattering waiters the appalling fear came over him – he could not feel. He could reason; he could read, Dante for example, quite easily ('Septimus, do put down your book,' said Rezia, gently shutting the *Inferno*), he could add up his bill; his brain was perfect; it must be the fault of the world then – that he could not feel.

'The English are so silent,' Rezia said. She liked it, she said. She respected these Englishmen, and wanted to see London, and the English horses, and the tailor-made suits, and could remember hearing how wonderful the shops were, from an aunt who had married and lived in Soho.

It might be possible, Septimus thought, looking at England from the train window, as they left Newhaven; it might be possible that the world itself is without meaning.

At the office they advanced him to a post of considerable responsibility. They were proud of him; he had won crosses. 'You have done your duty; it is up to us——' began Mr. Brewer; and could not finish, so pleasurable was his emotion. They took admirable lodgings off the Tottenham Court Road.

Here he opened Shakespeare once more. That boy's business of the intoxication of language – *Antony and Cleopatra* – had shrivelled utterly. How Shakespeare loathed humanity – the putting on of clothes, the getting of children, the sordidity of the mouth and the belly! This was now revealed to Septimus; the message hidden in the beauty of words. The secret signal which one generation passes, under disguise, to the next is loathing, hatred, despair. Dante the same. Aeschylus (translated) the same. There Rezia sat at the table trimming hats. She trimmed hats for Mrs. Filmer's friends; she trimmed hats by the hour. She looked pale, mysterious, like a lily, drowned, under water, he thought.

'The English are so serious,' she would say, putting her arms round Septimus, her cheek against his.

Love between man and woman was repulsive to Shakespeare. The business of copulation was filth to him before the end. But, Rezia said, she must have children. They had been married five years.

They went to the Tower together; to the Victoria and Albert Museum; stood in the crowd to see the King open Parliament. And there were the shops – hat shops, dress shops, shops with leather bags in the window, where she would stand staring. But she must have a boy.

She must have a son like Septimus, she said. But nobody could be like Septimus; so gentle; so serious; so clever. Could she not read Shakespeare too? Was Shakespeare a difficult author? she asked.

One cannot bring children into a world like this. One cannot perpetuate suffering, or increase the breed of these lustful animals, who have no lasting emotions, but only whims and vanities, eddying them now this way, now that.

He watched her snip, shape, as one watches a bird hop, flit in the grass, without daring to move a finger. For the truth is (let her ignore it) that human beings have neither kindness, nor faith, nor charity beyond what serves to increase the pleasure of the moment. They hunt in packs. Their packs scour the desert and vanish screaming into the wilderness. They desert the fallen. They are plastered over with grimaces. There was Brewer at the office, with his waxed moustache, coral tie-pin, white slip, and pleasurable emotions – all coldness and clamminess within, – his geraniums ruined in the War – his cook's nerves destroyed; or

Amelia Whatshername, handing round cups of tea punctually at five – a leering, sneering obscene little harpy; and the Toms and Berties in their starched shirt fronts oozing thick drops of vice. They never saw him drawing pictures of them naked at their antics in his notebook. In the street, vans roared past him; brutality blared out on placards; men were trapped in mines; women burnt alive; and once a maimed file of lunatics being exercised or displayed for the diversion of the populace (who laughed aloud), ambled and nodded and grinned past him, in the Tottenham Court Road, each half apologetically, yet triumphantly, inflicting his hopeless woe. And would *he* go mad?

At tea Rezia told him that Mrs. Filmer's daughter was expecting a baby. *She* could not grow old and have no children! She was very lonely, she was very unhappy! She cried for the first time since they were married. Far away he heard her sobbing; he heard it accurately, he noticed it distinctly; he compared it to a piston thumping. But he felt nothing.

His wife was crying, and he felt nothing; only each time she sobbed in this profound, this silent, this hopeless way, he descended another step into the pit.

At last, with a melodramatic gesture which he assumed mechanically and with complete consciousness of its insincerity, he dropped his head on his hands. Now he had surrendered; now other people must help him. People must be sent for. He gave in.

Nothing could rouse him. Rezia put him to bed. She sent for a doctor – Mrs. Filmer's Dr. Holmes. Dr. Holmes examined him. There was nothing whatever the matter, said Dr. Holmes. Oh, what a relief! What a kind man, what a good man! thought Rezia. When he felt like that he went to the music hall, said Dr. Holmes. He took a day off with his wife and played golf. Why not try two tabloids of bromide dissolved in a glass of water at bedtime? These old Bloomsbury houses, said Dr. Holmes, tapping the wall, are often full of very fine panelling, which the landlords have the folly to paper over. Only the other day, visiting a patient, Sir Somebody Something, in Bedford Square——

So there was no excuse; nothing whatever the matter, except the sin for which human nature had condemned him to death;

that he did not feel. He had not cared when Evans was killed; that was worst; but all the other crimes raised their heads and shook their fingers and jeered and sneered over the rail of the bed in the early hours of the morning at the prostrate body which lay realising its degradation; how he had married his wife without loving her; had lied to her; seduced her; outraged Miss Isabel Pole, and was so pocked and marked with vice that women shuddered when they saw him in the street. The verdict of human nature on such a wretch was death.

Dr. Holmes came again. Large, fresh-coloured, handsome, flicking his boots, looking in the glass, he brushed it all aside – headaches, sleeplessness, fears, dreams – nerve symptoms and nothing more, he said. If Dr. Holmes found himself even half a pound below eleven stone six, he asked his wife for another plate of porridge at breakfast. (Rezia would learn to cook porridge.) But, he continued, health is largely a matter in our own control. Throw yourself into outside interests; take up some hobby. He opened Shakespeare – *Antony and Cleopatra*; pushed Shakespeare aside. Some hobby, said Dr. Holmes, for did he not owe his own excellent health (and he worked as hard as any man in London) to the fact that he could always switch off from his patients on to old furniture? And what a very pretty comb, if he might say so, Mrs. Warren Smith was wearing!

When the damned fool came again, Septimus refused to see him. Did he indeed? said Dr. Holmes, smiling agreeably. Really he had to give that charming little lady, Mrs. Smith, a friendly push before he could get past her into her husband's bedroom.

'So you're in a funk,' he said agreeably, sitting down by his patient's side. He had actually talked of killing himself to his wife, quite a girl, a foreigner, wasn't she? Didn't that give her a very odd idea of English husbands? Didn't one owe perhaps a duty to one's wife? Wouldn't it be better to do something instead of lying in bed? For he had had forty years' experience behind him; and Septimus could take Dr. Holmes's word for it – there was nothing whatever the matter with him. And next time Dr. Holmes came he hoped to find Smith out of bed and not making that charming little lady his wife anxious about him.

Human nature, in short, was on him – the repulsive brute, with the blood-red nostrils. Holmes was on him. Dr. Holmes came quite regularly every day. Once you stumble, Septimus wrote on the back of a postcard, human nature is on you. Holmes is on you. Their only chance was to escape, without letting Holmes know; to Italy – anywhere, anywhere, away from Dr. Holmes.

But Rezia could not understand him. Dr. Holmes was such a kind man. He was so interested in Septimus. He only wanted to help them, he said. He had four little children and he had asked her to tea, she told Septimus.

So he was deserted. The whole world was clamouring: Kill yourself, kill yourself, for our sakes. But why should he kill himself for their sakes? Food was pleasant; the sun hot; and this killing oneself, how does one set about it, with a table knife, uglily, with floods of blood, – by sucking a gaspipe? He was too weak; he could scarcely raise his hand. Besides, now that he was quite alone, condemned, deserted, as those who are about to die are alone, there was a luxury in it, an isolation full of sublimity; a freedom which the attached can never know. Holmes had won of course; the brute with the red nostrils had won. But even Holmes himself could not touch this last relic straying on the edge of the world, this outcast, who gazed back at the inhabited regions, who lay, like a drowned sailor, on the shore of the world.

It was at that moment (Rezia had gone shopping) that the great revelation took place. A voice spoke from behind the screen. Evans was speaking. The dead were with him.

'Evans, Evans!' he cried.

Mr. Smith was talking aloud to himself, Agnes the servant girl cried to Mrs. Filmer in the kitchen. 'Evans, Evans!' he had said as she brought in the tray. She jumped, she did. She scuttled downstairs.

And Rezia came in, with her flowers, and walked across the room, and put the roses in a vase, upon which the sun struck directly, and it went laughing, leaping round the room.

She had had to buy the roses, Rezia said, from a poor man in the street. But they were almost dead already, she said, arranging the roses.

So there was a man outside; Evans presumably; and the roses, which Rezia said were half dead, had been picked by him in the fields of Greece. Communication is health; communication is happiness. Communication, he muttered.

'What are you saying, Septimus?' Rezia asked, wild with terror, for he was talking to himself.

She sent Agnes running for Dr. Holmes. Her husband, she said, was mad. He scarcely knew her.

'You brute! You brute!' cried Septimus, seeing human nature, that is Dr. Holmes, enter the room.

'Now what's all this about,' said Dr. Holmes in the most amiable way in the world. 'Talking nonsense to frighten your wife?' But he would give him something to make him sleep. And if they were rich people, said Dr. Holmes, looking ironically round the room, by all means let them go to Harley Street; if they had no confidence in him, said Dr. Holmes, looking not quite so kind.

It was precisely twelve o'clock; twelve by Big Ben; whose stroke was wafted over the northern part of London; blent with that of other clocks, mixed in a thin ethereal way with the clouds and wisps of smoke and died up there among the seagulls – twelve o'clock struck as Clarissa Dalloway laid her green dress on her bed, and the Warren Smiths walked down Harley Street. Twelve was the hour of their appointment. Probably, Rezia thought, that was Sir William Bradshaw's house[48] with the grey motor car in front of it. (The leaden circles dissolved in the air.)

Indeed it was – Sir William Bradshaw's motor car; low, powerful, grey with plain initials interlocked on the panel, as if the pomps of heraldry were incongruous, this man being the ghostly helper, the priest of science; and, as the motor car was grey, so to match its sober suavity, grey furs, silver grey rugs were heaped in it, to keep her ladyship warm while she waited. For often Sir William would travel sixty miles or more down into the country to visit the rich, the afflicted, who could afford the very large fee which Sir William very properly charged for his advice. Her ladyship waited with the rugs about her knees an hour or more, leaning back, thinking sometimes of the patient, sometimes, excusably, of the wall of gold, mounting minute by minute while she waited; the wall of gold that was mounting between them and all shifts and anxieties (she had borne them bravely; they had had their struggles) until she felt wedged on a calm ocean, where only spice winds blow; respected, admired, envied, with scarcely anything left to wish for, though she regretted her stoutness; large dinner-parties every Thursday night to the profession; an occasional bazaar to be opened; Royalty greeted; too little time, alas, with her husband, whose work grew and grew; a boy doing well at Eton; she would have liked a daughter too; interests she had, however, in plenty; child welfare; the aftercare of the epileptic, and photography, so that if there was a church building, or a church decaying, she bribed the sexton, got the key and took photographs, which were scarcely to be distinguished from the work of professionals, while she waited.

Sir William himself was no longer young. He had worked very hard; he had won his position by sheer ability (being the son of a shopkeeper); loved his profession; made a fine figurehead at ceremonies and spoke well – all of which had by the time he was knighted given him a heavy look, a weary look (the stream of patients being so incessant, the responsibilities and privileges of his profession so onerous), which weariness, together with his grey hairs, increased the extraordinary distinction of his presence and gave him the reputation (of the utmost importance in dealing with nerve cases) not merely of lightning skill and almost infallible accuracy in diagnosis, but of sympathy; tact; understanding of the human soul. He could see the first moment they came into the room (the Warren Smiths they were called); he was certain directly he saw the man; it was a case of extreme gravity. It was a case of complete breakdown – complete physical and nervous breakdown, with every symptom in an advanced stage, he ascertained in two or three minutes (writing answers to questions, murmured discreetly, on a pink card).

How long had Dr. Holmes been attending him?

Six weeks.

Prescribed a little bromide? Said there was nothing the matter? Ah yes (those general practitioners! thought Sir William. It took half his time to undo their blunders. Some were irreparable).

'You served with great distinction in the War?'

The patient repeated the word 'war' interrogatively.

He was attaching meanings to words of a symbolical kind. A serious symptom to be noted on the card.

'The War?' the patient asked. The European War – that little shindy of schoolboys with gunpowder? Had he served with distinction? He really forgot. In the War itself he had failed.

'Yes, he served with the greatest distinction,' Rezia assured the doctor; 'he was promoted.'

'And they have the very highest opinion of you at your office?' Sir William murmured, glancing at Mr. Brewer's very generously worded letter. 'So that you have nothing to worry you, no financial anxiety, nothing?'

He had committed an appalling crime and been condemned to death by human nature.

'I have – I have,' he began, 'committed a crime——'

'He has done nothing wrong whatever,' Rezia assured the doctor. If Mr. Smith would wait, said Sir William, he would speak to Mrs. Smith in the next room. Her husband was very seriously ill, Sir William said. Did he threaten to kill himself?

Oh, he did, she cried. But he did not mean it, she said. Of course not. It was merely a question of rest, said Sir William; of rest, rest, rest; a long rest in bed. There was a delightful home down in the country where her husband would be perfectly looked after. Away from her? she asked. Unfortunately, yes; the people we care for most are not good for us when we are ill. But he was not mad, was he? Sir William said he never spoke of 'madness'; he called it not having a sense of proportion. But her husband did not like doctors. He would refuse to go there. Shortly and kindly Sir William explained to her the state of the case. He had threatened to kill himself. There was no alternative. It was a question of law. He would lie in bed in a beautiful house in the country. The nurses were admirable. Sir William would visit him once a week. If Mrs. Warren Smith was quite sure she had no more questions to ask – he never hurried his patients – they would return to her husband. She had nothing more to ask – not of Sir William.

So they returned to the most exalted of mankind; the criminal who faced his judges; the victim exposed on the heights; the fugitive; the drowned sailor; the poet of the immortal ode; the Lord who had gone from life to death; to Septimus Warren Smith, who sat in the armchair under the skylight staring at a photograph of Lady Bradshaw in Court dress, muttering messages about beauty.

'We have had our little talk,' said Sir William.

'He says you are very, very ill,' Rezia cried.

'We have been arranging that you should go into a home,' said Sir William.

'One of Holmes's homes?' sneered Septimus.

The fellow made a distasteful impression. For there was in Sir William, whose father had been a tradesman, a natural respect for breeding and clothing, which shabbiness nettled; again, more profoundly, there was in Sir William, who had never had time for reading, a grudge, deeply buried, against cultivated people who came into his room and intimated that doctors, whose profession is a constant strain upon all the highest faculties, are not educated men.

'One of *my* homes, Mr. Warren Smith,' he said, 'where we will teach you to rest.'

And there was just one thing more.

He was quite certain that when Mr. Warren Smith was well he was the last man in the world to frighten his wife. But he had talked of killing himself.

'We all have our moments of depression,' said Sir William.

Once you fall, Septimus repeated to himself, human nature is on you. Holmes and Bradshaw are on you. They scour the desert. They fly screaming into the wilderness. The rack and the thumbscrew are applied. Human nature is remorseless.

'Impulses came upon him sometimes?' Sir William asked, with his pencil on a pink card.

That was his own affair, said Septimus.

'Nobody lives for himself alone,' said Sir William, glancing at the photograph of his wife in Court dress.

'And you have a brilliant career before you,' said Sir William. There was Mr. Brewer's letter on the table. 'An exceptionally brilliant career.'

But if he confessed? If he communicated? Would they let him off then, Holmes and Bradshaw?

'I – I——' he stammered.

But what was his crime? He could not remember it.

'Yes?' Sir William encouraged him. (But it was growing late.)

Love, trees, there is no crime – what was his message?

He could not remember it.

'I – I——' Septimus stammered.

'Try to think as little about yourself as possible,' said Sir William kindly. Really, he was not fit to be about.

Was there anything else they wished to ask him? Sir William would make all arrangements (he murmured to Rezia) and he would let her know between five and six that evening.

'Trust everything to me,' he said, and dismissed them.

Never, never had Rezia felt such agony in her life! She had asked for help and been deserted! He had failed them! Sir William Bradshaw was not a nice man.

The upkeep of that motor car alone must cost him quite a lot, said Septimus, when they got out into the street.

She clung to his arm. They had been deserted.

But what more did she want?

To his patients he gave three-quarters of an hour; and if in this exacting science which has to do with what, after all, we know nothing about – the nervous system, the human brain – a doctor loses his sense of proportion, as a doctor he fails. Health we must have; and health is proportion; so that when a man comes into your room and says he is Christ (a common delusion), and has a message, as they mostly have, and threatens, as they often do, to kill himself, you invoke proportion; order rest in bed; rest in solitude; silence and rest; rest without friends, without books, without messages; six months' rest; until a man who went in weighing seven stone six comes out weighing twelve.

Proportion, divine proportion, Sir William's goddess, was acquired by Sir William walking hospitals, catching salmon, begetting one son in Harley Street by Lady Bradshaw, who caught salmon herself and took photographs scarcely to be distinguished from the work of professionals. Worshipping proportion, Sir William not only prospered himself but made England prosper, secluded her lunatics, forbade childbirth, penalised despair, made it impossible for the unfit to propagate their views until they, too, shared his sense of proportion – his, if they were men, Lady Bradshaw's if they were women (she embroidered, knitted, spent four nights out of seven at home with her son), so that not only did his colleagues respect him, his subordinates fear him, but the friends and relations of his patients felt for him the keenest gratitude for insisting that these prophetic Christs and Christesses, who prophesied the end of the world, or the advent of God, should drink milk in bed, as Sir William ordered; Sir William with his thirty years' experience of these kinds of cases, and his infallible instinct, this is madness, this sense; in fact his sense of proportion.

But Proportion has a sister, less smiling, more formidable, a Goddess even now engaged – in the heat and sands of India, the mud and swamp of Africa, the purlieus of London, wherever in short the climate or the devil tempts men to fall from the true belief which is her own – even now engaged in dashing down shrines, smashing idols, and setting up in their place her own stern countenance. Conversion is her name and she feasts on the wills of the weakly, loving to impress, to impose, adoring her own features stamped on the face of the populace. At Hyde Park Corner on a tub she stands preaching; shrouds herself in white and walks penitentially disguised as brotherly love through factories and parliaments; offers help, but desires power; smites out of her way roughly the dissentient, or dissatisfied; bestows her blessing on those who, looking upward, catch submissively from her eyes the light of their own. This lady too (Rezia Warren Smith divined it) had her dwelling in Sir William's heart, though concealed, as she mostly is, under some plausible disguise; some venerable name; love, duty, self-sacrifice. How he would work – how toil to raise funds, propagate reforms, initiate institutions! But Conversion, fastidious Goddess, loves blood better than brick, and feasts most subtly on the human will. For example, Lady Bradshaw. Fifteen years ago she had gone under. It was nothing you could put your finger on; there had been no scene, no snap; only the slow sinking, water-logged, of her will into his. Sweet was her smile, swift her submission; dinner in Harley Street, numbering eight or nine courses, feeding ten or fifteen guests of the professional classes, was smooth and urbane. Only as the evening wore on a very slight dulness, or uneasiness perhaps, a nervous twitch, fumble, stumble and confusion indicated, what it was really painful to believe – that the poor lady lied. Once, long ago, she had caught salmon freely: now, quick to minister to the craving which lit her husband's eye so oilily for dominion, for power, she cramped, squeezed, pared, pruned, drew back, peeped through; so that without knowing precisely what made the evening disagreeable, and caused this pressure on the top of the head (which might well be imputed to the professional conversation, or the fatigue of a great doctor whose life, Lady Bradshaw said, 'is not his own but his patients'), disagreeable it was: so that guests, when the clock struck ten, breathed in the air of Harley Street even with rapture; which relief, however, was denied to his patients.

There in the grey room, with the pictures on the wall, and the valuable furniture, under the ground glass skylight, they learnt the extent of their transgressions; huddled up in arm-chairs, they watched him go through, for their benefit, a curious exercise with the arms, which he shot out, brought sharply back to his hip, to prove (if the patient was obstinate) that Sir William was master of his own actions, which the patient was not. There some weakly broke down; sobbed, submitted; others, inspired by Heaven knows what intemperate madness, called Sir William to his face a damnable humbug; questioned, even more impiously, life itself. Why live? they demanded. Sir William replied that life was good. Certainly Lady Bradshaw in ostrich feathers hung over the mantelpiece, and as for his income it was quite twelve thousand a year. But to us, they protested, life has given no such bounty. He acquiesced. They lacked a sense of proportion. And perhaps, after all, there is no God? He shrugged his shoulders. In short, this living or not living is an affair of our own? But there they were mistaken. Sir William had a friend in Surrey where they taught, what Sir William frankly admitted was a difficult art – a sense of proportion. There were, moreover, family affection; honour; courage; and a brilliant career. All of these had in Sir William a resolute champion. If they failed, he had to support him police and the good of society, which, he remarked very quietly, would take care, down in Surrey, that these unsocial impulses, bred more than anything by the lack of good blood, were held in control. And then stole out from her hiding-place and mounted her throne that Goddess whose lust is to override opposition, to stamp indelibly in the sanctuaries of others the image of herself. Naked, defenceless, the exhausted, the friendless received the impress of Sir William's will. He swooped; he devoured. He shut people up. It was this combination of decision and humanity that endeared Sir William so greatly to the relations of his victims.

But Rezia Warren Smith cried, walking down Harley Street, that she did not like that man.

Shredding and slicing, dividing and subdividing, the clocks of Harley Street nibbled at the June day, counselled submission, upheld authority, and pointed out in chorus the supreme advantages of a sense of proportion, until the mound of time was so far diminished that a commercial clock, suspended above a shop in Oxford Street, announced, genially and fraternally, as if it were a pleasure to Messrs. Rigby and Lowndes to give the information gratis, that it was half-past one.

Looking up, it appeared that each letter of their names stood for one of the hours; subconsciously one was grateful to Rigby and Lowndes for giving one time ratified by Greenwich; and this gratitude (so Hugh Whitbread ruminated, dallying there in front of the shop window) naturally took the form later of buying off Rigby and Lowndes socks or shoes. So he ruminated. It was his habit. He did not go deeply. He brushed surfaces; the dead languages, the living, life in Constantinople, Paris, Rome; riding, shooting, tennis, it had been once. The malicious asserted that he now kept guard at Buckingham Palace, dressed in silk stockings and knee-breeches, over what nobody knew. But he did it extremely efficiently. He had been afloat on the cream of English society for fifty-five years. He had known Prime Ministers. His affections were understood to be deep. And if it were true that he had not taken part in any of the great movements of the time or held important office, one or two humble reforms stood to his credit; an improvement in public shelters was one; the protection of owls in Norfolk another; servant girls had reason to be grateful to him; and his name at the end of letters to the *Times*, asking for funds, appealing to the public to protect, to preserve, to clear up litter, to abate smoke, and stamp out immorality in parks, commanded respect.

A magnificent figure he cut too, pausing for a moment (as the sound of the half-hour died away) to look critically, magisterially, at socks and shoes; impeccable, substantial, as if he beheld the world from a certain eminence, and dressed to match; but realised the obligations which size, wealth, health entail, and observed punctiliously even when not absolutely necessary, little courtesies, old-fashioned ceremonies which gave a quality to his manner, something to imitate, something to remember him by, for he would never lunch, for example, with Lady Bruton, whom he had known these twenty years, without bringing her in his outstretched hand a bunch of carnations and asking Miss Brush, Lady Bruton's secretary, after her brother in South Africa, which, for some reason, Miss Brush, deficient though she was in every attribute of female charm, so much resented that she said 'Thank you, he's doing very well in South Africa,' when, for half-a-dozen years, he had been doing badly in Portsmouth.

Lady Bruton herself preferred Richard Dalloway, who arrived at the same moment. Indeed they met on the doorstep.

Lady Bruton preferred Richard Dalloway of course. He was made of much finer material. But she wouldn't let them run down her poor dear Hugh. She could never forget his kindness – he had been really remarkably kind – she forgot precisely upon what occasion. But he had been – remarkably kind. Anyhow, the difference between one man and another does not amount to much. She had never seen the sense of cutting people up, as Clarissa Dalloway did – cutting them up and sticking them together again; not at any rate when one was sixty-two. She took Hugh's carnations with her angular grim smile. There was nobody else coming, she said. She had got them there on false pretences, to help her out of a difficulty –

'But let us eat first,' she said.

And so there began a soundless and exquisite passing to and fro through swing doors of aproned white-capped maids, handmaidens not of necessity, but adepts in a mystery or grand deception practised by hostesses in Mayfair from one-thirty to two, when, with a wave of the hand, the traffic ceases, and there rises instead this profound illusion in the first place about the food – how it is not paid for; and then that the table spreads itself voluntarily with glass and silver, little mats, saucers of red fruit; films of brown cream mask turbot; in casseroles severed chickens swim; coloured, undomestic, the fire burns; and with the wine and the coffee (not paid for) rise jocund visions before musing eyes; gently speculative eyes; eyes to whom life appears musical, mysterious; eyes now kindled to observe genially the beauty of the red carnations which Lady Bruton (whose movements were always angular) had laid beside her plate, so that Hugh Whitbread, feeling at peace with the entire universe and at the same time completely sure of his standing, said, resting his fork:

'Wouldn't they look charming against your lace?'

Miss Brush resented this familiarity intensely. She thought him an underbred fellow. She made Lady Bruton laugh.

Lady Bruton raised the carnations, holding them rather stiffly with much the same attitude with which the General held the scroll in the picture behind her; she remained fixed, tranced.

Which was she now, the General's great-grand-daughter? great-great grand-daughter? Richard Dalloway asked himself. Sir Roderick, Sir Miles, Sir Talbot – that was it. It was remarkable how in that family the likeness persisted in the women. She should have been a general of dragoons herself. And Richard would have served under her, cheerfully; he had the greatest respect for her; he cherished these romantic views about well-set-up old women of pedigree, and would have liked, in his good-humoured way, to bring some young hot-heads of his acquaintance to lunch with her; as if a type like hers could be bred of amiable tea-drinking enthusiasts! He knew her country. He knew her people. There was a vine, still bearing, which either Lovelace or Herrick[49] – she never read a word of poetry herself, but so the story ran – had sat under. Better wait to put before them the question that bothered her (about making an appeal to the public; if so, in what terms and so on), better wait until they have had their coffee, Lady Bruton thought; and so laid the carnations down beside her plate.

'How's Clarissa?' she asked abruptly.

Clarissa always said that Lady Bruton did not like her. Indeed, Lady Bruton had the reputation of being more interested in politics than people; of talking like a man; of having had a finger in some notorious intrigue of the eighties, which was now beginning to be mentioned in memoirs. Certainly there was an alcove in her drawing-room, and a table in that alcove, and a photograph upon that table of General Sir Talbot Moore, now deceased, who had written there (one evening in the eighties) in Lady Bruton's presence, with her cognisance, perhaps advice, a telegram ordering the British troops to advance upon an historical occasion. (She kept the pen and told the story.) Thus, when she said in her offhand way 'How's Clarissa?' husbands had difficulty in persuading their wives and indeed, however devoted, were secretly doubtful themselves, of her interest in women who often got in their husbands' way, prevented them from accepting posts abroad, and had to be taken to the sea-side in the middle of the session to recover from influenza. Nevertheless her inquiry, 'How's Clarissa?' was known by women infallibly to be a signal from a well-wisher, from an almost silent companion, whose utterances (half a dozen perhaps in the course of a lifetime) signified recognition of some feminine comradeship which went beneath masculine lunch parties and united Lady Bruton and Mrs. Dalloway, who seldom met, and appeared when they did meet indifferent and even hostile, in a singular bond.

'I met Clarissa in the Park this morning,' said Hugh Whitbread, diving into the casserole, anxious to pay himself this little tribute, for he had only to come to London and he met everybody at once; but greedy, one of the greediest men she had ever known, Milly Brush thought, who observed men with unflinching rectitude, and was capable of everlasting devotion, to her own sex in particular, being knobbed, scraped, angular, and entirely without feminine charm.

'D'you know who's in town?' said Lady Bruton suddenly bethinking her. 'Our old friend, Peter Walsh.'

They all smiled. Peter Walsh! And Mr. Dalloway was genuinely glad, Milly Brush thought; and Mr. Whitbread thought only of his chicken.

Peter Walsh! All three, Lady Bruton, Hugh Whitbread, and Richard Dalloway, remembered the same thing – how passionately Peter had been in love; been rejected; gone to India; come a cropper; made a mess of things; and Richard Dalloway had a very great liking for the dear old fellow too. Milly Brush saw that; saw a depth in the brown of his eyes; saw him hesitate; consider; which interested her, as Mr. Dalloway always interested her, for what was he thinking, she wondered, about Peter Walsh?

That Peter Walsh had been in love with Clarissa; that he would go back directly after lunch and find Clarissa; that he would tell her, in so many words, that he loved her. Yes, he would say that.

Milly Brush once might almost have fallen in love with these silences; and Mr. Dalloway was always so dependable; such a gentleman too. Now, being forty, Lady Bruton had only to nod, or turn her head a little abruptly, and Milly Brush took the

signal, however deeply she might be sunk in these reflections of
a detached spirit, of an uncorrupted soul whom life could not
bamboozle, because life had not offered her a trinket of the
slightest value; not a curl, smile, lip, cheek, nose; nothing whatever; Lady Bruton had only to nod, and Perkins was instructed
to quicken the coffee.

'Yes; Peter Walsh has come back,' said Lady Bruton. It was
vaguely flattering to them all. He had come back, battered, un-
successful, to their secure shores. But to help him, they reflected,
was impossible; there was some flaw in his character. Hugh
Whitbread said one might of course mention his name to So-
and-so. He wrinkled lugubriously, consequentially, at the thought
of the letters he would write to the heads of Government offices
about 'my old friend, Peter Walsh,' and so on. But it wouldn't
lead to anything – not to anything permanent, because of his
character.

'In trouble with some woman,' said Lady Bruton. They had
all guessed that *that* was at the bottom of it.

'However,' said Lady Bruton, anxious to leave the subject,
'we shall hear the whole story from Peter himself.'

(The coffee was very slow in coming.)

'The address?' murmured Hugh Whitbread; and there was at
once a ripple in the grey tide of service which washed round
Lady Bruton day in, day out, collecting, intercepting, enveloping
her in a fine tissue which broke concussions, mitigated interrup-
tions, and spread round the house in Brook Street a fine net
where things lodged and were picked out accurately, instantly,
by grey-haired Perkins, who had been with Lady Bruton these
thirty years and now wrote down the address; handed it to Mr.
Whitbread, who took out his pocket-book, raised his eyebrows,
and slipping it in among documents of the highest importance,
said that he would get Evelyn to ask him to lunch.

(They were waiting to bring the coffee until Mr. Whitbread
had finished.)

Hugh was very slow, Lady Bruton thought. He was getting fat,
she noticed. Richard always kept himself in the pink of condition.
She was getting impatient; the whole of her being was setting

positively, undeniably, domineeringly brushing aside all this unnecessary trifling (Peter Walsh and his affairs) upon that subject
which engaged her attention, and not merely her attention, but
that fibre which was the ramrod of her soul, that essential part
of her without which Millicent Bruton would not have been Millicent Bruton; that project for emigrating young people of both
sexes born of respectable parents and setting them up with a fair
prospect of doing well in Canada.⁵⁰ She exaggerated. She had
perhaps lost her sense of proportion. Emigration was not to others the obvious remedy, the sublime conception. It was not to them
(not to Hugh, or Richard, or even to devoted Miss Brush) the
liberator of the pent egotism, which a strong martial woman, well
nourished, well descended, of direct impulses, downright feelings,
and little introspective power (broad and simple – why could not
every one be broad and simple? she asked) feels rise within her,
once youth is past, and must eject upon some object – it may be
Emigration, it may be Emancipation; but whatever it be, this object round which the essence of her soul is daily secreted becomes
inevitably prismatic, lustrous, half looking-glass, half precious
stone; now carefully hidden in case people should sneer at it; now
proudly displayed. Emigration had become, in short, largely Lady
Bruton.

But she had to write. And one letter to the *Times*, she used to
say to Miss Brush, cost her more than to organise an expedition
to South Africa (which she had done in the war). After a morning's battle beginning, tearing up, beginning again, she used to
feel the futility of her own womanhood as she felt it on no other
occasion, and would turn gratefully to the thought of Hugh
Whitbread who possessed – no one could doubt it – the art of
writing letters to the *Times*.

A being so differently constituted from herself, with such a
command of language; able to put things as editors liked them
put; had passions which one could not call simply greed. Lady
Bruton often suspended judgement upon men in deference to the
mysterious accord in which they, but no woman, stood to the
laws of the universe; knew how to put things; knew what was
said; so that if Richard advised her, and Hugh wrote for her,

she was sure of being somehow right. So she let Hugh eat his soufflé; asked after poor Evelyn; waited until they were smoking, and then said,

'Milly, would you fetch the papers?'

And Miss Brush went out, came back; laid papers on the table; and Hugh produced his fountain pen; his silver fountain pen, which had done twenty years' service, he said, unscrewing the cap. It was still in perfect order; he had shown it to the makers; there was no reason, they said, why it should ever wear out; which was somehow to Hugh's credit, and to the credit of the sentiments which his pen expressed (so Richard Dalloway felt) as Hugh began carefully writing capital letters with rings round them in the margin, and thus marvellously reduced Lady Bruton's tangles to sense, to grammar such as the editor of the *Times*, Lady Bruton felt, watching the marvellous transformation, must respect. Hugh was slow. Hugh was pertinacious. Richard said one must take risks. Hugh proposed modifications in deference to people's feelings, which, he said rather tartly when Richard laughed, 'had to be considered,' and read out 'how, therefore, we are of opinion that the times are ripe . . . the superfluous youth of our ever-increasing population . . . what we owe to the dead . . . ' which Richard thought all stuffing and bunkum, but no harm in it, of course, and Hugh went on drafting sentiments in alphabetical order of the highest nobility, brushing the cigar ash from his waistcoat, and summing up now and then the progress they had made until, finally, he read out the draft of a letter which Lady Bruton felt certain was a masterpiece. Could her own meaning sound like that?

Hugh could not guarantee that the editor would put it in; but he would be meeting somebody at luncheon.

Whereupon Lady Bruton, who seldom did a graceful thing, stuffed all Hugh's carnations into the front of her dress, and flinging her hands out called him 'My Prime Minister!' What she would have done without them both she did not know. They rose. And Richard Dalloway strolled off as usual to have a look at the General's portrait, because he meant, whenever he had a moment of leisure, to write a history of Lady Bruton's family.

And Millicent Bruton was very proud of her family. But they could wait, they could wait, she said, looking at the picture; meaning that her family, of military men, administrators, admirals, had been men of action, who had done their duty; and Richard's first duty was to his country, but it was a fine face, she said; and all the papers were ready for Richard down at Aldmixton whenever the time came; the Labour Government she meant.[51] 'Ah, the news from India!' she cried.

And then, as they stood in the hall taking yellow gloves from the bowl on the malachite table and Hugh was offering Miss Brush with quite unnecessary courtesy some discarded ticket or other compliment, which she loathed from the depths of her heart and blushed brick red, Richard turned to Lady Bruton, with his hat in his hand, and said,

'We shall see you at our party to-night?' whereupon Lady Bruton resumed the magnificence which letter-writing had shattered. She might come; or she might not come. Clarissa had wonderful energy. Parties terrified Lady Bruton. But then, she was getting old. So she intimated, standing at her doorway; handsome; very erect; while her chow stretched behind her, and Miss Brush disappeared into the background with her hands full of papers.

And Lady Bruton went ponderously, majestically, up to her room, lay, one arm extended, on the sofa. She sighed, she snored, not that she was asleep, only drowsy and heavy, drowsy and heavy, like a field of clover in the sunshine this hot June day, with the bees going round and about and the yellow butterflies. Always she went back to those fields down in Devonshire, where she had jumped the brooks on Patty, her pony, with Mortimer and Tom, her brothers. And there were the dogs; there were the rats; there were her father and mother on the lawn under the trees, with the tea-things out, and the beds of dahlias, the hollyhocks, the pampas grass; and they, little wretches, always up to some mischief! stealing back through the shrubbery, so as not to be seen, all bedraggled from some roguery. What old nurse used to say about her frocks!

Ah dear, she remembered – it was Wednesday in Brook Street.

Those kind good fellows, Richard Dalloway, Hugh Whitbread, had gone this hot day through the streets whose growl came up to her lying on the sofa. Power was hers, position, income. She had lived in the forefront of her time. She had had good friends; known the ablest men of her day. Murmuring London flowed up to her, and her hand, lying on the sofa back, curled upon some imaginary baton such as her grandfathers might have held, holding which she seemed, drowsy and heavy, to be commanding battalions marching to Canada, and those good fellows walking across London, that territory of theirs, that little bit of carpet, Mayfair.

And they went further and further from her, being attached to her by a thin thread (since they had lunched with her) which would stretch and stretch, get thinner and thinner as they walked across London; as if one's friends were attached to one's body, after lunching with them, by a thin thread, which (as she dozed there) became hazy with the sound of bells, striking the hour or ringing to service, as a single spider's thread is blotted with rain-drops, and, burdened, sags down. So she slept.

And Richard Dalloway and Hugh Whitbread hesitated at the corner of Conduit Street at the very moment that Millicent Bruton, lying on the sofa, let the thread snap; snored. Contrary winds buffeted at the street corner. They looked in at a shop window; they did not wish to buy or to talk but to part, only with contrary winds buffeting the street corner, with some sort of lapse in the tides of the body, two forces meeting in a swirl, morning and afternoon, they paused. Some newspaper placard went up in the air, gallantly, like a kite at first, then paused, swooped, fluttered; and a lady's veil hung. Yellow awnings trembled. The speed of the morning traffic slackened, and single carts rattled carelessly down half-empty streets. In Norfolk, of which Richard Dalloway was half thinking, a soft warm wind blew back the petals; confused the waters; ruffled the flowering grasses. Haymakers, who had pitched beneath hedges to sleep away the morning toil, parted curtains of green blades; moved trembling globes of cow parsley to see the sky; the blue, the steadfast, the blazing summer sky.

Aware that he was looking at a silver two-handled Jacobean mug, and that Hugh Whitbread admired condescendingly, with airs of connoisseurship, a Spanish necklace which he thought of asking the price of in case Evelyn might like it – still Richard was torpid; could not think or move. Life had thrown up this wreckage; shop windows full of coloured paste, and one stood stark with the lethargy of the old, stiff with the rigidity of the old, looking in. Evelyn Whitbread might like to buy this Spanish necklace – so she might. Yawn he must. Hugh was going into the shop.

'Right you are!' said Richard, following.

Goodness knows he didn't want to go buying necklaces with Hugh. But there are tides in the body. Morning meets afternoon. Borne like a frail shallop on deep, deep floods, Lady Bruton's great-grandfather and his memoir and his campaigns in North America were whelmed and sunk. And Millicent Bruton too. She went under. Richard didn't care a straw what became of Emigration; about that letter, whether the editor put it in or not. The necklace hung stretched between Hugh's admirable fingers. Let him give it to a girl, if he must buy jewels – any girl, any girl in the street. For the worthlessness of this life did strike Richard pretty forcibly – buying necklaces for Evelyn. If he'd had a boy he'd have said, Work, work. But he had his Elizabeth; he adored his Elizabeth.

'I should like to see Mr. Dubonnet,' said Hugh in his curt worldly way. It appeared that this Dubonnet had the measurements of Mrs. Whitbread's neck, or, more strangely still, knew her views upon Spanish jewellery and the extent of her possessions in that line (which Hugh could not remember). All of which seemed to Richard Dalloway awfully odd. For he never gave Clarissa presents, except a bracelet two or three years ago, which had not been a success. She never wore it. It pained him to remember that she never wore it. And as a single spider's thread after wavering here and there attaches itself to the point of a leaf, so Richard's mind, recovering from its lethargy, set now on his wife, Clarissa, whom Peter Walsh had loved so passionately; and Richard had had a sudden vision of her there at luncheon; of himself and Clarissa; of their life together; and he drew the tray of old jewels towards him, and taking up first this brooch then that ring, 'How much is that?' he asked, but doubted his own taste. He wanted to open the drawing-room door and come in holding out something; a present for Clarissa. Only what? But Hugh was on his legs again. He was unspeakably pompous. Really, after dealing here for thirty-five years he was not going to be put off by a mere boy who did not know his business. For Dubonnet, it seemed, was out, and Hugh would not buy anything until Mr. Dubonnet chose to be in; at which the youth flushed and bowed his correct little bow. It was all perfectly correct. And yet Richard couldn't have said that to save his life! Why these people stood that damned insolence he could not conceive. Hugh was becoming an intolerable ass. Richard Dalloway could not stand more than an hour of his society. And, flicking his bowler hat by way of farewell, Richard turned at the corner of Conduit Street eager, yes, very eager, to travel that spider's thread of attachment between himself and Clarissa; he would go straight to her, in Westminster.

But he wanted to come in holding something. Flowers? Yes, flowers, since he did not trust his taste in gold; any number of flowers, roses, orchids, to celebrate what was, reckoning things as you will, an event; this feeling about her when they spoke of Peter Walsh at luncheon; and they never spoke of it; not for years had they spoken of it; which, he thought, grasping his red and white roses together (a vast bunch in tissue paper), is the greatest mistake in the world. The time comes when it can't be said; one's too shy to say it, he thought, pocketing his sixpence or two of change, setting off with his great bunch held against his body to Westminster to say straight out in so many words (whatever she might think of him), holding out his flowers, 'I love you.' Why not? Really it was a miracle thinking of the war, and thousands of poor chaps, with all their lives before them, shovelled together, already half forgotten; it was a miracle. Here he was walking across London to say to Clarissa in so many words that he loved her. Which one never does say, he thought. Partly one's lazy; partly one's shy. And Clarissa – it was difficult to think of her;

except in starts, as at luncheon, when he saw her quite distinctly; their whole life. He stopped at the crossing; and repeated – being simple by nature, and undebauched, because he had tramped, and shot; being pertinacious and dogged, having championed the downtrodden and followed his instincts in the House of Commons; being preserved in his simplicity yet at the same time grown rather speechless, rather stiff – he repeated that it was a miracle, that he should have married Clarissa; a miracle – his life had been a miracle, he thought; hesitating to cross. But it did make his blood boil to see little creatures of five or six crossing Piccadilly alone. The police ought to have stopped the traffic at once. He had no illusions about the London police. Indeed, he was collecting evidence of their malpractices; and those costermongers, not allowed to stand their barrows in the streets; and prostitutes, good Lord, the fault wasn't in them, nor in young men either, but in our detestable social system and so forth; all of which he considered, could be seen considering, grey, dogged, dapper, clean, as he walked across the Park to tell his wife that he loved her.

For he would say it in so many words, when he came into the room. Because it is a thousand pities never to say what one feels, he thought, crossing the Green Park and observing with pleasure how in the shade of the trees whole families, poor families, were sprawling; children kicking up their legs; sucking milk; paper bags thrown about, which could easily be picked up (if people objected) by one of those fat gentlemen in livery; for he was of opinion that every park, and every square, during the summer months should be open to children (the grass of the park flushed and faded, lighting up the poor mothers of Westminster and their crawling babies, as if a yellow lamp were moved beneath). But what could be done for female vagrants like that poor creature, stretched on her elbow (as if she had flung herself on the earth, rid of all ties, to observe curiously, to speculate boldly, to consider the whys and the wherefores, impudent, loose-lipped, humorous), he did not know. Bearing his flowers like a weapon, Richard Dalloway approached her; intent he passed her; still there was time for a spark between them – she laughed at the sight of him, he smiled good-humouredly, considering the problem of the female vagrant; not that they would ever speak. But he would tell Clarissa that he loved her, in so many words. He had, once upon a time, been jealous of Peter Walsh; jealous of him and Clarissa. But she had often said to him that she had been right not to marry Peter Walsh; which, knowing Clarissa, was obviously true; she wanted support. Not that she was weak; but she wanted support.

As for Buckingham Palace (like an old prima donna facing the audience all in white) you can't deny it a certain dignity, he considered, nor despise what does, after all, stand to millions of people (a little crowd was waiting at the gate to see the King drive out) for a symbol, absurd though it is; a child with a box of bricks could have done better, he thought; looking at the memorial to Queen Victoria (whom he could remember in her horn spectacles driving through Kensington), its white mound, its billowing motherliness; but he liked being ruled by the descendant of Horsa;[52] he liked continuity; and the sense of handing on the traditions of the past. It was a great age in which to have lived. Indeed, his own life was a miracle; let him make no mistake about it; here he was, in the prime of life, walking to his house in Westminster to tell Clarissa that he loved her. Happiness is this, he thought.

It is this, he said, as he entered Dean's Yard. Big Ben was beginning to strike, first the warning, musical; then the hour, irrevocable. Lunch parties waste the entire afternoon, he thought, approaching his door.

The sound of Big Ben flooded Clarissa's drawing-room, where she sat, ever so annoyed, at her writing-table; worried; annoyed. It was perfectly true that she had not asked Ellie Henderson to her party; but she had done it on purpose. Now Mrs. Marsham wrote: 'She had told Ellie Henderson she would ask Clarissa – Ellie so much wanted to come.'

But why should she invite all the dull women in London to her parties? Why should Mrs. Marsham interfere? And there was Elizabeth closeted all this time with Doris Kilman. Anything more nauseating she could not conceive. Prayer at this

hour with that woman. And the sound of the bell flooded the
room with its melancholy wave; which receded, and gathered
itself together to fall once more, when she heard, distractingly,
something fumbling, something scratching at the door. Who at
this hour? Three, good Heavens! Three already! For with overpowering directness and dignity the clock struck three; and she
heard nothing else; but the door handle slipped round and in
came Richard! What a surprise! In came Richard, holding out
flowers. She had failed him, once at Constantinople; and Lady
Bruton, whose lunch parties were said to be extraordinarily
amusing, had not asked her. He was holding out flowers – roses,
red and white roses. (But he could not bring himself to say he
loved her; not in so many words.)

But how lovely, she said, taking his flowers. She understood;
she understood without his speaking; his Clarissa. She put them
in vases on the mantelpiece. How lovely they looked! she said.
And was it amusing, she asked? Had Lady Bruton asked after
her? Peter Walsh was back. Mrs. Marsham had written. Must
she ask Ellie Henderson? That woman Kilman was upstairs.

'But let us sit down for five minutes,' said Richard.

It all looked so empty. All the chairs were against the wall.
What had they been doing? Oh, it was for the party; no, he had
not forgotten the party. Peter Walsh was back. Oh yes; she had
had him. And he was going to get a divorce; and he was in love
with some woman out there. And he hadn't changed in the
slightest. There she was, mending her dress . . .

'Thinking of Bourton,' she said.

'Hugh was at lunch,' said Richard. She had met him too!
Well, he was getting absolutely intolerable. Buying Evelyn necklaces; fatter than ever; an intolerable ass.

'And it came over me "I might have married you",' she said,
thinking of Peter sitting there in his little bow-tie; with that
knife, opening it, shutting it. 'Just as he always was, you know.'

They were talking about him at lunch, said Richard. (But he
could not tell her he loved her. He held her hand. Happiness is
this, he thought.) They had been writing a letter to the *Times*
for Millicent Bruton. That was about all Hugh was fit for.

'And our dear Miss Kilman?' he asked. Clarissa thought the roses absolutely lovely; first bunched together; now of their own accord starting apart.

'Kilman arrives just as we've done lunch,' she said. 'Elizabeth turns pink. They shut themselves up. I suppose they're praying.'

Lord! He didn't like it; but these things pass over if you let them.

'In a mackintosh with an umbrella,' said Clarissa.

He had not said 'I love you'; but he held her hand. Happiness is this, is this, he thought.

'But why should I ask all the dull women in London to my parties?' said Clarissa. And if Mrs. Marsham gave a party, did *she* invite her guests?

'Poor Ellie Henderson,' said Richard – it was a very odd thing how much Clarissa minded about her parties, he thought.

But Richard had no notion of the look of a room. However – what was he going to say?

If she worried about these parties he would not let her give them. Did she wish she had married Peter? But he must go.

He must be off, he said, getting up. But he stood for a moment as if he were about to say something; and she wondered what? Why? There were the roses.

'Some Committee?' she asked, as he opened the door.

'Armenians,' he said; or perhaps it was 'Albanians.'

And there is a dignity in people; a solitude; even between husband and wife a gulf; and that one must respect, thought Clarissa, watching him open the door; for one would not part with it oneself, or take it, against his will, from one's husband, without losing one's independence, one's self-respect – something, after all, priceless.

He returned with a pillow and a quilt.

'An hour's complete rest after luncheon,' he said. And he went.

How like him! He would go on saying 'An hour's complete rest after luncheon' to the end of time, because a doctor had ordered it once. It was like him to take what doctors said literally; part of his adorable, divine simplicity, which no one had to the same extent; which made him go and do the thing while she and Peter frittered their time away bickering. He was already halfway to the House of Commons, to his Armenians, his Albanians, having settled her on the sofa, looking at his roses. And people would say, 'Clarissa Dalloway is spoilt.' She cared much more for her roses than for the Armenians. Hunted out of existence, maimed, frozen, the victims of cruelty and injustice (she had heard Richard say so over and over again) – no, she could feel nothing for the Albanians, or was it the Armenians? but she loved her roses (didn't that help the Armenians?) – the only flowers she could bear to see cut. But Richard was already at the House of Commons; at his Committee, having settled all her difficulties. But no; alas, that was not true. He did not see the reasons against asking Ellie Henderson. She would do it, of course, as he wished it. Since he had brought the pillows, she would lie down . . . But – but – why did she suddenly feel, for no reason that she could discover, desperately unhappy? As a person who has dropped some grain of pearl or diamond into the grass and parts the tall blades very carefully, this way and that, and searches here and there vainly, and at last spies it there at the roots, so she went through one thing and another; no, it was not Sally Seton saying that Richard would never be in the Cabinet because he had a second-class brain (it came back to her); no, she did not mind that; nor was it to do with Elizabeth either and Doris Kilman; those were facts. It was a feeling, some unpleasant feeling, earlier in the day perhaps; something that Peter had said, combined with some depression of her own, in her bedroom, taking off her hat; and what Richard had said had added to it, but what had he said? There were his roses. Her parties! That was it! Her parties! Both of them criticised her very unfairly, laughed at her very unjustly, for her parties. That was it! That was it!

Well, how was she going to defend herself? Now that she knew what it was, she felt perfectly happy. They thought, or Peter at any rate thought, that she enjoyed imposing herself; liked to have famous people about her; great names; was simply a snob in short. Well, Peter might think so. Richard merely thought it foolish of her to like excitement when she knew it was bad for her heart. It was childish, he thought. And both were quite wrong. What she liked was simply life.

'That's what I do it for,' she said, speaking aloud, to life.

Since she was lying on the sofa, cloistered, exempt, the presence of this thing which she felt to be so obvious became physically existent; with robes of sound from the street, sunny, with hot breath, whispering, blowing out the blinds. But suppose Peter said to her, 'Yes, yes, but your parties – what's the sense of your parties?' all she could say was (and nobody could be expected to understand): They're an offering; which sounded horribly vague. But who was Peter to make out that life was all plain sailing? – Peter always in love, always in love with the wrong woman? What's your love? she might say to him. And she knew his answer; how it is the most important thing in the world and no woman could possibly understand it. Very well. But could any man understand what she meant either? about life? She could not imagine Peter or Richard taking the trouble to give a party for no reason whatever.

But to go deeper, beneath what people said (and these judgements, how superficial, how fragmentary they are!) in her own mind now, what did it mean to her, this thing she called life? Oh, it was very queer. Here was So-and-so in South Kensington; some one up in Bayswater; and somebody else, say, in Mayfair. And she felt quite continuously a sense of their existence; and she felt what a waste; and she felt what a pity; and she felt if only they could be brought together; so she did it. And it was an offering; to combine, to create; but to whom?

An offering for the sake of offering, perhaps. Anyhow, it was her gift. Nothing else had she of the slightest importance; could not think, write, even play the piano. She muddled Armenians and Turks; loved success; hated discomfort; must be liked; talked oceans of nonsense: and to this day, ask her what the Equator was, and she did not know.

All the same, that one day should follow another; Wednesday, Thursday, Friday, Saturday; that one should wake up in the morning; see the sky; walk in the park; meet Hugh Whitbread;

then suddenly in came Peter; then these roses; it was enough. After that, how unbelievable death was! – that it must end; and no one in the whole world would know how she had loved it all; how, every instant . . .

The door opened. Elizabeth knew that her mother was resting. She came in very quietly. She stood perfectly still. Was it that some Mongol had been wrecked on the coast of Norfolk (as Mrs. Hilbery said),[53] had mixed with the Dalloway ladies, perhaps a hundred years ago? For the Dalloways, in general, were fair-haired; blue-eyed; Elizabeth, on the contrary, was dark; had Chinese eyes in a pale face; an Oriental mystery; was gentle, considerate, still. As a child, she had had a perfect sense of humour; but now at seventeen, why, Clarissa could not in the least understand, she had become very serious; like a hyacinth sheathed in glossy green, with buds just tinted, a hyacinth which has had no sun.

She stood quite still and looked at her mother; but the door was ajar, and outside the door was Miss Kilman, as Clarissa knew; Miss Kilman in her mackintosh, listening to whatever they said.

Yes, Miss Kilman stood on the landing, and wore a mackintosh; but had her reasons. First, it was cheap; second, she was over forty; and did not, after all, dress to please. She was poor, moreover; degradingly poor. Otherwise she would not be taking jobs from people like the Dalloways; from rich people, who liked to be kind. Mr. Dalloway, to do him justice, had been kind. But Mrs. Dalloway had not. She had been merely condescending. She came from the most worthless of all classes – the rich, with a smattering of culture. They had expensive things everywhere; pictures, carpets, lots of servants. She considered that she had a perfect right to anything that the Dalloways did for her.

She had been cheated. Yes, the word was no exaggeration, for surely a girl has a right to some kind of happiness? And she had never been happy, what with being so clumsy and so poor. And then, just as she might have had a chance at Miss Dolby's school, the war came; and she had never been able to tell lies. Miss Dolby thought she would be happier with people who shared her views about the Germans. She had had to go. It was true that the family was of German origin; spelt the name Kiehlman in the eighteenth century; but her brother had been killed. They turned her out because she would not pretend that the Germans were all villains – when she had German friends, when the only happy days of her life had been spent in Germany! And after all, she could read history. She had had to take whatever she could get. Mr. Dalloway had come across her working for the Friends. He had allowed her (and that was really generous of him) to teach his daughter history. Also she did a little Extension lecturing and so on. Then Our Lord had come to her (and here she always bowed her head). She had seen the light two years and three months ago. Now she did not envy women like Clarissa Dalloway; she pitied them.

She pitied and despised them from the bottom of her heart, as she stood on the soft carpet, looking at the old engraving of a little girl with a muff. With all this luxury going on, what hope was there for a better state of things? Instead of lying on a sofa – 'My mother is resting,' Elizabeth had said – she should have been in a factory; behind a counter; Mrs. Dalloway and all the other fine ladies!

Bitter and burning, Miss Kilman had turned into a church two years three months ago. She had heard the Rev. Edward Whittaker preach; the boys sing; had seen the solemn lights descend, and whether it was the music, or the voices (she herself when alone in the evening found comfort in a violin; but the sound was excruciating; she had no ear), the hot and turbulent feelings which boiled and surged in her had been assuaged as she sat there, and she had wept copiously, and gone to call on Mr. Whittaker at his private house in Kensington. It was the hand of God, he said. The Lord had shown her the way. So now, whenever the hot and painful feelings boiled within her, this hatred of Mrs. Dalloway, this grudge against the world, she thought of God. She thought of Mr. Whittaker. Rage was succeeded by calm. A sweet savour filled her veins, her lips parted, and, standing formidable upon the landing in her mackintosh, she looked with steady and sinister serenity at Mrs. Dalloway, who came out with her daughter.

Elizabeth said she had forgotten her gloves. That was because Miss Kilman and her mother hated each other. She could not bear to see them together. She ran upstairs to find her gloves.

But Miss Kilman did not hate Mrs. Dalloway. Turning her large gooseberry-coloured eyes upon Clarissa, observing her small pink face, her delicate body, her air of freshness and fashion, Miss Kilman felt, Fool! Simpleton! You who have known neither sorrow nor pleasure; who have trifled your life away! And there rose in her an overmastering desire to overcome her; to unmask her. If she could have felled her it would have eased her. But it was not the body; it was the soul and its mockery that she wished to subdue; make feel her mastery. If only she could make her weep; could ruin her; humiliate her; bring her to her knees crying, You are right! But this was God's will, not Miss Kilman's. It was to be a religious victory. So she glared; so she glowered.

Clarissa was really shocked. This a Christian – this woman! This woman had taken her daughter from her! She in touch with invisible presences! Heavy, ugly, commonplace, without kindness or grace, she know the meaning of life!

'You are taking Elizabeth to the Stores?'⁵⁴ Mrs. Dalloway said.

Miss Kilman said she was. They stood there. Miss Kilman was not going to make herself agreeable. She had always earned her living. Her knowledge of modern history was thorough in the extreme. She did out of her meagre income set aside so much for causes she believed in; whereas this woman did nothing, believed nothing; brought up her daughter – but here was Elizabeth, rather out of breath, the beautiful girl.

So they were going to the Stores. Odd it was, as Miss Kilman stood there (and stand she did, with the power and taciturnity of some prehistoric monster armoured for primeval warfare), how, second by second, the idea of her diminished, how hatred (which was for ideas, not people) crumbled, how she lost her malignity, her size, became second by second merely Miss Kilman, in a mackintosh, whom Heaven knows Clarissa would have liked to help.

At this dwindling of the monster, Clarissa laughed. Saying good-bye, she laughed.

Off they went together, Miss Kilman and Elizabeth, down-stairs.

With a sudden impulse, with a violent anguish, for this woman was taking her daughter from her, Clarissa leant over the banis-ters and cried out, 'Remember the party! Remember our party to-night!'

But Elizabeth had already opened the front door; there was a van passing; she did not answer.

Love and religion! thought Clarissa, going back into the drawing-room, tingling all over. How detestable, how detest-able they are! For now that the body of Miss Kilman was not before her, it overwhelmed her – the idea. The cruellest things in the world, she thought, seeing them clumsy, hot, domineer-ing, hypocritical, eavesdropping, jealous, infinitely cruel and unscrupulous dressed in a mackintosh coat, on the landing; love and religion. Had she ever tried to convert any one herself? Did she not wish everybody merely to be themselves? And she watched out of the window the old lady opposite climbing up-stairs.[55] Let her climb upstairs if she wanted to; let her stop; then let her, as Clarissa had often seen her, gain her bedroom, part her curtains, and disappear again into the background. Some-how one respected that – that old woman looking out of the window, quite unconscious that she was being watched. There was something solemn in it – but love and religion would destroy that, whatever it was, the privacy of the soul. The odious Kilman would destroy it. Yet it was a sight that made her want to cry.

Love destroyed too. Everything that was fine, everything that was true went. Take Peter Walsh now. There was a man, charm-ing, clever, with ideas about everything. If you wanted to know about Pope, say, or Addison, or just to talk nonsense, what people were like, what things meant, Peter knew better than any one. It was Peter who had helped her; Peter who had lent her books. But look at the women he loved – vulgar, trivial, commonplace. Think of Peter in love – he came to see her after all these years, and what did he talk about? Himself. Horrible passion! she thought. Degrading passion! she thought, thinking of Kilman and her Elizabeth walking to the Army and Navy Stores.

Big Ben struck the half-hour.

How extraordinary it was, strange, yes touching to see the old lady (they had been neighbours ever so many years) move away from the window, as if she were attached to that sound, that string. Gigantic as it was, it had something to do with her. Down, down, into the midst of ordinary things the finger fell making the moment solemn. She was forced, so Clarissa imagined, by that sound, to move, to go – but where? Clarissa tried to follow her as she turned and disappeared, and could still just see her white cap moving at the back of the bedroom. She was still there moving about at the other end of the room. Why creeds and prayers and mackintoshes? when, thought Clarissa, that's the miracle, that's the mystery; that old lady, she meant, whom she could see going from chest of drawers to dressing-table. She could still see her. And the supreme mystery which Kilman might say she had solved, or Peter might say he had solved, but Clarissa didn't believe either of them had the ghost of an idea of solving, was simply this: here was one room; there another. Did religion solve that, or love?

Love – but here the other clock, the clock which always struck two minutes after Big Ben, came shuffling in with its lap full of odds and ends, which it dumped down as if Big Ben were all very well with his majesty laying down the law, so solemn, so just, but she must remember all sorts of little things besides – Mrs. Marsham, Ellie Henderson, glasses for ices – all sorts of little things came flooding and lapping and dancing in on the wake of that solemn stroke which lay flat like a bar of gold on the sea. Mrs. Marsham, Ellie Henderson, glasses for ices. She must telephone now at once.

Volubly, troublously, the late clock sounded, coming in on the wake of Big Ben, with its lap full of trifles. Beaten up, broken up by the assault of carriages, the brutality of vans, the eager advance of myriads of angular men, of flaunting women, the domes and spires of offices and hospitals, the last relics of this lap full of odds and ends seemed to break, like the spray of an exhausted wave, upon the body of Miss Kilman standing still in the street for a moment to mutter 'It is the flesh.'

It was the flesh that she must control. Clarissa Dalloway had insulted her. That she expected. But she had not triumphed; she had not mastered the flesh. Ugly, clumsy, Clarissa Dalloway had laughed at her for being that; and had revived the fleshly desires, for she minded looking as she did beside Clarissa. Nor could she talk as she did. But why wish to resemble her? Why? She despised Mrs. Dalloway from the bottom of her heart. She was not serious. She was not good. Her life was a tissue of vanity and deceit. Yet Doris Kilman had been overcome. She had, as a matter of fact, very nearly burst into tears when Clarissa Dalloway laughed at her. 'It is the flesh, it is the flesh,' she muttered (it being her habit to talk aloud), trying to subdue this turbulent and painful feeling as she walked down Victoria Street. She prayed to God. She could not help being ugly; she could not afford to buy pretty clothes. Clarissa Dalloway had laughed – but she would concentrate her mind upon something else until she had reached the pillar-box. At any rate she had got Elizabeth. But she would think of something else; she would think of Russia; until she reached the pillar-box.

How nice it must be, she said, in the country, struggling, as Mr. Whittaker had told her, with that violent grudge against the world which had scorned her, sneered at her, cast her off, beginning with this indignity – the infliction of her unlovable body which people could not bear to see. Do her hair as she might, her forehead remained like an egg, bald, white. No clothes suited her. She might buy anything. And for a woman, of course, that meant never meeting the opposite sex. Never would she come first with any one. Sometimes lately it had seemed to her that, except for Elizabeth, her food was all that she lived for; her comforts; her dinner, her tea; her hot-water bottle at night. But one must fight; vanquish; have faith in God. Mr. Whittaker had said she was there for a purpose. But no one knew the agony! He said, pointing to the crucifix, that God knew. But why should she have to suffer when other women, like Clarissa Dalloway, escaped? Knowledge comes through suffering, said Mr. Whittaker.

She had passed the pillar-box, and Elizabeth had turned into the cool brown tobacco department of the Army and Navy Stores while she was still muttering to herself what Mr. Whittaker had said about knowledge coming through suffering and the flesh. 'The flesh,' she muttered.

What department did she want? Elizabeth interrupted her.

'Petticoats,' she said abruptly, and stalked straight on to the lift.

Up they went. Elizabeth guided her this way and that; guided her in her abstraction as if she had been a great child, an unwieldy battleship. There were the petticoats, brown, decorous, striped, frivolous, solid, flimsy; and she chose, in her abstraction, portentously, and the girl serving thought her mad.

Elizabeth rather wondered, as they did up the parcel, what Miss Kilman was thinking. They must have their tea, said Miss Kilman, rousing, collecting herself. They had their tea.

Elizabeth rather wondered whether Miss Kilman could be hungry. It was her way of eating, eating with intensity, then looking, again and again, at a plate of sugared cakes on the table next them; then, when a lady and a child sat down and the child took the cake, could Miss Kilman really mind it? Yes, Miss Kilman did mind it. She had wanted that cake – the pink one. The pleasure of eating was almost the only pure pleasure left her, and then to be baffled even in that!

When people are happy they have a reserve, she had told Elizabeth, upon which to draw, whereas she was like a wheel without a tyre (she was fond of such metaphors), jolted by every pebble – so she would say staying on after the lesson, standing by the fire-place with her bag of books, her 'satchel', she called it, on a Tuesday morning, after the lesson was over. And she talked too about the war. After all, there were people who did not think the English invariably right. There were books. There were meetings. There were other points of view. Would Elizabeth like to come with her to listen to So-and-so? (a most extraordinary-looking old man). Then Miss Kilman took her to some church in Kensington and they had tea with a clergyman. She had lent her books. Law, medicine, politics, all professions are open to women of your generation, said Miss Kilman. But for herself, her career was absolutely ruined, and was it her fault? Good gracious, said Elizabeth, no.

And her mother would come calling to say that a hamper had come from Bourton and would Miss Kilman like some flowers? To Miss Kilman she was always very, very nice, but Miss Kilman squashed the flowers all in a bunch, and hadn't any small talk, and what interested Miss Kilman bored her mother, and Miss Kilman and she were terrible together; and Miss Kilman swelled and looked very plain, but Miss Kilman was frightfully clever. Elizabeth had never thought about the poor. They lived with everything they wanted, – her mother had breakfast in bed every day; Lucy carried it up; and she liked old women because they were Duchesses, and being descended from some Lord. But Miss Kilman said (one of those Tuesday mornings when the lesson was over), 'My grandfather kept an oil and colour shop[56] in Kensington.' Miss Kilman was quite different from any one she knew; she made one feel so small.

Miss Kilman took another cup of tea. Elizabeth, with her oriental bearing, her inscrutable mystery, sat perfectly upright; no, she did not want anything more. She looked for her gloves – her white gloves. They were under the table. Ah, but she must not go! Miss Kilman could not let her go! this youth, that was so beautiful; this girl, whom she genuinely loved! Her large hand opened and shut on the table.

But perhaps it was a little flat somehow, Elizabeth felt. And really she would like to go.

But said Miss Kilman, 'I've not quite finished yet.'

Of course, then, Elizabeth would wait. But it was rather stuffy in here.

'Are you going to the party to-night?' Miss Kilman said. Elizabeth supposed she was going; her mother wanted her to go. She must not let parties absorb her, Miss Kilman said, fingering the last two inches of a chocolate éclair.

She did not much like parties, Elizabeth said. Miss Kilman opened her mouth, slightly projected her chin, and swallowed down the last inches of the chocolate éclair, then wiped her fingers, and washed the tea round in her cup.

She was about to split asunder, she felt. The agony was so terrific. If she could grasp her, if she could clasp her, if she could make her hers absolutely and for ever and then die; that was all she wanted. But to sit here, unable to think of anything to say; to see Elizabeth turning against her; to be felt repulsive even by her – it was too much; she could not stand it. The thick fingers curled inwards.

'I never go to parties,' said Miss Kilman, just to keep Elizabeth from going. 'People don't ask me to parties' – and she knew as she said it that it was this egotism that was her undoing; Mr. Whittaker had warned her; but she could not help it. She had suffered so horribly. 'Why should they ask me?' she said. 'I'm plain, I'm unhappy.' She knew it was idiotic. But it was all those people passing – people with parcels who despised her – who made her say it. However, she was Doris Kilman. She had her degree. She was a woman who had made her way in the world. Her knowledge of modern history was more than respectable.

'I don't pity myself,' she said. 'I pity' – she meant to say 'your mother,' but no, she could not, not to Elizabeth. 'I pity other people much more.'

Like some dumb creature who has been brought up to a gate for an unknown purpose, and stands there longing to gallop away, Elizabeth Dalloway sat silent. Was Miss Kilman going to say anything more?

'Don't quite forget me,' said Doris Kilman; her voice quivered. Right away to the end of the field the dumb creature galloped in terror.

The great hand opened and shut.

Elizabeth turned her head. The waitress came. One had to pay at the desk, Elizabeth said, and went off, drawing out, so Miss Kilman felt, the very entrails in her body, stretching them as she crossed the room, and then, with a final twist, bowing her head very politely, she went.

She had gone. Miss Kilman sat at the marble table among the éclairs, stricken once, twice, thrice by shocks of suffering. She had gone. Mrs. Dalloway had triumphed. Elizabeth had gone. Beauty had gone; youth had gone.

So she sat. She got up, blundered off among the little tables, rocking slightly from side to side, and somebody came after her with her petticoat, and she lost her way, and was hemmed in by trunks specially prepared for taking to India; next got among the accouchement sets and baby linen; through all the commodities of the world, perishable and permanent, hams, drugs, flowers, stationery, variously smelling, now sweet, now sour, she lurched; saw herself thus lurching with her hat askew, very red in the face, full length in a looking-glass; and at last came out into the street.

The tower of Westminster Cathedral[57] rose in front of her, the habitation of God. In the midst of the traffic, there was the habitation of God. Doggedly she set off with her parcel to that other sanctuary, the Abbey, where, raising her hands in a tent before her face, she sat beside those driven into shelter too; the variously assorted worshippers, now divested of social rank, almost of sex, as they raised their hands before their faces; but once they removed them, instantly reverent, middle-class, English men and women, some of them desirous of seeing the wax works.

But Miss Kilman held her tent before her face. Now she was deserted; now rejoined. New worshippers came in from the street to replace the strollers, and still, as people gazed round and shuffled past the tomb of the Unknown Warrior, still she barred her eyes with her fingers and tried in this double darkness, for the light in the Abbey was bodiless, to aspire above the vanities, the desires, the commodities, to rid herself both of hatred and of love. Her hands twitched. She seemed to struggle. Yet to others God was accessible and the path to Him smooth. Mr. Fletcher, retired, of the Treasury, Mrs. Gorham, widow of the famous K.C., approached Him simply, and having done their praying, leant back, enjoyed the music (the organ pealed sweetly), and saw Miss Kilman at the end of the row, praying, praying,

and, being still on the threshold of their underworld, thought of
her sympathetically as a soul haunting the same territory; a soul
cut out of immaterial substance; not a woman, a soul.

But Mr. Fletcher had to go. He had to pass her, and being
himself neat as a new pin, could not help being a little distressed
by the poor lady's disorder; her hair down; her parcel on the
floor. She did not at once let him pass. But, as he stood gazing
about him, at the white marbles, grey window panes, and accumulated treasures (for he was extremely proud of the Abbey),
her largeness, robustness, and power as she sat there shifting her
knees from time to time (it was so rough the approach to her
God – so tough her desires) impressed him, as they had impressed Mrs. Dalloway (she could not get the thought of her out
of her mind that afternoon), the Rev. Edward Whittaker, and
Elizabeth too.

And Elizabeth waited in Victoria Street for an omnibus. It
was so nice to be out of doors. She thought perhaps she need not
go home just yet. It was so nice to be out in the air. So she would
get on to an omnibus. And already, even as she stood there, in
her very well-cut clothes, it was beginning . . . People were beginning to compare her to poplar trees, early dawn, hyacinths,
fawns, running water, and garden lilies; and it made her life a
burden to her, for she so much preferred being left alone to do
what she liked in the country, but they would compare her to
lilies, and she had to go to parties, and London was so dreary
compared with being alone in the country with her father and
the dogs.

Buses swooped, settled, were off – garish caravans, glistening
with red and yellow varnish. But which should she get on to?
She had no preferences. Of course, she would not push her way.
She inclined to be passive. It was expression she needed, but her
eyes were fine, Chinese, oriental, and, as her mother said, with
such nice shoulders and holding herself so straight, she was always charming to look at; and lately, in the evening especially,
when she was interested, for she never seemed excited, she
looked almost beautiful, very stately, very serene. What could
she be thinking? Every man fell in love with her, and she was

really awfully bored. For it was beginning. Her mother could
see that – the compliments were beginning. That she did not care
more about it – for instance for her clothes – sometimes worried
Clarissa, but perhaps it was as well with all those puppies and
guinea pigs about having distemper, and it gave her a charm.
And now there was this odd friendship with Miss Kilman. Well,
thought Clarissa about three o'clock in the morning, reading
Baron Marbot for she could not sleep, it proves she has a heart.

Suddenly Elizabeth stepped forward and most competently
boarded the omnibus, in front of everybody. She took a seat on
top. The impetuous creature – a pirate – started forward, sprang
away; she had to hold the rail to steady herself, for a pirate it
was, reckless, unscrupulous, bearing down ruthlessly, circum-
venting dangerously, boldly snatching a passenger, or ignoring
a passenger, squeezing eel-like and arrogant in between, and
then rushing insolently all sails spread up Whitehall. And did
Elizabeth give one thought to poor Miss Kilman who loved her
without jealousy, to whom she had been a fawn in the open, a
moon in a glade? She was delighted to be free. The fresh air was
so delicious. It had been so stuffy in the Army and Navy Stores.
And now it was like riding, to be rushing up Whitehall; and to
each movement of the omnibus the beautiful body in the fawn-
coloured coat responded freely like a rider, like the figure-head
of a ship, for the breeze slightly disarrayed her; the heat gave her
cheeks the pallor of white painted wood; and her fine eyes, having no eyes to meet, gazed ahead, blank, bright, with the staring
incredible innocence of sculpture.

It was always talking about her own sufferings that made
Miss Kilman so difficult. And was she right? If it was being
on committees and giving up hours and hours every day (she
hardly ever saw him in London) that helped the poor, her father
did that, goodness knows – if that was what Miss Kilman
meant about being a Christian; but it was so difficult to say. Oh,
she would like to go a little farther. Another penny was it to the
Strand? Here was another penny, then. She would go up the
Strand.

She liked people who were ill. And every profession is open

to the women of your generation, said Miss Kilman. So she might be a doctor. She might be a farmer. Animals are often ill. She might own a thousand acres and have people under her. She would go and see them in their cottages. This was Somerset House. One might be a very good farmer – and that, strangely enough, though Miss Kilman had her share in it, was almost entirely due to Somerset House.[58] It looked so splendid, so serious, that great grey building. And she liked the feeling of people working. She liked those churches, like shapes of grey paper, breasting the stream of the Strand. It was quite different here from Westminster, she thought, getting off at Chancery Lane. It was so serious; it was so busy. In short, she would like to have a profession. She would become a doctor, a farmer, possibly go into Parliament if she found it necessary, all because of the Strand.

The feet of those people busy about their activities, hands putting stone to stone, minds eternally occupied not with trivial chatterings (comparing women to poplars – which was rather exciting, of course, but very silly), but with thoughts of ships, of business, of law, of administration, and with it all so stately (she was in the Temple), gay (there was the river), pious (there was the Church), made her quite determined, whatever her mother might say, to become either a farmer or a doctor. But she was, of course, rather lazy.

And it was much better to say nothing about it. It seemed so silly. It was the sort of thing that did sometimes happen, when one was alone – buildings without architects' names, crowds of people coming back from the city having more power than single clergymen in Kensington, than any of the books Miss Kilman had lent her, to stimulate what lay slumbrous, clumsy, and shy on the mind's sandy floor, to break surface, as a child suddenly stretches its arms; it was just that, perhaps, a sigh, a stretch of the arms, an impulse, a revelation, which has its effects for ever, and then down again it went to the sandy floor. She must go home. She must dress for dinner. But what was the time? – where was a clock?

She looked up Fleet Street. She walked just a little way

towards St. Paul's, shyly, like some one penetrating on tiptoe, exploring a strange house by night with a candle, on edge lest the owner should suddenly fling wide his bedroom door and ask her business, nor did she dare wander off into queer alleys, tempting bystreets, any more than in a strange house open doors which might be bedroom doors, or sitting-room doors, or lead straight to the larder. For no Dalloways came down the Strand daily; she was a pioneer, a stray, venturing, trusting.

In many ways, her mother felt, she was extremely immature, like a child still, attached to dolls, to old slippers; a perfect baby; and that was charming. But then, of course, there was in the Dalloway family the tradition of public service. Abbesses, principals, head mistresses, dignitaries, in the republic of women – without being brilliant, any of them, they were that. She penetrated a little farther in the direction of St. Paul's. She liked the geniality, sisterhood, motherhood, brotherhood of this uproar. It seemed to her good. The noise was tremendous; and suddenly there were trumpets (the unemployed) blaring, rattling about in the uproar; military music; as if people were marching; yet had they been dying – had some woman breathed her last, and whoever was watching, opening the window of the room where she had just brought off that act of supreme dignity, looked down on Fleet Street, that uproar, that military music would have come triumphing up to him, consolatory, indifferent.

It was not conscious. There was no recognition in it of one's fortune, or fate, and for that very reason even to those dazed with watching for the last shivers of consciousness on the faces of the dying, consoling.

Forgetfulness in people might wound, their ingratitude corrode, but this voice, pouring endlessly, year in year out, would take whatever it might be; this vow; this van; this life; this procession, would wrap them all about and carry them on, as in the rough stream of a glacier the ice holds a splinter of bone, a blue petal, some oak trees, and rolls them on.

But it was later than she thought. Her mother would not like her to be wandering off alone like this. She turned back down the Strand.

A puff of wind (in spite of the heat, there was quite a wind) blew a thin black veil over the sun and over the Strand. The faces faded; the omnibuses suddenly lost their glow. For although the clouds were of mountainous white so that one could fancy hacking hard chips off with a hatchet, with broad golden slopes, lawns of celestial pleasure gardens, on their flanks, and had all the appearance of settled habitations assembled for the conference of gods above the world, there was a perpetual movement among them. Signs were interchanged, when, as if to fulfil some scheme arranged already, now a summit dwindled, now a whole block of pyramidal size which had kept its station inalterably advanced into the midst or gravely led the procession to fresh anchorage. Fixed though they seemed at their posts, at rest in perfect unanimity, nothing could be fresher, freer, more sensitive superficially than the snow-white or gold-kindled surface; to change, to go, to dismantle the solemn assemblage was immediately possible; and in spite of the grave fixity, the accumulated robustness and solidity, now they struck light to the earth, now darkness.

Calmly and competently, Elizabeth Dalloway mounted the Westminster omnibus.

Going and coming, beckoning, signalling, so the light and shadow, which now made the wall grey, now the bananas bright yellow, now made the Strand grey, now made the omnibuses bright yellow, seemed to Septimus Warren Smith lying on the sofa in the sitting-room; watching the watery gold glow and fade with the astonishing sensibility of some live creature on the roses, on the wall-paper. Outside the trees dragged their leaves like nets through the depths of the air; the sound of water was in the room, and through the waves came the voices of birds singing. Every power poured its treasures on his head, and his hand lay there on the back of the sofa, as he had seen his hand lie when he was bathing, floating, on the top of the waves, while far away on shore he heard dogs barking and barking far away. Fear no more, says the heart in the body; fear no more.

He was not afraid. At every moment Nature signified by some laughing hint like that gold spot which went round the wall –

there, there, there – her determination to show, by brandishing her plumes, shaking her tresses, flinging her mantle this way and that, beautifully, always beautifully, and standing close up to breathe through her hollowed hands Shakespeare's words, her meaning.

Rezia, sitting at the table twisting a hat in her hands, watched him; saw him smiling. He was happy then. But she could not bear to see him smiling. It was not marriage; it was not being one's husband to look strange like that, always to be starting, laughing, sitting hour after hour silent, or clutching her and telling her to write. The table drawer was full of those writings; about war; about Shakespeare; about great discoveries; how there is no death. Lately he had become excited suddenly for no reason (and both Dr. Holmes and Sir William Bradshaw said excitement was the worst thing for him), and waved his hands and cried out that he knew the truth! He knew everything! That man, his friend who was killed, Evans, had come, he said. He was singing behind the screen. She wrote it down just as he spoke it. Some things were very beautiful; others sheer nonsense. And he was always stopping in the middle, changing his mind; wanting to add something; hearing something new; listening with his hand up. But she heard nothing.

And once they found the girl who did the room reading one of these papers in fits of laughter. It was a dreadful pity. For that made Septimus cry out about human cruelty – how they tear each other to pieces. The fallen, he said, they tear to pieces. 'Holmes is on us,' he would say, and he would invent stories about Holmes; Holmes eating porridge; Holmes reading Shakespeare – making himself roar with laughter or rage, for Dr. Holmes seemed to stand for something horrible to him. 'Human nature', he called him. Then there were the visions. He was drowned, he used to say, and lying on a cliff with the gulls screaming over him. He would look over the edge of the sofa down into the sea. Or he was hearing music. Really it was only a barrel organ or some man crying in the street. But 'Lovely!' he used to cry, and the tears would run down his cheeks, which was to her the most dreadful thing of all, to see a man like Septimus, who had fought,

who was brave, crying. And he would lie listening until suddenly
he would cry that he was falling down, down into the flames!
Actually she would look for flames, it was so vivid. But there was
nothing. They were alone in the room. It was a dream, she would
tell him, and so quiet him at last, but sometimes she was fright-
ened too. She sighed as she sat sewing.

Her sigh was tender and enchanting, like the wind outside a
wood in the evening. Now she put down her scissors; now she
turned to take something from the table. A little stir, a little
crinkling, a little tapping built up something on the table there,
where she sat sewing. Through his eyelashes he could see her
blurred outline; her little black body; her face and hands; her
turning movements at the table, as she took up a reel, or looked
(she was apt to lose things) for her silk. She was making a hat
for Mrs. Filmer's married daughter, whose name was – he had
forgotten her name.

'What is the name of Mrs. Filmer's married daughter?' he
asked.

'Mrs. Peters,' said Rezia. She was afraid it was too small, she
said, holding it before her. Mrs. Peters was a big woman; but
she did not like her. It was only because Mrs. Filmer had been so
good to them – 'She gave me grapes this morning,' she said – that
Rezia wanted to do something to show that they were grateful.
She had come into the room the other evening and found Mrs.
Peters, who thought they were out, playing the gramophone.

'Was it true?' he asked. She was playing the gramophone?
Yes; she had told him about it at the time; she had found Mrs.
Peters playing the gramophone.

He began, very cautiously, to open his eyes, to see whether a
gramophone was really there. But real things – real things were
too exciting. He must be cautious. He would not go mad. First
he looked at the fashion papers on the lower shelf, then gradually at the gramophone with the green trumpet. Nothing could
be more exact. And so, gathering courage, he looked at the sideboard; the plate of bananas; the engraving of Queen Victoria
and the Prince Consort; at the mantelpiece, with the jar of roses.
None of these things moved. All were still; all were real.

'She is a woman with a spiteful tongue,' said Rezia.

'What does Mr. Peters do?' Septimus asked.

'Ah,' said Rezia, trying to remember. She thought Mrs. Filmer had said that he travelled for some company. 'Just now he is in Hull,' she said.

'Just now!' She said that with her Italian accent. She said that herself. He shaded his eyes so that he might see only a little of her face at a time, first the chin, then the nose, then the forehead, in case it were deformed, or had some terrible mark on it. But no, there she was, perfectly natural, sewing, with the pursed lips that women have, the set, the melancholy expression, when sewing. But there was nothing terrible about it, he assured himself, looking a second time, a third time at her face, her hands, for what was frightening or disgusting in her as she sat there in broad daylight, sewing? Mrs. Peters had a spiteful tongue. Mr. Peters was in Hull. Why then rage and prophesy? Why fly scourged and outcast? Why be made to tremble and sob by the clouds? Why seek truths and deliver messages when Rezia sat sticking pins into the front of her dress, and Mr. Peters was in Hull? Miracles, revelations, agonies, loneliness, falling through the sea, down, down into the flames, all were burnt out, for he had a sense, as he watched Rezia trimming the straw hat for Mrs. Peters, of a coverlet of flowers.

'It's too small for Mrs. Peters,' said Septimus.

For the first time for days he was speaking as he used to do! Of course it was – absurdly small, she said. But Mrs. Peters had chosen it.

He took it out of her hands. He said it was an organ grinder's monkey's hat.

How it rejoiced her that! Not for weeks had they laughed like this together, poking fun privately like married people. What she meant was that if Mrs. Filmer had come in, or Mrs. Peters or anybody, they would not have understood what she and Septimus were laughing at.

'There,' she said, pinning a rose to one side of the hat. Never had she felt so happy! Never in her life!

But that was still more ridiculous, Septimus said. Now the

poor woman looked like a pig at a fair. (Nobody ever made her laugh as Septimus did.)

What had she got in her work-box? She had ribbons and beads, tassels, artificial flowers. She tumbled them out on the table. He began putting odd colours together – for though he had no fingers, could not even do up a parcel, he had a wonderful eye, and often he was right, sometimes absurd, of course, but sometimes wonderfully right.

'She shall have a beautiful hat!' he murmured, taking up this and that, Rezia kneeling by his side, looking over his shoulder. Now it was finished – that is to say the design; she must stitch it together. But she must be very, very careful, he said, to keep it just as he had made it.

So she sewed. When she sewed, he thought, she made a sound like a kettle on the hob; bubbling, murmuring, always busy, her strong little pointed fingers pinching and poking; her needle flashing straight. The sun might go in and out, on the tassels, on the wall-paper, but he would wait, he thought, stretching out his feet, looking at his ringed sock at the end of the sofa; he would wait in this warm place, this pocket of still air, which one comes on at the edge of a wood sometimes in the evening, when, because of a fall in the ground, or some arrangement of the trees (one must be scientific above all, scientific), warmth lingers, and the air buffets the cheek like the wing of a bird.

'There it is,' said Rezia, twirling Mrs. Peters' hat on the tips of her fingers. 'That'll do for the moment. Later . . .' her sentence bubbled away drip, drip, drip, like a contented tap left running.

It was wonderful. Never had he done anything which made him feel so proud. It was so real, it was so substantial, Mrs. Peters' hat.

'Just look at it,' he said.

Yes, it would always make her happy to see that hat. He had become himself then, he had laughed then. They had been alone together. Always she would like that hat.

He told her to try it on.

'But I must look so queer!' she cried, running over to the glass and looking first this side, then that. Then she snatched it off again, for there was a tap at the door. Could it be Sir William Bradshaw? Had he sent already?

No! it was only the small girl with the evening paper.

What always happened, then happened – what happened every night of their lives. The small girl sucked her thumb at the door; Rezia went down on her knees; Rezia cooed and kissed; Rezia got a bag of sweets out of the table drawer. For so it always happened. First one thing, then another. So she built it up, first one thing and then another. Dancing, skipping, round and round the room they went. He took the paper. Surrey was all out, he read. There was a heat-wave. Rezia repeated: Surrey was all out.[59] There was a heat-wave, making it part of the game she was playing with Mrs. Filmer's grandchild, both of them laughing, chattering at the same time, at their game. He was very tired. He was very happy. He would sleep. He shut his eyes. But directly he saw nothing the sounds of the game became fainter and stranger and sounded like the cries of people seeking and not finding, and passing farther and farther away. They had lost him!

He started up in terror. What did he see? The plate of bananas on the sideboard. Nobody was there (Rezia had taken the child to its mother; it was bedtime). That was it: to be alone for ever. That was the doom pronounced in Milan when he came into the room and saw them cutting out buckram shapes with their scissors; to be alone for ever.

He was alone with the sideboard and the bananas. He was alone, exposed on this bleak eminence, stretched out – but not on a hill-top; not on a crag; on Mrs. Filmer's sitting-room sofa. As for the visions, the faces, the voices of the dead, where were they? There was a screen in front of him, with black bulrushes and blue swallows. Where he had once seen mountains, where he had seen faces, where he had seen beauty, there was a screen.

'Evans!' he cried. There was no answer. A mouse had squeaked, or a curtain rustled. Those were the voices of the dead. The screen, the coal-scuttle, the sideboard remained to him. Let him then face the screen, the coal-scuttle and the sideboard . . . but Rezia burst into the room chattering.

Some letter had come. Everybody's plans were changed. Mrs. Filmer would not be able to go to Brighton after all. There was no time to let Mrs. Williams know, and really Rezia thought it very, very annoying, when she caught sight of the hat and thought . . . perhaps . . . she . . . might just make a little . . . Her voice died out in contented melody.

'Ah, damn!' she cried (it was a joke of theirs, her swearing); the needle had broken. Hat, child, Brighton, needle. She built it up; first one thing, then another, she built it up, sewing.

She wanted him to say whether by moving the rose she had improved the hat. She sat on the end of the sofa.

They were perfectly happy now, she said suddenly, putting the hat down. For she could say anything to him now. She could say whatever came into her head. That was almost the first thing she had felt about him, that night in the café when he had come in with his English friends. He had come in, rather shyly, looking round him, and his hat had fallen when he hung it up. That she could remember. She knew he was English, though not one of the large Englishmen her sister admired, for he was always thin; but he had a beautiful fresh colour; and with his big nose, his bright eyes, his way of sitting a little hunched, made her think, she had often told him, of a young hawk, that first evening she saw him, when they were playing dominoes, and he had come in – of a young hawk; but with her he was always very gentle. She had never seen him wild or drunk, only suffering sometimes through this terrible war, but even so, when she came in, he would put it all away. Anything, anything in the whole world, any little bother with her work, anything that struck her to say she would tell him, and he understood at once. Her own family even were not the same. Being older than she was and being so clever – how serious he was, wanting her to read Shakespeare before she could even read a child's story in English! – being so much more experienced, he could help her. And she, too, could help him.

But this hat now. And then (it was getting late) Sir William Bradshaw.

She held her hands to her head, waiting for him to say did he like the hat or not, and as she sat there, waiting, looking down, he could feel her mind, like a bird, falling from branch to branch, and always alighting, quite rightly; he could follow her mind, as she sat there in one of those loose lax poses that came to her naturally, and, if he should say anything, at once she smiled, like a bird alighting with all its claws firm upon the bough.

But he remembered. Bradshaw said, 'The people we are most fond of are not good for us when we are ill.' Bradshaw said he must be taught to rest. Bradshaw said they must be separated.

'Must,' 'must,' why 'must'? What power had Bradshaw over him? 'What right has Bradshaw to say "must" to me?' he demanded.

'It is because you talked of killing yourself,' said Rezia. (Mercifully, she could now say anything to Septimus.)

So he was in their power! Holmes and Bradshaw were on him! The brute with the red nostrils was snuffing into every secret place! 'Must' it could say! Where were his papers? the things he had written?

She brought him his papers, the things he had written, things she had written for him. She tumbled them out on to the sofa. They looked at them together. Diagrams, designs, little men and women brandishing sticks for arms, with wings – were they? – on their backs; circles traced round shillings and sixpences – the suns and stars; zigzagging precipices with mountaineers ascending roped together, exactly like knives and forks; sea pieces with little faces laughing out of what might perhaps be waves: the map of the world. Burn them! he cried. Now for his writings; how the dead sing behind rhododendron bushes; odes to Time; conversations with Shakespeare; Evans, Evans, Evans – his messages from the dead; do not cut down trees; tell the Prime Minister. Universal love: the meaning of the world. Burn them! he cried.

But Rezia laid her hands on them. Some were very beautiful, she thought. She would tie them up (for she had no envelope) with a piece of silk.

Even if they took him, she said, she would go with him. They could not separate them against their wills, she said.

Shuffling the edges straight, she did up the papers, and tied the parcel almost without looking, sitting close, sitting beside him, he thought, as if all her petals were about her. She was a flowering tree; and through her branches looked out the face of a lawgiver, who had reached a sanctuary where she feared no one; not Holmes; not Bradshaw; a miracle, a triumph, the last and greatest. Staggering he saw her mount the appalling staircase, laden with Holmes and Bradshaw, men who never weighed less than eleven stone six, who sent their wives to Court, men who made ten thousand a year and talked of proportion; who differed in their verdicts (for Holmes said one thing, Bradshaw another), yet judges they were; who mixed the vision and the sideboard; saw nothing clear, yet ruled, yet inflicted. Over them she triumphed.

'There!' she said. The papers were tied up. No one should get at them. She would put them away.

And, she said, nothing should separate them. She sat down beside him and called him by the name of that hawk or crow which being malicious and a great destroyer of crops was precisely like him. No one could separate them, she said.

Then she got up to go into the bedroom to pack their things, but hearing voices downstairs and thinking that Dr. Holmes had perhaps called, ran down to prevent him coming up.

Septimus could hear her talking to Holmes on the staircase.

'My dear lady, I have come as a friend,' Holmes was saying.

'No. I will not allow you to see my husband,' she said.

He could see her, like a little hen, with her wings spread barring his passage. But Holmes persevered.

'My dear lady, allow me . . . ' Holmes said, putting her aside (Holmes was a powerfully built man).

Holmes was coming upstairs. Holmes would burst open the door. Holmes would say, 'In a funk, eh?' Holmes would get him. But no; not Holmes; not Bradshaw. Getting up rather unsteadily, hopping indeed from foot to foot, he considered Mrs. Filmer's nice clean bread-knife with 'Bread' carved on the handle. Ah, but one mustn't spoil that. The gas fire? But it was too late now. Holmes was coming. Razors he might have got, but Rezia, who always did that sort of thing, had packed them. There remained only the window, the large Bloomsbury lodging-house window; the tiresome, the troublesome, and rather melodramatic business of opening the window and throwing himself out. It was their idea of tragedy, not his or Rezia's (for she was with him). Holmes and Bradshaw liked that sort of thing. (He sat on the sill.) But he would wait till the very last moment. He did not want to die. Life was good. The sun hot. Only human beings? Coming down the staircase opposite an old man stopped and stared at him. Holmes was at the door. 'I'll give it you!' he cried, and flung himself vigorously, violently down on to Mrs. Filmer's area railings.

'The coward!' cried Dr. Holmes, bursting the door open. Rezia ran to the window, she saw; she understood. Dr. Holmes and Mrs. Filmer collided with each other. Mrs. Filmer flapped her apron and made her hide her eyes in the bedroom. There was a great deal of running up and down stairs. Dr. Holmes came in – white as a sheet, shaking all over, with a glass in his hand. She must be brave and drink something, he said (What was it? Something sweet), for her husband was horribly mangled, would not recover consciousness, she must not see him, must be spared as much as possible, would have the inquest to go through, poor young woman. Who could have foretold it? A sudden impulse, no one was in the least to blame (he told Mrs. Filmer). And why the devil he did it, Dr. Holmes could not conceive.

It seemed to her as she drank the sweet stuff that she was opening long windows, stepping out into some garden. But where? The clock was striking – one, two, three: how sensible the sound was; compared with all this thumping and whispering; like Septimus himself. She was falling asleep. But the clock went on striking, four, five, six and Mrs. Filmer waving her apron (they wouldn't bring the body in here, would they?) seemed part of that garden; or a flag. She had once seen a flag slowly rippling out from a mast when she stayed with her aunt at Venice. Men killed in battle were thus saluted, and Septimus had been through the War. Of her memories, most were happy.

She put on her hat, and ran through cornfields – where could it have been? – on to some hill, somewhere near the sea, for there were ships, gulls, butterflies; they sat on a cliff. In London, too, there they sat, and, half dreaming, came to her through the bedroom door, rain falling, whisperings, stirrings among dry corn, the caress of the sea, as it seemed to her, hollowing them in its arched shell and murmuring to her laid on shore, strewn she felt, like flying flowers over some tomb.

'He is dead,' she said, smiling at the poor old woman who guarded her with her honest light-blue eyes fixed on the door. (They wouldn't bring him in here, would they?) But Mrs. Filmer pooh-poohed. Oh no, oh no! They were carrying him away now. Ought she not to be told? Married people ought to be together, Mrs. Filmer thought. But they must do as the doctor said.

'Let her sleep,' said Dr. Holmes, feeling her pulse. She saw the large outline of his body dark against the window. So that was Dr. Holmes.

One of the triumphs of civilisation, Peter Walsh thought. It is one of the triumphs of civilisation, as the light high bell of the ambulance sounded. Swiftly, cleanly, the ambulance sped to the hospital, having picked up instantly, humanely, some poor devil; some one hit on the head, struck down by disease, knocked over perhaps a minute or so ago at one of these crossings, as might happen to oneself. That was civilisation. It struck him coming back from the East – the efficiency, the organisation, the communal spirit of London. Every cart or carriage of its own accord drew aside to let the ambulance pass. Perhaps it was morbid; or was it not touching rather, the respect which they showed this ambulance with its victim inside – busy men hurrying home, yet instantly bethinking them as it passed of some wife; or presumably how easily it might have been them there, stretched on a shelf with a doctor and a nurse . . . Ah, but thinking became morbid, sentimental, directly one began conjuring up doctors, dead bodies; a little glow of pleasure, a sort of lust, too, over the visual impression warned one not to go on with that sort of thing any more – fatal to art, fatal to friendship. True. And yet, thought Peter Walsh, as the ambulance turned the corner, though the light high bell could be heard down the next street and still farther as it crossed the Tottenham Court Road, chiming constantly, it is the privilege of loneliness; in privacy one may do as one chooses. One might weep if no one saw. It had been his undoing – this susceptibility – in Anglo-Indian society; not weeping at the right time, or laughing either. I have that in me, he thought, standing by the pillar-box, which could now dissolve in tears. Why, heaven knows. Beauty of some sort probably, and the weight of the day, which, beginning with that visit to Clarissa, had exhausted him with its heat, its intensity, and the drip, drip of one impression after another down into that cellar where they stood, deep, dark, and no one would ever know. Partly for that reason, its secrecy, complete and inviolable, he had found life like an unknown garden, full of turns and corners, surprising, yes; really it took one's breath away, these moments; there coming to him by the pillar-box opposite the British Museum one of them, a moment, in which things came together; this ambulance; and life and death. It was as if he were sucked up to some very high roof by that rush of emotion, and the rest of him, like a white shell-sprinkled beach, left bare. It had been his undoing in Anglo-Indian society – this susceptibility.

Clarissa once, going on top of an omnibus with him somewhere, Clarissa superficially at least, so easily moved, now in despair, now in the best of spirits, all aquiver in those days and such good company, spotting queer little scenes, names, people from the top of a bus, for they used to explore London and bring back bags full of treasures from the Caledonian market – Clarissa had a theory in those days – they had heaps of theories, always theories, as young people have. It was to explain the feeling they had of dissatisfaction; not knowing people; not being known. For how could they know each other? You met every day; then not for six months, or years. It was unsatisfactory, they agreed, how little one knew people. But she said, sitting on the bus going

up Shaftesbury Avenue, she felt herself everywhere; not 'here,
here, here'; and she tapped the back of the seat; but everywhere.
She waved her hand, going up Shaftesbury Avenue. She was all
that. So that to know her, or any one, one must seek out the
people who completed them; even the places. Odd affinities she
had with people she had never spoken to, some woman in the
street, some man behind a counter – even trees, or barns. It ended
in a transcendental theory which, with her horror of death, allowed her to believe, or say that she believed (for all her scepti-
cism), that since our apparitions, the part of us which appears,
are so momentary compared with the other, the unseen part of
us, which spreads wide, the unseen might survive, be recovered
somehow attached to this person or that, or even haunting certain places, after death. Perhaps – perhaps.

Looking back over that long friendship of almost thirty years
her theory worked to this extent. Brief, broken, often painful as
their actual meetings had been, what with his absences and in-
terruptions (this morning, for instance, in came Elizabeth, like
a long-legged colt, handsome, dumb, just as he was beginning
to talk to Clarissa), the effect of them on his life was immeasurable. There was a mystery about it. You were given a sharp,
acute, uncomfortable grain – the actual meeting; horribly painful as often as not; yet in absence, in the most unlikely places, it
would flower out, open, shed its scent, let you touch, taste, look
about you, get the whole feel of it and understanding, after years
of lying lost. Thus she had come to him; on board ship; in the
Himalayas; suggested by the oddest things (so Sally Seton, generous, enthusiastic goose! thought of *him* when she saw blue
hydrangeas). She had influenced him more than any person he
had ever known. And always in this way coming before him
without his wishing it, cool, lady-like, critical; or ravishing, romantic, recalling some field or English harvest. He saw her most
often in the country, not in London. One scene after another at
Bourton . . .

He had reached his hotel. He crossed the hall, with its mounds
of reddish chairs and sofas, its spike-leaved, withered-looking
plants. He got his key off the hook. The young lady handed him

some letters. He went upstairs – he saw her most often at Bourton, in the late summer, when he stayed there for a week, or fortnight even, as people did in those days. First on top of some hill there she would stand, hands clapped to her hair, her cloak blowing out, pointing, crying to them – She saw the Severn beneath. Or in a wood, making the kettle boil – very ineffective with her fingers; the smoke curtseying, blowing in their faces; her little pink face showing through; begging water from an old woman in a cottage, who came to the door to watch them go. They walked always; the others drove. She was bored driving, disliked all animals, except that dog. They tramped miles along roads. She would break off to get her bearings, pilot him back across country; and all the time they argued, discussed poetry, discussed people, discussed politics (she was a Radical then); never noticing a thing except when she stopped, cried out at a view or a tree, and made him look with her; and so on again, through stubble fields, she walking ahead, with a flower for her aunt, never tired of walking for all her delicacy; to drop down on Bourton in the dusk. Then, after dinner, old Breitkopf would open the piano and sing without any voice, and they would lie sunk in arm-chairs, trying not to laugh, but always breaking down and laughing, laughing – laughing at nothing. Breitkopf was supposed not to see. And then in the morning, flirting up and down like a wagtail in front of the house . . .

Oh it was a letter from her! This blue envelope; that was her hand. And he would have to read it. Here was another of those meetings, bound to be painful! To read her letter needed the devil of an effort. 'How heavenly it was to see him. She must tell him that.' That was all.

But it upset him. It annoyed him. He wished she hadn't written it. Coming on top of his thoughts, it was like a nudge in the ribs. Why couldn't she let him be? After all, she had married Dalloway, and lived with him in perfect happiness all these years.

These hotels are not consoling places. Far from it. Any number of people had hung up their hats on those pegs. Even the flies, if you thought of it, had settled on other people's noses. As for the cleanliness which hit him in the face, it wasn't cleanliness, so much as bareness, frigidity; a thing that had to be. Some arid matron made her rounds at dawn sniffing, peering, causing blue-nosed maids to scour, for all the world as if the next visitor were a joint of meat to be served on a perfectly clean platter. For sleep, one bed; for sitting in, one armchair; for cleaning one's teeth and shaving one's chin, one tumbler, one looking-glass. Books, letters, dressing-gown, slipped about on the impersonality of the horsehair like incongruous impertinences. And it was Clarissa's letter that made him see all this. 'Heavenly to see you. She must say so!' He folded the paper; pushed it away; nothing would induce him to read it again!

To get that letter to him by six o'clock she must have sat down and written it directly he left her; stamped it; sent somebody to the post. It was, as people say, very like her. She was upset by his visit. She had felt a great deal; had for a moment, when she kissed his hand, regretted, envied him even, remembered possibly (for he saw her look it) something he had said – how they would change the world if she married him perhaps; whereas, it was this; it was middle age; it was mediocrity; then forced herself with her indomitable vitality to put all that aside, there being in her a thread of life which for toughness, endurance, power to overcome obstacles, and carry her triumphantly through he had never known the like of. Yes; but there would come a reaction directly he left the room. She would be frightfully sorry for him; she would think what in the world she could do to give him pleasure (short always of the one thing), and he could see her with the tears running down her cheeks going to her writing-table and dashing off that one line which he was to find greeting him . . .

'Heavenly to see you!' And she meant it.

Peter Walsh had now unlaced his boots.

But it would not have been a success, their marriage. The other thing, after all, came so much more naturally.

It was odd; it was true; lots of people felt it. Peter Walsh, who had done just respectably, filled the usual posts adequately, was liked, but thought a little cranky, gave himself airs – it was odd that *he* should have had, especially now that his hair was grey, a contented look; a look of having reserves. It was this that made him attractive to women, who liked the sense that he was not altogether manly. There was something unusual about him, or something behind him. It might be that he was bookish – never came to see you without taking up the book on the table (he was now reading, with his bootlaces trailing on the floor); or that he was a gentleman, which showed itself in the way he knocked the ashes out of his pipe, and in his manners of course to women. For it was very charming and quite ridiculous how easily some girl without a grain of sense could twist him round her finger. But at her own risk. That is to say, though he might be ever so easy, and indeed with his gaiety and good-breeding fascinating to be with, it was only up to a point. She said something – no, no; he saw through that. He wouldn't stand that – no, no. Then he could shout and rock and hold his sides together over some joke with men. He was the best judge of cooking in India. He was a man. But not the sort of man one had to respect – which was a mercy; not like Major Simmons, for instance; not in the least, Daisy thought, when in spite of her two small children, she used to compare them.

He pulled off his boots. He emptied his pockets. Out came with his pocket-knife a snapshot of Daisy on the verandah; Daisy all in white, with a fox-terrier on her knee; very charming, very dark; the best he had ever seen of her. It did come, after all, so naturally; so much more naturally than Clarissa. No fuss. No bother. No finicking and fidgeting. All plain sailing. And the dark, adorably pretty girl on the verandah exclaimed (he could hear her) Of course, of course she would give him everything! she cried (she had no sense of discretion), everything he wanted! she cried, running to meet him, whoever might be looking. And she was only twenty-four. And she had two children. Well, well!

Well indeed he had got himself into a mess at his age. And it came over him when he woke in the night pretty forcibly. Suppose they did marry? For him it would be all very well, but what about her? Mrs. Burgess, a good sort and no chatterbox, in whom he had confided, thought this absence of his in England, ostensibly to see lawyers, might serve to make Daisy reconsider, think what it meant. It was a question of her position, Mrs. Burgess said; the social barrier; giving up her children. She'd be a widow with a past one of these days, draggling about in the suburbs, or more likely, indiscriminate (you know, she said, what such women get like, with too much paint). But Peter Walsh pooh-poohed all that. He didn't mean to die yet. Anyhow, she must settle for herself; judge for herself, he thought, padding about the room in his socks, smoothing out his dress-shirt, for he might go to Clarissa's party, or he might go to one of the Halls, or he might settle in and read an absorbing book written by a man he used to know at Oxford. And if he did retire, that's what he'd do – write books. He would go to Oxford and poke about in the Bodleian. Vainly the dark, adorably pretty girl ran to the end of the terrace; vainly waved her hand; vainly cried she didn't care a straw what people said. There he was, the man she thought the world of, the perfect gentleman, the fascinating, the distinguished (and his age made not the least difference to her), padding about a room in an hotel in Bloomsbury, shaving, washing, continuing, as he took up cans, put down razors, to poke about in the Bodleian, and get at the truth about one or two little matters that interested him. And he would have a chat with whoever it might be, and so come to disregard more and more precise hours for lunch, and miss engagements; and when Daisy asked him, as she would, for a kiss, a scene, fail to come up to the scratch[60] (though he was genuinely devoted to her) – in short it might be happier, as Mrs. Burgess said, that she should forget him, or merely remember him as he was in August 1922, like a figure standing at the cross roads at dusk, which grows more and more remote as the dog-cart spins away, carrying her securely fastened to the back seat, though her arms are outstretched, and as she sees the figure dwindle and disappear, still she cries out how she would do anything in the world, anything, anything, anything . . .

He never knew what people thought. It became more and more difficult for him to concentrate. He became absorbed; he became busied with his own concerns; now surly, now gay;

dependent on women, absent-minded, moody, less and less able (so he thought as he shaved) to understand why Clarissa couldn't simply find them a lodging and be nice to Daisy; introduce her. And then he could just – just do what? just haunt and hover (he was at the moment actually engaged in sorting out various keys, papers), swoop and taste, be alone, in short, sufficient to himself; and yet nobody of course was more dependent upon others (he buttoned his waistcoat); it had been his undoing. He could not keep out of smoking-rooms, liked colonels, liked golf, liked bridge, and above all women's society, and the fineness of their companionship, and their faithfulness and audacity and greatness in loving which, though it had its drawbacks, seemed to him (and the dark, adorably pretty face was on top of the envelopes) so wholly admirable, so splendid a flower to grow on the crest of human life, and yet he could not come up to the scratch, being always apt to see round things (Clarissa had sapped something in him permanently), and to tire very easily of mute devotion and to want variety in love, though it would make him furious if Daisy loved anybody else, furious! for he was jealous, uncontrollably jealous by temperament. He suffered tortures! But where was his knife; his watch; his seals, his note-case, and Clarissa's letter which he would not read again but liked to think of, and Daisy's photograph? And now for dinner.

They were eating.

Sitting at little tables round vases, dressed or not dressed, with their shawls and bags laid beside them, with their air of false composure, for they were not used to so many courses at dinner; and confidence, for they were able to pay for it; and strain, for they had been running about London all day shopping, sightseeing; and their natural curiosity, for they looked round and up as the nice-looking gentleman in horn-rimmed spectacles came in; and their good nature, for they would have been glad to do any little service, such as lend a time-table or impart useful information; and their desire, pulsing in them, tugging at them subterraneously, somehow to establish connections if it were only a birthplace (Liverpool, for example), in common or friends of the same name; with their furtive glances, odd silences, and sudden withdrawals into family jocularity and isolation; there they sat eating dinner when Mr. Walsh came in and took his seat at a little table by the curtain.

It was not that he said anything, for being solitary he could only address himself to the waiter; it was his way of looking at the menu, of pointing his forefinger to a particular wine, of hitching himself up to the table, of addressing himself seriously, not gluttonously to dinner, that won him their respect; which, having to remain unexpressed for the greater part of the meal, flared up at the table where the Morrises sat when Mr. Walsh was heard to say at the end of the meal, 'Bartlett pears.' Why he should have spoken so moderately yet firmly, with the air of a disciplinarian well within his rights which are founded upon justice, neither young Charles Morris, nor old Charles, neither Miss Elaine nor Mrs. Morris knew. But when he said, 'Bartlett pears,' sitting alone at his table, they felt that he counted on their support in some lawful demand; was champion of a cause which immediately became their own, so that their eyes met his eyes sympathetically, and when they all reached the smoking-room simultaneously, a little talk between them became inevitable.

It was not very profound – only to the effect that London was crowded; had changed in thirty years; that Mr. Morris preferred Liverpool; that Mrs. Morris had been to the Westminster flower-show, and that they had all seen the Prince of Wales. Yet, thought Peter Walsh, no family in the world can compare with the Morrises; none whatever; and their relations to each other are perfect, and they don't care a hang for the upper classes, and they like what they like, and Elaine is training for the family business, and the boy has won a scholarship at Leeds, and the old lady (who is about his own age) has three more children at home; and they have two motor cars, but Mr. Morris still mends the boots on Sunday; it is superb, it is absolutely superb, thought Peter Walsh, swaying a little backwards and forwards with his liqueur glass in his hand among the hairy red chairs and ash-trays, feeling very well pleased with himself, for the Morrises liked him. Yes, they liked a man who said 'Bartlett pears.' They liked him, he felt.

He would go to Clarissa's party. (The Morrises moved off; but they would meet again.) He would go to Clarissa's party, because he wanted to ask Richard what they were doing in India – the conservative duffers. And what's being acted? And music . . . Oh yes, and mere gossip.

For this is the truth about our soul, he thought, our self, who fish-like inhabits deep seas and plies among obscurities threading her way between the boles of giant weeds, over sun-flickered spaces and on and on into gloom, cold, deep, inscrutable; suddenly she shoots to the surface and sports on the wind-wrinkled waves; that is, has a positive need to brush, scrape, kindle herself, gossiping. What did the Government mean – Richard Dalloway would know – to do about India?

Since it was a very hot night and the paper boys went by with placards proclaiming in huge red letters that there was a heat-wave, wicker chairs were placed on the hotel steps and there, sipping, smoking, detached gentlemen sat. Peter Walsh sat there. One might fancy that day, the London day, was just beginning. Like a woman who had slipped off her print dress and white apron to array herself in blue and pearls, the day changed, put off stuff, took gauze, changed to evening, and with the same sigh of exhilaration that a woman breathes, tumbling petticoats on the floor, it too shed dust, heat, colour; the traffic thinned; motor cars, tinkling, darting, succeeded the lumber of vans; and here and there among the thick foliage of the squares an intense light hung. I resign, the evening seemed to say, as it paled and faded above the battlements and prominences, moulded, pointed, of hotel, flat, and block of shops, I fade, she was beginning, I disappear, but London would have none of it, and rushed her bayonets into the sky, pinioned her, constrained her to partnership in her revelry.

For the great revolution of Mr. Willett's summer time[61] had taken place since Peter Walsh's last visit to England. The prolonged evening was new to him. It was inspiriting, rather. For as the young people went by with their despatch-boxes, awfully glad to be free, proud too, dumbly, of stepping this famous pavement, joy of a kind, cheap, tinselly, if you like, but all the same

rapture, flushed their faces. They dressed well too; pink stockings; pretty shoes. They would now have two hours at the pictures. It sharpened, it refined them, the yellow-blue evening
light; and on the leaves in the square shone lurid, livid – they
looked as if dipped in sea water – the foliage of a submerged city.
He was astonished by the beauty; it was encouraging too, for
where the returned Anglo-Indian sat by rights (he knew crowds
of them) in the Oriental Club biliously summing up the ruin of
the world, here was he, as young as ever; envying young people
their summer time and the rest of it, and more than suspecting
from the words of a girl, from a housemaid's laughter – intangible
things you couldn't lay your hands on – that shift in the whole
pyramidal accumulation which in his youth had seemed immov-
able. On top of them it had pressed; weighed them down, the
women especially, like those flowers Clarissa's Aunt Helena
used to press between sheets of grey blotting-paper with Littré's
dictionary[62] on top, sitting under the lamp after dinner. She was
dead now. He had heard of her, from Clarissa, losing the sight
of one eye. It seemed so fitting – one of nature's masterpieces –
that old Miss Parry should turn to glass. She would die like some
bird in a frost gripping her perch. She belonged to a different
age, but being so entire, so complete, would always stand up on
the horizon, stone-white, eminent, like a lighthouse marking
some past stage on this adventurous, long, long voyage, this
interminable – (he felt for a copper to buy a paper and read
about Surrey and Yorkshire; he had held out that copper millions of times – Surrey was all out once more) – this interminable
life. But cricket was no mere game. Cricket was important. He
could never help reading about cricket. He read the scores in the
stop press first, then how it was a hot day; then about a murder
case. Having done things millions of times enriched them,
though it might be said to take the surface off. The past enriched, and experience, and having cared for one or two people,
and so having acquired the power which the young lack, of cutting short, doing what one likes, not caring a rap what people
say and coming and going without any very great expectations
(he left his paper on the table and moved off), which however

(and he looked for his hat and coat) was not altogether true of him, not to-night, for here he was starting to go to a party, at his age, with the belief upon him, that he was about to have an experience. But what?

Beauty anyhow. Not the crude beauty of the eye. It was not beauty pure and simple – Bedford Place leading into Russell Square. It was straightness and emptiness of course; the symmetry of a corridor; but it was also windows lit up, a piano, a gramophone sounding; a sense of pleasure-making hidden, but now and again emerging when, through the uncurtained window, the window left open, one saw parties sitting over tables, young people slowly circling, conversations between men and women, maids idly looking out (a strange comment theirs, when work was done), stockings drying on top ledges, a parrot, a few plants. Absorbing, mysterious, of infinite richness, this life. And in the large square where the cabs shot and swerved so quick, there were loitering couples, dallying, embracing, shrunk up under the shower of a tree; that was moving; so silent, so absorbed, that one passed, discreetly, timidly, as if in the presence of some sacred ceremony to interrupt which would have been impious. That was interesting. And so on into the flare and glare.

His light overcoat blew open, he stepped with indescribable idiosyncrasy, leant a little forward, tripped, with his hands behind his back and his eyes still a little hawk-like; he tripped through London, towards Westminster, observing.

Was everybody dining out, then? Doors were being opened here by a footman to let issue a high-stepping old dame, in buckled shoes, with three purple ostrich feathers in her hair. Doors were being opened for ladies wrapped like mummies in shawls with bright flowers on them, ladies with bare heads. And in respectable quarters with stucco pillars through small front gardens, lightly swathed, with combs in their hair (having run up to see the children), women came; men waited for them, with their coats blowing open, and the motor started. Everybody was going out. What with these doors being opened, and the descent and the start, it seemed as if the whole of London were embarking in little boats moored to the bank, tossing on the waters, as if the whole place were floating off in carnival. And Whitehall was skated over, silver beaten as it was, skated over by spiders, and there was a sense of midges round the arc lamps; it was so hot that people stood about talking. And here in Westminster was a retired Judge, presumably, sitting four-square at his house door dressed all in white. An Anglo-Indian presumably.

And here a shindy of brawling women, drunken women; here only a policeman and looming houses, high houses, domed houses, churches, parliaments, and the hoot of a steamer on the river, a hollow misty cry. But it was her street, this, Clarissa's; cabs were rushing round the corner, like water round the piers of a bridge, drawn together, it seemed to him because they bore people going to her party, Clarissa's party.

The cold stream of visual impressions failed him now as if the eye were a cup that overflowed and let the rest run down its china walls unrecorded. The brain must wake now. The body must contract now, entering the house, the lighted house, where the door stood open, where the motor cars were standing, and bright women descending: the soul must brave itself to endure. He opened the big blade of his pocket-knife.

Lucy came running full tilt downstairs, having just nipped in to the drawing-room to smooth a cover, to straighten a chair, to pause a moment and feel whoever came in must think how clean, how bright, how beautifully cared for, when they saw the beautiful silver, the brass fire-irons, the new chair-covers, and the curtains of yellow chintz: she appraised each; heard a roar of voices; people already coming up from dinner; she must fly!

The Prime Minister was coming, Agnes said: so she had heard them say in the dining-room, she said, coming in with a tray of glasses. Did it matter, did it matter in the least, one Prime Minister more or less? It made no difference at this hour of the night to Mrs. Walker among the plates, saucepans, cullenders, frying-pans, chicken in aspic, ice-cream freezers, pared crusts of bread, lemons, soup tureens, and pudding basins which, however hard they washed up in the scullery, seemed to be all on top of her, on the kitchen table, on chairs, while the fire blared and roared, the electric lights glared, and still supper had to be laid. All she felt was, one Prime Minister more or less made not a scrap of difference to Mrs. Walker.

The ladies were going upstairs already, said Lucy; the ladies were going up, one by one, Mrs. Dalloway walking last and almost always sending back some message to the kitchen, 'My love to Mrs. Walker,' that was it one night. Next morning they would go over the dishes – the soup, the salmon; the salmon, Mrs. Walker knew, as usual underdone, for she always got nervous about the pudding and left it to Jenny; so it happened, the salmon was always underdone. But some lady with fair hair and silver ornaments had said, Lucy said, about the entrée, was it really made at home? But it was the salmon that bothered Mrs. Walker, as she spun the plates round and round, and pushed in dampers[63] and pulled out dampers; and there came a burst of laughter from the dining-room; a voice speaking; then another burst of laughter – the gentlemen enjoying themselves when the ladies had gone. The tokay, said Lucy running in. Mr. Dalloway had sent for the tokay, from the Emperor's cellars, the Imperial Tokay.

It was borne through the kitchen. Over her shoulder Lucy reported how Miss Elizabeth looked quite lovely; she couldn't take her eyes off her; in her pink dress, wearing the necklace Mr. Dalloway had given her. Jenny must remember the dog, Miss Elizabeth's fox-terrier, which, since it bit had to be shut up and might, Elizabeth thought, want something. Jenny must remember the dog. But Jenny was not going upstairs with all those people about. There was a motor at the door already! There was a ring at the bell – and the gentlemen still in the dining-room, drinking tokay!

There, they were going upstairs; that was the first to come, and now they would come faster and faster, so that Mrs. Parkinson (hired for parties) would leave the hall door ajar, and the hall would be full of gentlemen waiting (they stood waiting, sleeking down their hair) while the ladies took their cloaks off in the room along the passage; where Mrs. Barnet helped them, old Ellen Barnet, who had been with the family for forty years, and came every summer to help the ladies, and remembered mothers when they were girls, and though very unassuming did shake hands; said 'milady' very respectfully, yet had a humorous way with her, looking at the young ladies, and ever so tactfully helping Lady Lovejoy, who had some trouble with her under-bodice. And they could not help feeling, Lady Lovejoy and Miss Alice, that some little privilege in the matter of brush and comb, was awarded them having known Mrs. Barnet – 'thirty years, milady,' Mrs. Barnet supplied her. Young ladies did not use to rouge, said Lady Lovejoy, when they stayed at Bourton in the old days. And Miss Alice didn't need rouge, said Mrs. Barnet, looking at her fondly. There Mrs. Barnet would sit, in the cloak-room, patting down the furs, smoothing out the Spanish shawls, tidying the dressing-table, and knowing perfectly well, in spite of the furs and the embroideries, which were nice ladies, which were not. The dear old body, said Lady Lovejoy, mounting the stairs, Clarissa's old nurse.

And then Lady Lovejoy stiffened. 'Lady and Miss Lovejoy,' she said to Mr. Wilkins (hired for parties). He had an admirable manner, as he bent and straightened himself, bent and straightened himself and announced with perfect impartiality 'Lady and Miss Lovejoy ... Sir John and Lady Needham ... Miss Weld ... Mr. Walsh.' His manner was admirable; his family life must be irreproachable, except that it seemed impossible that a being with greenish lips and shaven cheeks could ever have blundered into the nuisance of children.

'How delightful to see you!' said Clarissa. She said it to every one. How delightful to see you! She was at her worst – effusive, insincere. It was a great mistake to have come. He should have stayed at home and read his book, thought Peter Walsh; should have gone to a music hall; he should have stayed at home, for he knew no one.

Oh dear, it was going to be a failure; a complete failure, Clarissa felt it in her bones as dear old Lord Lexham stood there apologising for his wife who had caught cold at the Buckingham

Palace garden party. She could see Peter out of the tail of her eye, criticising her, there, in that corner. Why, after all, did she do these things? Why seek pinnacles and stand drenched in fire? Might it consume her anyhow! Burn her to cinders! Better anything, better brandish one's torch and hurl it to earth than taper and dwindle away like some Ellie Henderson! It was extraordinary how Peter put her into these states just by coming and standing in a corner. He made her see herself; exaggerate. It was idiotic. But why did he come, then, merely to criticise? Why always take, never give? Why not risk one's one little point of view? There he was wandering off, and she must speak to him. But she would not get the chance. Life was that humiliation, renunciation. What Lord Lexham was saying was that his wife would not wear her furs at the garden party because 'my dear, you ladies are all alike' – Lady Lexham being seventy-five at least! It was delicious, how they petted each other, that old couple. She did like old Lord Lexham. She did think it mattered, her party, and it made her feel quite sick to know that it was all going wrong, all falling flat. Anything, any explosion, any horror was better than people wandering aimlessly, standing in a bunch at a corner like Ellie Henderson, not even caring to hold themselves upright.

Gently the yellow curtain with all the birds of Paradise blew out and it seemed as if there were a flight of wings into the room, right out, then sucked back. (For the windows were open.) Was it draughty, Ellie Henderson wondered? She was subject to chills. But it did not matter that she should come down sneezing to-morrow; it was the girls with their naked shoulders she thought of, being trained to think of others by an old father, an invalid, late vicar of Bourton, but he was dead now; and her chills never went to her chest, never. It was the girls she thought of, the young girls with their bare shoulders, she herself having always been a wisp of a creature, with her thin hair and meagre profile; though now, past fifty, there was beginning to shine through some mild beam, something purified into distinction by years of self-abnegation but obscured again, perpetually, by her distressing gentility, her panic fear, which arose from three

hundred pounds income, and her weaponless state (she could
not earn a penny) and it made her timid, and more and more
disqualified year by year to meet well-dressed people who did
this sort of thing every night of the season, merely telling their
maids 'I'll wear so and so,' whereas Ellie Henderson ran out
nervously and bought cheap pink flowers, half-a-dozen, and
then threw a shawl over her old black dress. For her invitation
to Clarissa's party had come at the last moment. She was not
quite happy about it. She had a sort of feeling that Clarissa had
not meant to ask her this year.

Why should she? There was no reason really, except that they
had always known each other. Indeed, they were cousins. But
naturally they had rather drifted apart, Clarissa being so sought
after. It was an event to her, going to a party. It was quite a treat
just to see the lovely clothes. Wasn't that Elizabeth, grown up,
with her hair done in the fashionable way, in the pink dress? Yet
she could not be more than seventeen. She was very, very handsome. But girls when they first came out didn't seem to wear
white as they used. (She must remember everything to tell Edith.)
Girls wore straight frocks, perfectly tight, with skirts well above
the ankles. It was not becoming, she thought.

So, with her weak eyesight, Ellie Henderson craned rather
forward, and it wasn't so much she who minded not having any
one to talk to (she hardly knew anybody there), for she felt that
they were all such interesting people to watch; politicians presumably; Richard Dalloway's friends; but it was Richard himself
who felt that he could not let the poor creature go on standing
there all the evening by herself.

'Well, Ellie, and how's the world treating *you*?' he said in his
genial way, and Ellie Henderson, getting nervous and flushing
and feeling that it was extraordinarily nice of him to come and
talk to her, said that many people really felt the heat more than
the cold.

'Yes, they do,' said Richard Dalloway. 'Yes.'

But what more did one say?

'Hullo, Richard,' said somebody, taking him by the elbow,

and, good Lord, there was old Peter, old Peter Walsh. He was delighted to see him – ever so pleased to see him! He hadn't changed a bit. And off they went together walking right across the room, giving each other little pats, as if they hadn't met for a long time, Ellie Henderson thought, watching them go, certain she knew that man's face. A tall man, middle aged, rather fine eyes, dark, wearing spectacles, with a look of John Burrows. Edith would be sure to know.

The curtain with its flight of birds of Paradise blew out again. And Clarissa saw – she saw Ralph Lyon beat it back, and go on talking. So it wasn't a failure after all! it was going to be all right now – her party. It had begun. It had started. But it was still touch and go. She must stand there for the present. People seemed to come in a rush.

'Colonel and Mrs. Garrod . . . Mr. Hugh Whitbread . . . Mr. Bowley . . . Mrs. Hilbery . . . Lady Mary Maddox . . . Mr. Quin . . . ' intoned Wilkins. She had six or seven words with each, and they went on, they went into the rooms; into something now, not nothing, since Ralph Lyon had beat back the curtain.

And yet for her own part, it was too much of an effort. She was not enjoying it. It was too much like being – just anybody, standing there; anybody could do it; yet this anybody she did a little admire, couldn't help feeling that she had, anyhow, made this happen, that it marked a stage, this post that she felt herself to have become, for oddly enough she had quite forgotten what she looked like, but felt herself a stake driven in at the top of her stairs. Every time she gave a party she had this feeling of being something not herself, and that every one was unreal in one way; much more real in another. It was, she thought, partly their clothes, partly being taken out of their ordinary ways, partly the background; it was possible to say things you couldn't say any-how else, things that needed an effort; possible to go much deeper. But not for her; not yet anyhow.

'How delightful to see you!' she said. Dear old Sir Harry! He would know every one.

And what was so odd about it was the sense one had as they came up the stairs one after another, Mrs. Mount and Celia, Herbert Ainsty, Mrs. Dakers – oh, and Lady Bruton!

'How awfully good of you to come!' she said, and she meant it – it was odd how standing there one felt them going on, going on, some quite old, some . . .

What name? Lady Rosseter? But who on earth was Lady Rosseter?

'Clarissa!' That voice! It was Sally Seton! Sally Seton! after all these years! She loomed through a mist. For she hadn't looked like *that*, Sally Seton, when Clarissa grasped the hot-water can. To think of her under this roof, under this roof! Not like that!

All on top of each other, embarrassed, laughing, words tumbled out – passing through London; heard from Clara Haydon; what a chance of seeing you! So I thrust myself in – without an invitation . . .

One might put down the hot-water can quite composedly. The lustre had left her. Yet it was extraordinary to see her again, older, happier, less lovely. They kissed each other, first this cheek, then that, by the drawing-room door, and Clarissa turned, with Sally's hand in hers, and saw her rooms full, heard the roar of voices, saw the candlesticks, the blowing curtains, and the roses which Richard had given her.

'I have five enormous boys,' said Sally.

She had the simplest egotism, the most open desire to be thought first always, and Clarissa loved her for being still like that. 'I can't believe it!' she cried, kindling all over with pleasure at the thought of the past.

But alas, Wilkins; Wilkins wanted her; Wilkins was emitting in a voice of commanding authority, as if the whole company must be admonished and the hostess reclaimed from frivolity, one name:

'The Prime Minister,' said Peter Walsh.

The Prime Minister? Was it really? Ellie Henderson marvelled. What a thing to tell Edith!

One couldn't laugh at him. He looked so ordinary. You might have stood him behind a counter and bought biscuits – poor chap, all rigged up in gold lace. And to be fair, as he went his rounds, first with Clarissa, then with Richard escorting him, he did it very well. He tried to look somebody. It was amusing to watch. Nobody looked at him. They just went on talking, yet it was perfectly plain that they all knew, felt to the marrow of their bones, this majesty passing; this symbol of what they all stood for, English society. Old Lady Bruton, and she looked very fine too, very stalwart in her lace, swam up, and they withdrew into a little room which at once became spied upon, guarded, and a sort of stir and rustle rippled through every one openly: the Prime Minister!

Lord, lord, the snobbery of the English! thought Peter Walsh, standing in the corner. How they loved dressing up in gold lace and doing homage! There! That must be – by Jove it was – Hugh Whitbread, snuffing round the precincts of the great, grown rather fatter, rather whiter, the admirable Hugh!

He looked always as if he were on duty, thought Peter, a privileged but secretive being, hoarding secrets which he would die to defend, though it was only some little piece of tittle-tattle dropped by a court footman which would be in all the papers to-morrow. Such were his rattles, his baubles, in playing with which he had grown white, come to the verge of old age, enjoying the respect and affection of all who had the privilege of knowing this type of the English public school man. Inevitably one made up things like that about Hugh; that was his style; the style of those admirable letters which Peter had read thousands of miles across the sea in the *Times*, and had thanked God he was out of that pernicious hubble-bubble if it were only to hear baboons chatter and coolies beat their wives. An olive-skinned youth from one of the Universities stood obsequiously by. Him he would patronise, initiate, teach how to get on. For he liked nothing better than doing kindnesses, making the hearts of old ladies palpitate with the joy of being thought of in their age, their affliction, thinking themselves quite forgotten, yet here was dear Hugh driving up and spending an hour talking of the past, remembering trifles, praising the home-made cake, though Hugh might eat cake with a Duchess any day of his life, and, to look at him, probably did spend a good deal of time in that agreeable occupation. The All-judging, the All-merciful, might excuse. Peter Walsh had no mercy. Villains there must be, and, God knows, the rascals who get hanged for battering the brains of a girl out in a train[64] do less harm on the whole than Hugh Whitbread and his kindness! Look at him now, on tiptoe, dancing forward, bowing and scraping, as the Prime Minister and Lady Bruton emerged, intimating for all the world to see that he was privileged to say something, something private, to Lady Bruton as she passed. She stopped. She wagged her fine old head. She was thanking him presumably for some piece of servility. She had her toadies, minor officials in Government offices who ran about putting through little jobs on her behalf, in return for which she gave them luncheon. But she derived from the eighteenth century. She was all right.

And now Clarissa escorted her Prime Minister down the room, prancing, sparkling, with the stateliness of her grey hair. She wore ear-rings, and a silver-green mermaid's dress. Lolloping on the waves and braiding her tresses she seemed, having that gift still; to be; to exist; to sum it all up in the moment as she passed; turned, caught her scarf in some other woman's dress, unhitched it, laughed, all with the most perfect ease and air of a creature floating in its element. But age had brushed her; even as a mermaid might behold in her glass the setting sun on some very clear evening over the waves. There was a breath of tenderness; her severity, her prudery, her woodenness were all warmed through now, and she had about her as she said goodbye to the thick gold-laced man who was doing his best, and good luck to him, to look important, an inexpressible dignity; an exquisite cordiality; as if she wished the whole world well, and must now, being on the very verge and rim of things, take her leave. So she made him think. (But he was not in love.)

Indeed, Clarissa felt, the Prime Minister had been good to come. And, walking down the room with him, with Sally there and Peter there and Richard very pleased, with all those people rather inclined, perhaps, to envy, she had felt that intoxication of the moment, that dilatation of the nerves of the heart itself till it seemed to quiver, steeped, upright; – yes, but after all it was what other people felt, that; for, though she loved it and felt it tingle and sting, still these semblances, these triumphs (dear old Peter, for example, thinking her so brilliant), had a hollowness; at arm's length they were, not in the heart; and it might be that she was growing old, but they satisfied her no longer as they used; and suddenly, as she saw the Prime Minister go down the stairs, the gilt rim of the Sir Joshua[65] picture of the little girl with a muff brought back Kilman with a rush; Kilman her enemy. That was satisfying; that was real. Ah, how she hated her – hot, hypocritical, corrupt; with all that power; Elizabeth's seducer; the woman who had crept in to steal and defile (Richard would say, What nonsense!). She hated her: she loved her. It was enemies one wanted, not friends – not Mrs. Durrant and Clara, Sir William and Lady Bradshaw, Miss Truelock and Eleanor Gibson (whom she saw coming upstairs). They must find her if they wanted her. She was for the party!

There was her old friend Sir Harry.

'Dear Sir Harry!' she said, going up to the fine old fellow who had produced more bad pictures than any other two Academicians in the whole of St. John's Wood (they were always of cattle, standing in sunset pools absorbing moisture, or signifying, for he had a certain range of gesture, by the raising of one foreleg and the toss of the antlers, 'the Approach of the Stranger' – all his activities, dining out, racing, were founded on cattle standing absorbing moisture in sunset pools).

'What are you laughing at?' she asked him. For Willie Titcomb and Sir Harry and Herbert Ainsty were all laughing. But no. Sir Harry could not tell Clarissa Dalloway (much though he liked her; of her type he thought her perfect, and threatened to paint her) his stories of the music hall stage. He chaffed her about her party. He missed his brandy. These circles, he said, were above him. But he liked her; respected her, in spite of her damnable, difficult, upper-class refinement, which made it impossible to ask Clarissa Dalloway to sit on his knee. And up came that wandering will-o'-the-wisp, that vagous phosphorescence, old Mrs. Hilbery, stretching her hands to the blaze of his laughter (about the Duke and the Lady), which, as she heard it across the room, seemed to reassure her on a point which sometimes bothered her if she woke early in the morning and did not like to call her maid for a cup of tea: how it is certain we must die.

'They won't tell us their stories,' said Clarissa.

'Dear Clarissa!' exclaimed Mrs. Hilbery. She looked to-night, she said, so like her mother as she first saw her walking in a garden in a grey hat.

And really Clarissa's eyes filled with tears. Her mother, walking in a garden! But alas, she must go.

For there was Professor Brierly, who lectured on Milton, talking to little Jim Hutton (who was unable even for a party like this to compass both tie and waistcoat or make his hair lie flat), and even at this distance they were quarrelling, she could see. For Professor Brierly was a very queer fish. With all those degrees, honours, lectureships between him and the scribblers, he suspected instantly an atmosphere not favourable to his queer compound; his prodigious learning and timidity; his wintry charm without cordiality; his innocence blent with snobbery; he quivered if made conscious, by a lady's unkempt hair, a youth's boots, of an underworld, very creditable doubtless, of rebels, of ardent young people; of would-be geniuses, and intimated with a little toss of the head, with a sniff – Humph! – the value of moderation; of some slight training in the classics in order to appreciate Milton. Professor Brierly (Clarissa could see) wasn't hitting it off with little Jim Hutton (who wore red socks, his black being at the laundry) about Milton. She interrupted.

She said she loved Bach. So did Hutton. That was the bond between them, and Hutton (a very bad poet) always felt that Mrs. Dalloway was far the best of the great ladies who took an interest in art. It was odd how strict she was. About music she was purely impersonal. She was rather a prig. But how charming to look at! She made her house so nice, if it weren't for her Professors. Clarissa had half a mind to snatch him off and set him down at the piano in the back room. For he played divinely.

'But the noise!' she said. 'The noise!'

'The sign of a successful party.' Nodding urbanely, the Professor stepped delicately off.

'He knows everything in the whole world about Milton,' said Clarissa.

'Does he indeed?' said Hutton, who would imitate the Professor throughout Hampstead: the Professor on Milton; the Professor on moderation; the Professor stepping delicately off.

But she must speak to that couple, said Clarissa, Lord Gayton and Nancy Blow.

Not that *they* added perceptibly to the noise of the party. They were not talking (perceptibly) as they stood side by side by the yellow curtains. They would soon be off elsewhere, together; and never had very much to say in any circumstances. They looked; that was all. That was enough. They looked so clean, so sound, she with an apricot bloom of powder and paint, but he scrubbed, rinsed, with the eyes of a bird, so that no ball could pass him or stroke surprise him. He struck, he leapt, accurately, on the spot. Ponies' mouths quivered at the end of his reins. He had his honours, ancestral monuments, banners hanging in the church at home. He had his duties; his tenants; a mother and sisters; had been all day at Lords, and that was what they were talking about – cricket, cousins, the movies – when Mrs. Dalloway came up. Lord Gayton liked her most awfully. So did Miss Blow. She had such charming manners.

'It is angelic – it is delicious of you to have come!' she said. She loved Lords; she loved youth, and Nancy, dressed at enormous expense by the greatest artists in Paris, stood there looking as if her body had merely put forth, of its own accord, a green frill.

'I had meant to have dancing,' said Clarissa.

For the young people could not talk. And why should they? Shout, embrace, swing, be up at dawn; carry sugar to ponies; kiss and caress the snouts of adorable chows; and then, all tingling and streaming, plunge and swim. But the enormous resources of the English language, the power it bestows, after all, of communicating feelings (at their age, she and Peter would have been arguing all the evening), was not for them. They would solidify young. They would be good beyond measure to the people on the estate, but alone, perhaps, rather dull.

'What a pity!' she said. 'I had hoped to have dancing.'

It was so extraordinarily nice of them to have come! But talk of dancing! The rooms were packed.

There was old Aunt Helena in her shawl. Alas, she must leave them – Lord Gayton and Nancy Blow. There was old Miss Parry, her aunt.

For Miss Helena Parry was not dead: Miss Parry was alive. She was past eighty. She ascended staircases slowly with a stick. She was placed in a chair (Richard had seen to it). People who had known Burma in the 'seventies were always led up to her. Where had Peter got to? They used to be such friends. For at the mention of India, or even Ceylon, her eyes (only one was glass) slowly deepened, became blue, beheld, not human beings – she had no tender memories, no proud illusions about Viceroys, Generals, Mutinies – it was orchids she saw, and mountain passes, and herself carried on the backs of coolies in the 'sixties over solitary peaks; or descending to uproot orchids (startling blossoms, never beheld before) which she painted in water-colour; an indomitable Englishwoman, fretful if disturbed by the war, say, which dropped a bomb at her very door, from her deep meditation over orchids and her own figure journeying in the 'sixties in India – but here was Peter.

'Come and talk to Aunt Helena about Burma,' said Clarissa.

And yet he had not had a word with her all the evening!

'We will talk later,' said Clarissa, leading him up to Aunt Helena, in her white shawl, with her stick.

'Peter Walsh,' said Clarissa.

That meant nothing.

Clarissa had asked her. It was tiring; it was noisy; but Clarissa had asked her. So she had come. It was a pity that they lived in London – Richard and Clarissa. If only for Clarissa's health it would have been better to live in the country. But Clarissa had always been fond of society.

'He has been in Burma,' said Clarissa.

Ah! She could not resist recalling what Charles Darwin had said about her little book on the orchids of Burma.

(Clarissa must speak to Lady Bruton.)

No doubt it was forgotten now, her book on the orchids of Burma, but it went into three editions before 1870, she told Peter. She remembered him now. He had been at Bourton (and he had left her, Peter Walsh remembered, without a word in the drawing-room that night when Clarissa had asked him to come boating).

'Richard so much enjoyed his lunch party,' said Clarissa to Lady Bruton.

'Richard was the greatest possible help,' Lady Bruton replied. 'He helped me to write a letter. And how are you?'

'Oh, perfectly well!' said Clarissa. (Lady Bruton detested illness in the wives of politicians.)

'And there's Peter Walsh!' said Lady Bruton (for she could never think of anything to say to Clarissa; though she liked her. She had lots of fine qualities; but they had nothing in common – she and Clarissa. It might have been better if Richard had married a woman with less charm, who would have helped him more in his work. He had lost his chance of the Cabinet). 'There's Peter Walsh!' she said, shaking hands with that agreeable sinner, that very able fellow who should have made a name for himself but hadn't (always in difficulties with women), and, of course, old Miss Parry. Wonderful old lady!

Lady Bruton stood by Miss Parry's chair, a spectral grenadier, draped in black, inviting Peter Walsh to lunch; cordial; but without small talk, remembering nothing whatever about the flora or fauna of India. She had been there, of course; had stayed with three Viceroys; thought some of the Indian civilians uncommonly fine fellows; but what a tragedy it was – the state of India! The Prime Minister had just been telling her (old Miss Parry, huddled up in her shawl, did not care what the Prime Minister had just been telling her), and Lady Bruton would like to have Peter Walsh's opinion, he being fresh from the centre, and she would get Sir Sampson to meet him, for really it prevented her from sleeping at night, the folly of it, the wickedness she might

say, being a soldier's daughter. She was an old woman now, not
good for much. But her house, her servants, her good friend
Milly Brush – did he remember her? – were all there only asking
to be used if – if they could be of help, in short. For she never
spoke of England, but this isle of men, this dear, dear land,[66] was
in her blood, (without reading Shakespeare), and if ever a woman
could have worn the helmet and shot the arrow, could have led
troops to attack, ruled with indomitable justice barbarian hordes
and lain under a shield noseless in a church, or made a green
grass mound on some primeval hillside, that woman was Millicent Bruton. Debarred by her sex, and some truancy too, of the
logical faculty (she found it impossible to write a letter to the
Times), she had the thought of Empire always at hand, and had
acquired from her association with that armoured goddess her
ramrod bearing, her robustness of demeanour, so that one could
not figure her even in death parted from the earth or roaming
territories over which, in some spiritual shape, the Union Jack
had ceased to fly. To be not English even among the dead – no,
no! Impossible!

But was it Lady Bruton? (whom she used to know). Was it
Peter Walsh grown grey? Lady Rosseter asked herself (who had
been Sally Seton). It was old Miss Parry certainly – the old aunt
who used to be so cross when she stayed at Bourton. Never
should she forget running along the passage naked, and being
sent for by Miss Parry! And Clarissa! oh Clarissa! Sally caught
her by the arm.

Clarissa stopped beside them.

'But I can't stay,' she said. 'I shall come later. Wait,' she said,
looking at Peter and Sally. They must wait, she meant, until all
these people had gone.

'I shall come back,' she said, looking at her old friends, Sally
and Peter, who were shaking hands, and Sally, remembering the
past no doubt, was laughing.

But her voice was wrung of its old ravishing richness; her eyes
not aglow as they used to be, when she smoked cigars, when she
ran down the passage to fetch her sponge bag without a stitch
of clothing on her, and Ellen Atkins asked, What if the gentle-

men had met her? But everybody forgave her. She stole a chicken
from the larder because she was hungry in the night; she smoked
cigars in her bedroom; she left a priceless book in the punt. But
everybody adored her (except perhaps Papa). It was her warmth;
her vitality – she would paint, she would write. Old women in
the village never to this day forgot to ask after 'your friend in
the red cloak who seemed so bright'. She accused Hugh Whitbread, of all people (and there he was, her old friend Hugh,
talking to the Portuguese Ambassador), of kissing her in the
smoking-room to punish her for saying that women should have
votes. Vulgar men did, she said. And Clarissa remembered having to persuade her not to denounce him at family prayers –
which she was capable of doing with her daring, her recklessness,
her melodramatic love of being the centre of everything and
creating scenes, and it was bound, Clarissa used to think, to end
in some awful tragedy; her death; her martyrdom; instead of
which she had married, quite unexpectedly, a bald man with a
large buttonhole who owned, it was said, cotton mills at Manchester. And she had five boys!

She and Peter had settled down together. They were talking:
it seemed so familiar – that they should be talking. They would
discuss the past. With the two of them (more even than with
Richard) she shared her past; the garden; the trees; old Joseph
Breitkopf singing Brahms without any voice; the drawing-room
wallpaper; the smell of the mats. A part of this Sally must always
be; Peter must always be. But she must leave them. There were
the Bradshaws, whom she disliked.

She must go up to Lady Bradshaw (in grey and silver, balanc-
ing like a sea-lion at the edge of its tank, barking for invitations,
Duchesses, the typical successful man's wife), she must go up to
Lady Bradshaw and say . . .

But Lady Bradshaw anticipated her.

'We are shockingly late, dear Mrs. Dalloway; we hardly dared
to come in,' she said.

And Sir William, who looked very distinguished, with his
grey hair and blue eyes, said yes; they had not been able to resist
the temptation. He was talking to Richard about that Bill

probably, which they wanted to get through the Commons. Why
did the sight of him, talking to Richard, curl her up? He looked
what he was, a great doctor. A man absolutely at the head of his
profession, very powerful, rather worn. For think what cases
came before him – people in the uttermost depths of misery;
people on the verge of insanity; husbands and wives. He had to
decide questions of appalling difficulty. Yet – what she felt was,
one wouldn't like Sir William to see one unhappy. No; not
that man.

'How is your son at Eton?' she asked Lady Bradshaw.

He had just missed his eleven, said Lady Bradshaw, because
of the mumps. His father minded even more than he did, she
thought, 'being,' she said, 'nothing but a great boy himself.'

Clarissa looked at Sir William, talking to Richard. He did not
look like a boy – not in the least like a boy.

She had once gone with some one to ask his advice. He had
been perfectly right; extremely sensible. But Heavens – what a
relief to get out to the street again! There was some poor wretch
sobbing, she remembered, in the waiting-room. But she did not
know what it was about Sir William; what exactly she disliked.
Only Richard agreed with her, 'didn't like his taste, didn't like
his smell.' But he was extraordinarily able. They were talking
about this Bill. Some case Sir William was mentioning, lowering
his voice. It had its bearing upon what he was saying about the
deferred effects of shell shock. There must be some provision in
the Bill.

Sinking her voice, drawing Mrs. Dalloway into the shelter of
a common femininity, a common pride in the illustrious qualities of husbands and their sad tendency to overwork, Lady Bradshaw (poor goose – one didn't dislike her) murmured how, 'just
as we were starting, my husband was called up on the telephone,
a very sad case. A young man (that is what Sir William is telling
Mr. Dalloway) had killed himself. He had been in the army.' Oh!
thought Clarissa, in the middle of my party, here's death, she
thought.

She went on, into the little room where the Prime Minister
had gone with Lady Bruton. Perhaps there was somebody there.

But there was nobody. The chairs still kept the impress of the Prime Minister and Lady Bruton, she turned deferentially, he sitting four-square, authoritatively. They had been talking about India. There was nobody. The party's splendour fell to the floor, so strange it was to come in alone in her finery.

What business had the Bradshaws to talk of death at her party? A young man had killed himself. And they talked of it at her party – the Bradshaws talked of death. He had killed himself – but how? Always her body went through it first, when she was told, suddenly, of an accident; her dress flamed, her body burnt. He had thrown himself from a window. Up had flashed the ground; through him, blundering, bruising, went the rusty spikes. There he lay with a thud, thud, thud in his brain, and then a suffocation of blackness. So she saw it. But why had he done it? And the Bradshaws talked of it at her party!

She had once thrown a shilling into the Serpentine, never anything more. But he had flung it away. They went on living (she would have to go back; the rooms were still crowded; people kept on coming). They (all day she had been thinking of Bourton, of Peter, of Sally), they would grow old. A thing there was that mattered; a thing, wreathed about with chatter, defaced, obscured in her own life, let drop every day in corruption, lies, chatter. This he had preserved. Death was defiance. Death was an attempt to communicate, people feeling the impossibility of reaching the centre which, mystically, evaded them; closeness drew apart; rapture faded; one was alone. There was an embrace in death.

But this young man who had killed himself – had he plunged holding his treasure? 'If it were now to die, 'twere now to be most happy,' she had said to herself once, coming down, in white.

Or there were the poets and thinkers. Suppose he had had that passion, and had gone to Sir William Bradshaw, a great doctor, yet to her obscurely evil, without sex or lust, extremely polite to women, but capable of some indescribable outrage – forcing your soul, that was it – if this young man had gone to him, and Sir William had impressed him, like that, with his power, might he not then have said (indeed she felt it now), Life is made intolerable; they make life intolerable, men like that?

Then (she had felt it only this morning) there was the terror; the overwhelming incapacity, one's parents giving it into one's hands, this life, to be lived to the end, to be walked with serenely; there was in the depths of her heart an awful fear. Even now, quite often if Richard had not been there reading the *Times*, so that she could crouch like a bird and gradually revive, send roaring up that immeasurable delight, rubbing stick to stick, one thing with another, she must have perished. She had escaped. But that young man had killed himself.

Somehow it was her disaster – her disgrace. It was her punishment to see sink and disappear here a man, there a woman, in this profound darkness, and she forced to stand here in her evening dress. She had schemed; she had pilfered. She was never wholly admirable. She had wanted success, Lady Bexborough and the rest of it. And once she had walked on the terrace at Bourton.

Odd, incredible; she had never been so happy. Nothing could be slow enough; nothing last too long. No pleasure could equal, she thought, straightening the chairs, pushing in one book on the shelf, this having done with the triumphs of youth, lost herself in the process of living, to find it, with a shock of delight, as the sun rose, as the day sank. Many a time had she gone, at Bourton when they were all talking, to look at the sky; or seen it between people's shoulders at dinner; seen it in London when she could not sleep. She walked to the window.

It held, foolish as the idea was, something of her own in it, this country sky, this sky above Westminster. She parted the curtains; she looked. Oh, but how surprising! – in the room opposite the old lady stared straight at her! She was going to bed. And the sky. It will be a solemn sky, she had thought, it will be a dusky sky, turning away its cheek in beauty. But there it was – ashen pale, raced over quickly by tapering vast clouds. It was new to her. The wind must have risen. She was going to bed, in the room opposite. It was fascinating to watch her, moving about, that old lady, crossing the room, coming to the window. Could she see her? It was fascinating, with people still laughing and shouting in the drawing-room, to watch that old woman, quite quietly, going to bed alone. She pulled the blind now. The clock began striking. The young man had killed himself; but she did not pity him; with the clock striking the hour, one, two, three, she did not pity him, with all this going on. There! the old lady had put out her light! the whole house was dark now with this going on, she repeated, and the words came to her, Fear no more the heat of the sun. She must go back to them. But what an extraordinary night! She felt somehow very like him – the young man who had killed himself. She felt glad that he had done it; thrown it away while they went on living. The clock was striking. The leaden circles dissolved in the air. But she must go back. She must assemble. She must find Sally and Peter. And she came in from the little room.

'But where is Clarissa?' said Peter. He was sitting on the sofa with Sally. (After all these years he really could not call her 'Lady Rosseter'.) 'Where's the woman gone to?' he asked. 'Where's Clarissa?'

Sally supposed, and so did Peter for the matter of that, that there were people of importance, politicians, whom neither of them knew unless by sight in the picture papers, whom Clarissa had to be nice to, had to talk to. She was with them. Yet there was Richard Dalloway not in the Cabinet. He hadn't been a success, Sally supposed? For herself, she scarcely ever read the papers. She sometimes saw his name mentioned. But then – well, she lived a very solitary life, in the wilds, Clarissa would say, among great merchants, great manufacturers, men, after all, who did things. She had done things too!

'I have five sons!' she told him.

Lord, lord, what a change had come over her! the softness of motherhood; its egotism too. Last time they met, Peter remembered, had been among the cauliflowers in the moonlight, the leaves 'like rough bronze' she had said, with her literary turn;

and she had picked a rose. She had marched him up and down
that awful night, after the scene by the fountain; he was to catch
the midnight train. Heavens, he had wept!

That was his old trick, opening a pocket-knife, thought Sally,
always opening and shutting a knife when he got excited. They
had been very, very intimate, she and Peter Walsh, when he was
in love with Clarissa, and there was that dreadful, ridiculous
scene over Richard Dalloway at lunch. She had called Richard
'Wickham'. Clarissa had flared up! and indeed they had never
seen each other since, she and Clarissa, not more than half-a-
dozen times perhaps in the last ten years. And Peter Walsh had
gone off to India, and she had heard vaguely that he had made
an unhappy marriage, and she didn't know whether he had any
children, and she couldn't ask him, for he had changed. He was
rather shrivelled-looking, but kinder, she felt, and she had a real
affection for him, for he was connected with her youth, and she
still had a little Emily Brontë he had given her, and he was to
write, surely? In those days he was to write.

'Have you written?' she asked him, spreading her hand, her
firm and shapely hand, on her knee in a way he recalled.

'Not a word!' said Peter Walsh, and she laughed.

She was still attractive, still a personage, Sally Seton. But who
was this Rosseter? He wore two camellias on his wedding day –
that was all Peter knew of him. 'They have myriads of servants,
miles of conservatories,' Clarissa wrote; something like that.
Sally owned it with a shout of laughter.

'Yes, I have ten thousand a year' – whether before the tax was
paid or after, she couldn't remember, for her husband, 'whom
you must meet,' she said, 'whom you would like,' she said, did
all that for her.

And Sally used to be in rags and tatters. She had pawned
her great-grandfather's ring which Marie Antoinette had given
him – had he got it right? – to come to Bourton.

Oh yes, Sally remembered; she had it still, a ruby ring which
Marie Antoinette had given her great-grandfather. She never
had a penny to her name in those days, and going to Bourton
always meant some frightful pinch. But going to Bourton had

meant so much to her – had kept her sane, she believed, so unhappy had she been at home. But that was all a thing of the past
– all over now, she said. And Mr. Parry was dead; and Miss
Parry was still alive. Never had he had such a shock in his life!
said Peter. He had been quite certain she was dead. And the
marriage had been, Sally supposed, a success? And that very
handsome, very self-possessed young woman was Elizabeth,
over there, by the curtains, in red.

(She was like a poplar, she was like a river, she was like a
hyacinth, Willie Titcomb was thinking. Oh how much nicer to
be in the country and do what she liked! She could hear her poor
dog howling, Elizabeth was certain.) She was not a bit like Clarissa, Peter Walsh said.

'Oh, Clarissa!' said Sally.

What Sally felt was simply this. She had owed Clarissa an
enormous amount. They had been friends, not acquaintances,
friends, and she still saw Clarissa all in white going about the
house with her hands full of flowers – to this day tobacco plants
made her think of Bourton. But – did Peter understand? – she
lacked something. Lacked what was it? She had charm; she had
extraordinary charm. But to be frank (and she felt that Peter was
an old friend, a real friend – did absence matter? did distance
matter? She had often wanted to write to him, but torn it up,
yet felt he understood, for people understand without things
being said, as one realises growing old, and old she was, had
been that afternoon to see her sons at Eton, where they had the
mumps), to be quite frank, then, how could Clarissa have done
it? – married Richard Dalloway? a sportsman, a man who cared
only for dogs. Literally, when he came into the room he smelt of
the stables. And then all this? She waved her hand.

Hugh Whitbread it was, strolling past in his white waistcoat,
dim, fat, blind, past everything he looked, except self-esteem
and comfort.

'He's not going to recognise *us*,' said Sally, and really she
hadn't the courage – so that was Hugh! the admirable Hugh!

'And what does he do?' she asked Peter.

He blacked the King's boots or counted bottles at Windsor,

Peter told her. Peter kept his sharp tongue still! But Sally must be frank, Peter said. That kiss now, Hugh's.

On the lips, she assured him, in the smoking-room one evening. She went straight to Clarissa in a rage. Hugh didn't do such things! Clarissa said, the admirable Hugh! Hugh's socks were without exception the most beautiful she had ever seen – and now his evening dress. Perfect! And had he children?

'Everybody in the room has six sons at Eton,' Peter told her, except himself. He, thank God, had none. No sons, no daughters, no wife. Well, he didn't seem to mind, said Sally. He looked younger, she thought, than any of them.

But it had been a silly thing to do, in many ways, Peter said, to marry like that; 'a perfect goose she was,' he said, but, he said, 'we had a splendid time of it.' But how could that be? Sally wondered; what did he mean? and how odd it was to know him and yet not know a single thing that had happened to him. And did he say it out of pride? Very likely, for after all it must be galling for him (though he was an oddity, a sort of sprite, not at all an ordinary man), it must be lonely at his age to have no home, nowhere to go to. But he must stay with them for weeks and weeks. Of course he would; he would love to stay with them, and that was how it came out. All these years the Dalloways had never been once. Time after time they had asked them. Clarissa (for it was Clarissa of course) would not come. For, said Sally, Clarissa was at heart a snob – one had to admit it, a snob. And it was that that was between them, she was convinced. Clarissa thought she had married beneath her, her husband being – she was proud of it – a miner's son. Every penny they had he had earned. As a little boy (her voice trembled) he had carried great sacks.

(And so she would go on, Peter felt, hour after hour; the miner's son; people thought she had married beneath her; her five sons; and what was the other thing – plants, hydrangeas, syringas, very very rare hibiscus lilies that never grow north of the Suez Canal, but she, with one gardener in a suburb near Manchester, had beds of them, positively beds! Now all that Clarissa had escaped, unmaternal as she was.)

A snob was she? Yes, in many ways. Where was she, all this time? It was getting late.

'Yet,' said Sally, 'when I heard Clarissa was giving a party, I felt I couldn't *not* come – must see her again (and I'm staying in Victoria Street, practically next door). So I just came without an invitation. But,' she whispered, 'tell me, do. Who is this?'

It was Mrs. Hilbery, looking for the door. For how late it was getting! And, she murmured, as the night grew later, as people went, one found old friends; quiet nooks and corners; and the loveliest views. Did they know, she asked, that they were surrounded by an enchanted garden? Lights and trees and wonderful gleaming lakes and the sky. Just a few fairy lamps, Clarissa Dalloway had said, in the back garden![67] But she was a magician! It was a park . . . And she didn't know their names, but friends she knew they were, friends without names, songs without words, always the best. But there were so many doors, such unexpected places, she could not find her way.

'Old Mrs. Hilbery,' said Peter; but who was that? that lady standing by the curtain all the evening, without speaking? He knew her face; connected her with Bourton. Surely she used to cut up underclothes at the large table in the window? Davidson, was that her name?

'Oh, that is Ellie Henderson,' said Sally. Clarissa was really very hard on her. She was a cousin, very poor. Clarissa *was* hard on people.

She was rather, said Peter. Yet, said Sally, in her emotional way, with a rush of that enthusiasm which Peter used to love her for, yet dreaded a little now, so effusive she might become – how generous to her friends Clarissa was! and what a rare quality one found it, and how sometimes at night or on Christmas Day, when she counted up her blessings, she put that friendship first. They were young; that was it. Clarissa was pure-hearted; that was it. Peter would think her sentimental. So she was. For she had come to feel that it was the only thing worth saying – what one felt. Cleverness was silly. One must say simply what one felt.

'But I do not know,' said Peter Walsh, 'what I feel.'

Poor Peter, thought Sally. Why did not Clarissa come and talk

to them? That was what he was longing for. She knew it. All the
time he was thinking only of Clarissa, and was fidgeting with
his knife.

He had not found life simple, Peter said. His relations with
Clarissa had not been simple. It had spoilt his life, he said. (They
had been so intimate – he and Sally Seton, it was absurd not to
say it.) One could not be in love twice, he said. And what could
she say? Still, it is better to have loved (but he would think her
sentimental – he used to be so sharp). He must come and stay
with them in Manchester. That is all very true, he said. All very
true. He would love to come and stay with them, directly he had
done what he had to do in London.

And Clarissa had cared for him more than she had ever cared
for Richard, Sally was positive of that.

'No, no, no!' said Peter (Sally should not have said that – she
went too far). That good fellow – there he was at the end of the
room, holding forth, the same as ever, dear old Richard. Who
was he talking to? Sally asked, that very distinguished-looking
man? Living in the wilds as she did, she had an insatiable curiosity to know who people were. But Peter did not know. He did
not like his looks, he said, probably a Cabinet Minister. Of them
all, Richard seemed to him the best, he said – the most disinterested.

'But what has he done?' Sally asked. Public work, she supposed. And were they happy together? Sally asked (she herself
was extremely happy); for, she admitted, she knew nothing
about them, only jumped to conclusions, as one does, for what
can one know even of the people one lives with every day? she
asked. Are we not all prisoners? She had read a wonderful play
about a man who scratched on the wall of his cell, and she had
felt that was true of life – one scratched on the wall. Despairing
of human relationships (people were so difficult), she often went
into her garden and got from her flowers a peace which men and
women never gave her. But no; he did not like cabbages; he preferred human beings, Peter said. Indeed, the young are beautiful,
Sally said, watching Elizabeth cross the room. How unlike Clarissa at her age! Could he make anything of her? She would not

open her lips. Not much, not yet, Peter admitted. She was like a lily, Sally said, a lily by the side of a pool. But Peter did not agree that we know nothing. We know everything, he said; at least he did.

But these two, Sally whispered, these two coming now (and really she must go, if Clarissa did not come soon), this distinguished-looking man and his rather common-looking wife who had been talking to Richard – what could one know about people like that?

'That they're damnable humbugs,' said Peter, looking at them casually. He made Sally laugh.

But Sir William Bradshaw stopped at the door to look at a picture. He looked in the corner for the engraver's name. His wife looked too. Sir William Bradshaw was so interested in art.

When one was young, said Peter, one was too much excited to know people. Now that one was old, fifty-two to be precise (Sally was fifty-five, in body, she said, but her heart was like a girl's of twenty); now that one was mature then, said Peter, one could watch, one could understand, and one did not lose the power of feeling, he said. No, that is true, said Sally. She felt more deeply, more passionately, every year. It increased, he said, alas, perhaps, but one should be glad of it – it went on increasing in his experience. There was some one in India. He would like to tell Sally about her. He would like Sally to know her. She was married, he said. She had two small children. They must all come to Manchester, said Sally – he must promise before they left.

'There's Elizabeth,' he said, 'she feels not half what we feel, not yet.' 'But,' said Sally, watching Elizabeth go to her father, 'one can see they are devoted to each other.' She could feel it by the way Elizabeth went to her father.

For her father had been looking at her, as he stood talking to the Bradshaws, and he had thought to himself, who is that lovely girl? And suddenly he realised that it was his Elizabeth, and he had not recognised her, she looked so lovely in her pink frock! Elizabeth had felt him looking at her as she talked to Willie Titcomb. So she went to him and they stood together, now that the party was almost over, looking at the people going, and the rooms getting emptier and emptier, with things scattered on the floor. Even Ellie Henderson was going, nearly last of all, though no one had spoken to her, but she had wanted to see everything, to tell Edith. And Richard and Elizabeth were rather glad it was over, but Richard was proud of his daughter. And he had not meant to tell her, but he could not help telling her. He had looked at her, he said, and he had wondered, who is that lovely girl? and it was his daughter! That did make her happy. But her poor dog was howling.

'Richard has improved. You are right,' said Sally. 'I shall go and talk to him. I shall say good-night. What does the brain matter,' said Lady Rosseter, getting up, 'compared with the heart?'

'I will come,' said Peter, but he sat on for a moment. What is this terror? what is this ecstasy? he thought to himself. What is it that fills me with extraordinary excitement?

It is Clarissa, he said.

For there she was.

THE END

Notes

1. **Bourton:** the country house where Clarissa Parry had grown up, probably located in the west country since Peter Walsh remembers her looking down at the Severn river. See p. 131.
2. **grown very white since her illness:** Scrope Purvis refers to her hair. In 'Mrs. Dalloway in Bond Street' she is seen as 'strangely white-haired for her pink cheeks' (Susan Dick, ed.: *The Complete Shorter Fiction*, p. 206). See also p. 30.
3. **Lords, Ascot, Ranelagh:** Lords is the cricket ground at St John's Wood, home to the Marylebone Cricket Club. A week of horse-racing at Ascot in June culminates in Cup day; Woolf described it as marking 'the highest tide of the finest societies greatest season – all superlatives that mean little to me' (*Diary*, II, 17 June 1920, p. 48). Ranelagh, like Hurlingham (see p. 13), was a London polo club. On Bank Holiday Monday, 24 May 1920, Leonard and Virginia went to watch polo at Hurlingham Park and her account of it is distantly echoed in the passage that follows (*Diary*, II, pp. 41–42).
4. **Messages . . . the Fleet to the Admiralty:** at the top of the Mall stands Admiralty Arch, put up in 1887 to connect the Old Admiralty with the New. A recently installed radio mast on the roof of the new building kept the authorities in touch with the British fleet at sea. In *Jacob's Room* (1922) 'The wires of the Admiralty shivered with some far-away communication' (Penguin Books 1992, p. 151).
5. **Wagner, Pope's poetry:** the operas of Richard Wagner (1813–83) represent an extreme of high romanticism, in contrast to the formal, urbane and neo-classical poetry of Alexander Pope (1688–1744). The presence of the musician Joseph Breitkopf seems to have occasioned the discussion of Wagner – see p. 29.
6. **Devonshire House, Bath House:** walking up Piccadilly, Clarissa would have passed Bath House, on the corner of Bolton Street,

and Devonshire House on the corner of Berkeley Street, the town
house of the Duke of Devonshire until 1919.

7. **throwing a shilling into the Serpentine:** her gesture is recalled at
    the end of the novel in relation to Septimus's act of sacrifice (pp.
    157, 159), and is paralleled by the childhood memory of throw-
    ing bread to the ducks, p. 35.

8. **Hatchards' shop window:** Hatchards' is a bookshop in Picca-
    dilly, opened in 1757 and still in business. In the book in the
    window, she reads the first two lines of the song from Shake-
    speare's *Cymbeline* (IV. ii. 258–59). This is the dirge sung over
    the grave of 'Fidele' who is actually the fugitive Imogen, in a
    drugged trance-state. The words 'fear no more' recur through
    the novel and come to be associated with the rhythm of the heart
    beat. They are repeated by Clarissa at pp. 24, 32 and 159, and
    by Septimus Smith at p. 118 (see also Introduction, p. xxxvii).

9. **Jorrocks'. . . Nigeria:** *Jorrocks' Jaunts and Jollities* (1838) is the
    best known of R. S. Surtees' comic novels of English sporting
    life; *Soapy Sponge* (i.e. *Mr Sponge's Sporting Tour*, 1853), is a
    later novel of the same type. Margot Asquith's *Memoirs* (entitled
    Autobiography) were published in October 1920; excerpts from
    them appeared in August in the *Sunday Times*, and Woolf gos-
    siped with her friend Lady Cecil about 'Mrs Asquith and her
    inaccuracies' (*Diary*, II, 19 August 1920, p. 60). *Big Game
    Shooting in Nigeria* is apparently an invented title, but in keeping
    with the other hunting, sporting and society books in Hatchards'
    window.

10. **Grizzle:** Grizzle was the name of Woolf's own dog in the twen-
    ties. In *MD* it is Elizabeth's fox-terrier (see p. 141). Distemper is
    a disease of dogs, sometimes treated with tar.

11. **a pistol shot in the street outside:** a car has backfired, causing a
    sound like a gun going off.

12. **the Prince of Wales's, the Queen's, the Prime Minister's:** at this
    time, Edward was Prince of Wales, later to become (very briefly)
    Edward VIII, while King George V's consort was Queen Mary
    (see note to p. 15, note 20 below). On the identity of the Prime
    Minister, see Introduction, p. xiv; he later puts in an undistin-
    guished appearance at Clarissa's party (see p. 146).

13. **Lords, Ascot, Hurlingham:** see note 3 above.

14. **stiff with oak leaves:** oak leaves are military badges worn by
    servicemen mentioned in dispatches (the implication may be that
    the wearers had fought in the First World War without distin-
    guishing themselves).

15. **the House of Windsor:** i.e. the British royal family. A shindy is a
    fuss or brawl. Septimus later thinks of the European war as 'that
    little shindy of schoolboys with gunpowder' (p. 81).

16. **White's:** Woolf originally put 'Brooks's' – this club, built by Henry Holland in 1777–78, occupies no. 60, St James's Street. Woolf subsequently changed this to 'White's' Club, on the other side, at no. 37, when she found that Brooks's did not have a bow window, whereas White's did (see A Note on the Text).

17. **the *Tatler*:** in 1923 this was a magazine devoted to the activities of high society, though Woolf may also have recalled that the essayist Richard Steele, who lodged next to White's in 1709, had written many of the original numbers.

18. **St. James's . . . Queen Alexandra's policeman approved:** i.e. the sentries at St James's Palace where 'the Prince [of Wales] lived'. Queen Alexandra was the widow of Edward VII, and the mother of King George V (who came to the throne in 1910). She died in 1925.

19. **Victoria, billowing on her mound:** the memorial to Queen Victoria in front of Buckingham Palace was designed by Sir Thomas Brock and unveiled by George V in 1911.

20. **the Queen's old doll's house . . . :** Queen Mary's magnificent doll's house is now exhibited at Windsor Castle. At this time the royal family consisted of George V, Queen Mary, and their four sons of whom Edward was the eldest and heir to the throne. Their only daughter, Princess Mary, had married 'an Englishman', Henry Lascelles, in 1922. Later Clarissa's maid Lucy imagines herself as attending Princess Mary (p. 31).

21. **Little Mr. Bowley . . . the Albany:** Mr. Bowley had earlier appeared in chapter 13 of Woolf's previous novel, *Jacob's Room*, where he takes Clara Durrant and her dog for a walk: 'kind little Bowley – Bowley who had rooms in the Albany, Bowley who wrote letters to the *Times* . . .' (1922, Penguin Books 1992, p. 145). The Albany is an eighteenth-century mansion on the north side of Piccadilly, close to Burlington House, converted into bachelor chambers in 1802; it became a fashionable address for men of letters throughout the nineteenth and twentieth centuries.

22. **The sound of an aeroplane . . . in the sky!:** see Introduction, pp. xxxi–xxxii.

23. **its ancient shape . . . such was her darkness:** in Joseph Conrad's *Heart of Darkness* (1902) the narrator Marlow imagines the Roman conquest of the Thames valley: 'When the Romans first came here . . . darkness was here yesterday.' (Penguin Books, 1989, p. 30) Woolf's essay 'Mr Conrad: A Conversation' was published in the *Nation & Athenaeum*, 1 September 1923 (*Essays* III, pp. 376–79).

24. **in Greek words:** after her first suicide attempt in 1904, Woolf imagined she heard the birds singing in Greek (Bell: *VWI*, p. 90).

25. **the Mendelian theory:** named after Gregor Mendel (1822–84), who founded the modern science of genetics.

26. **a child exploring a tower:** enlarged upon later – see pp. 38–39 and accompanying note.

27. **Baron Marbot's** *Memoirs*: Jean Baptiste Antoine Marcelin, Baron de Marbot (1782–1854) was an officer in Napoleon's army. His *Memoirs* were translated into English several times. Phyllis Rose argues that the book is a metaphor for Clarissa's frigidity. According to Rose, Clarissa's 'choice of reading matter (the retreat from Moscow) suggests her enjoyment of the pattern of aggressors repelled, of a city resisting takeover by a foreign tyrant and triumphing partly by sheer will to maintain its integrity and partly because of the coldness of its winters.' (*Woman of Letters*, O.U.P., 1978, p. 144) – see Introduction, p. xxxix. On a more literal level, Clarissa's reading matter is not at all what we might expect from her self-description as a badly educated, frivolous woman.

28. **William Morris:** i.e. Morris's radical and socialist writings such as *A Dream of John Ball* (1886–87), *Signs of Change* (1888), *News from Nowhere* (1890), or *Socialism, Its Growth and Outcome* (1893).

29. **hollyhocks, dahlias . . . in bowls:** Vanessa Bell arranged flowers in this way. On a visit to Charleston in August 1923, Woolf noted 'Hollyhocks, decapitated, swam in a bowl' (*Diary*, II, p. 260).

30. **'She is beneath this roof!':** Quentin Bell describes Woolf in the nineties: 'gripping the handle of the water-jug in the top room at Hyde Park Gate, she exclaimed to herself: "Madge is here; at this moment she is actually under this roof,"' and a footnote gives Vita Sackville-West's confirmation that 'Madge Symonds . . . is Sally in Mrs. Dalloway' (Bell: *VW* I, pp. 60–61). See also Introduction, p. xl.

31. **'if it were now to die, 'twere now to be most happy':** *Othello*, II. i. 189–90 (spoken by Othello as he lands at Cyprus and is restored to Desdemona). Clarissa recalls this moment again at the end of the book, p. 157.

32. **Leith Hill:** four miles south-west of Dorking, Leith Hill is the highest point in south-east England; the Gothic tower (built in 1766) brings its total height to a thousand feet. It was a favourite spot for outings. See also Introduction, p. xxvii.

33. **St. Margaret's:** Peter Walsh passing St. Margaret's, the parish church of the House of Commons, associates it with Clarissa in her role as hostess.

34. **the Duke of Cambridge:** his equestrian statue (put up in 1907) is outside the War Office, half-way down Whitehall.

35. **the empty tomb:** i.e. the Cenotaph (literally 'empty tomb' in Greek), the memorial in Whitehall commemorating the dead of the First World War. The cadets have marched with their wreath from Finsbury Pavement at Moorgate, in the City of London.

36. **Nelson, Gordon, Havelock:** all military heroes with memorial statues in Trafalgar Square at this time: Horatio Nelson died fighting against the French and Spanish fleets at the battle of Trafalgar in 1805 and is commemorated by Nelson's column. Charles George Gordon was killed at Khartoum during a revolt in the Sudan in 1885. Henry Havelock was a hero of the Indian Mutiny who died at Lucknow in 1857.

37. **air-balls:** i.e. balloons.

38. **an old nurse . . . they called her:** in fact Clarissa's old nurse is called Ellen Barnet, and she later turns up to help with the party – see pp. 141–2. Peter Walsh later recalls Clarissa's Aunt Helena as having died (p. 138), though she too comes to the party (p. 152).

39. **Wickham:** the name of the officer who elopes with Lydia Bennet but is reluctant to marry her, in Jane Austen's *Pride and Prejudice* (1813).

40. **women's rights . . . topic:** 'antediluvian' since the suffragettes' immediate aim was satisfied when women over thirty gained the vote in January 1918. Women's political oppression is connected with their economic oppression through the issue of prostitution, a connection also made by Evelyn M. in Chapter 19 of *The Voyage Out* (1915, Penguin Books 1992, p. 235). Hugh's kiss (see pp. 61, 155, 'to punish her for saying that women should have votes') recalls Richard Dalloway's kissing of Rachel, which prompts her to ask Helen 'What are those women in Piccadilly?' (Chapter 6, *The Voyage Out*, p. 72).

41. **tariff-reform:** the policy of those conservatives who were opposed to free trade and supported differential charges on imports (especially of agricultural produce) in order to protect home and British empire goods from open competition on a free market.

42. **Morning Post:** owned by Lady Bathurst, this was a publication of the extreme right which had published violent anti-Semitic propaganda in 1920. Peter Walsh is greatly exaggerating Richard Dalloway's political conservatism; Dalloway actually reads *The Times*.

43. **Huxley and Tyndall:** Thomas Henry Huxley (1825–95) was a biologist who defended Darwin's theory of evolution against orthodox religious positions. John Tyndall (1820–93) was a natural philosopher.

44. **A sound interrupted him:** this episode seems to have had its origin in an incident of 8 June 1920: 'An old beggar woman, blind,

sat against a stone wall in Kingsway holding a brown mongrel
in her arms and sang aloud . . . Perhaps it was the song at night
that seemed strange; she was singing shrilly, but for her own
amusement, not begging . . . It was gay, & yet terrible & fear-
fully vivid. Nowadays I'm often overcome by London; even
think of the dead who have walked in the city.' (*Diary*, II, p. 47)
Woolf used the incident more directly in *Jacob's Room* (1922,
Penguin Books 1992, p. 56), but in this version the singer is at
once archetypal, singing in an unknown, perhaps archaic language yet the words are also identifiable as those of a particular
lied by Richard Strauss.

45. **singing of love:** this song was identified by J. Hillis Miller as
'Allerseelen', set by Richard Strauss to words by Hermann von
Gilm. It evokes All Souls' Day, when dead lovers return. Miller
could not find a translation that corresponded to Woolf's version
(the middle stanza of which rhymes), so provided the following
version:

> Place on the table the perfuming heather,
> Bring here the last red aster,
> And let us speak of love,
> As once in May.
> Give me your hand, that I may secretly press it,
> And if someone sees, it's all the same to me;
> Give me but one of your sweet glances,
> As once in May.
> It is blooming and breathing perfume today on every grave,
> One day in the year is free to the dead,
> Come to my heart that I may have you again,
> As once in May.

Miller writes, 'Like Strauss's song, *Mrs. Dalloway* has the form
of an All Souls' Day in which Peter Walsh, Sally Seton, and the
rest rise from the dead to come to Clarissa's party.' (*Fiction and
Repetition: Seven English Novels*, Basil Blackwell, 1982, p. 190).

46. **lecturing in the Waterloo Road:** the site of Morley College where
Virginia Woolf taught adult evening courses to working men and
women from 1905 to 1907. Isabel Pole might have thought Smith
resembled Keats in having little education and wanting to be a
poet.

47. *The History of Civilisation*, **and Bernard Shaw:** The first and
more important volume of Thomas Henry Buckle's *History of
Civilisation in England* (1857) argued for the influence of envi-
ronment on the intellectual progress of mankind. Shaw was read
for his socialist opinions as well as for his plays.

48. **Sir William Bradshaw's house**: Woolf's portrait exposes Bradshaw's complacency, and may include elements of Sir George Savage, who, as an old family friend of the Stephens, had treated her when she was ill, but later came to be distrusted by both Leonard and Virginia (Bell, *VW* I, p. 90; II, pp. 8, 14). Bradshaw seems to arouse an instinctive dislike in people as different as Rezia (p. 86) and the Dalloways (p. 156). See Introduction, p. xlvi.

49. **Lovelace or Herrick**: Richard Lovelace (1618–58) and Robert Herrick (1591–1674) were cavalier poets.

50. **that project . . . Canada**: Lady Bruton's adopted cause is 'a way of handling the massive unemployment of the period', as Alex Zwerdling explains (*Virginia Woolf and the Real World*, University of California Press, 1986, p. 129).

51. **the Labour Government she meant**: it came within seven months – see Introduction, p. xxiv.

52. **the descendant of Horsa**: with his brother Hengist, the leader of a group of Anglo-Saxon invaders of England in the fifth century.

53. **as Mrs. Hilbery said**: Mrs. Hilbery is a major figure in Woolf's second novel *Night and Day* (1919), mother of the heroine and daughter of a great poet, she is a somewhat eccentric figure. Later she appears as a guest at the party (pp. 145, 149), making a gnomic little speech as she leaves (p. 163).

54. **the Stores**: i.e. the Army and Navy department stores in Victoria Street.

55. **the old lady . . . upstairs**: this mysterious yet close and familiar figure, who reappears at the end (p. 158) at once focuses Clarissa's sense of solitude, or perhaps of her own futurity, while also being associated with the unknown, like the singer in Regent's Park (pp. 68–9) or Mrs. Brown in the railway carriage in the essay 'Mr. Bennett and Mrs. Brown', on which see Introduction, pp. xxv–xxvi. ('Mr Bennett and Mrs Brown', retitled 'Character in Fiction', *Essays*, III, pp. 423–25).

56. **oil and colour shop**: i.e. a shop selling oil paints.

57. **Westminster Cathedral . . . Abbey**: the Cathedral is Roman Catholic, built at the end of the nineteenth century in Byzantine style; the Abbey Anglican and much of it is Early English in style. A stone slab in the nave marks the tomb of the Unknown Warrior, brought from Flanders and interred in the Abbey in November 1920, as a representative of the nameless British servicemen killed in the War. While Miss Kilman visits the Abbey, Elizabeth is drawn towards London's other great cathedral, St Paul's, but turns back, deciding 'it was later than she thought' (p. 117).

58. **Somerset House**: a long mainly eighteenth-century mansion standing between the Strand and Waterloo Bridge; at this time

it housed various government activities, but particularly the principal tax and public record offices.

59. **Surrey was all out:** i.e. the county cricket team. Shortly afterwards (p. 138) Peter Walsh buys a newspaper for the cricket scores and reads the same item: 'Surrey was all out once more . . . But cricket was no mere game. Cricket was important' (p. 138).

60. **come up to the scratch:** to do what is expected of one (the scratch is the line from which a race begins).

61. **Mr. Willett's summer time:** after the war, the British retained the daylight saving time advocated by the English builder William Willett, and moved the clocks forward an hour during summer months.

62. **Littré's dictionary:** Emile Littrés monumental French dictionary was published 1863–72.

63. **dampers:** used to control the heat of the oven.

64. **the rascals who get hanged . . . train:** earlier (p. 138) Peter Walsh had read 'about a murder case' in the evening paper.

65. **Sir Joshua:** i.e. Reynolds (1723–92), English portraitist.

66. **this isle of men . . . land:** this passage suggests John of Gaunt's apostrophe to England in Shakespeare's *Richard II*:

> 'This happy breed of men, this little world,
> This precious stone set in a silver sea' (II. i. 45–6)

Lady Bruton 'never read a word of poetry herself' (p. 89).

67. **an enchanted garden . . . in the back garden!:** at Lady Sybil Colefax's summer parties at Argyll House, 'The doors which led from the large room into the garden were open, and the guests strolled about the garden, which was lit by garlands of fairy lamps.' Leonard Woolf, *An Autobiography* II (1964–69, O.U.P., 1980, p. 263). Although Woolf drew on parties at Argyll House in describing Clarissa's, Lady Sybil Colefax is probably the model for Lady Bruton rather than for Clarissa, who was partly based on the Stephens' old friend Kitty Maxse.

Appendix

Substantive emendations adopted or conjectured in this edition.

The first reading is the one printed in this edition. The italic entry immediately following the square bracket indicates whether this reading is that of the first British edition (*1925*), its revised second impression (*1925 ii*), later British editions (*1929, 1942, 1947*), the first American edition (*A 1925*), G. Patton Wright's edition in The Definitive Collected Edition of the Novels of Virginia Woolf, 1990 (*Wright*), or the present edition (*this edn*). When an emendation has been adopted in this edition, the original reading of *1925* is also given for purposes of comparison. When the present editor has allowed the reading of *1925* to stand but conjectures an emendation, the formula *conj. this edn* is used. The readings of Virginia Woolf's corrected proofs for *A 1925*, of her corrected proofs for Jacques Raverat, and of any part of her unpublished holograph material are indicated by *APR, JR*, and *Holograph* respectively.

14.15   White's] *1925 ii*; Brooks's *1925*
         The bow window was at White's Club (37–38 St. James's Street), not at Brooks's Club (60 St. James's Street).
18.29   sister] *Wright*; sisters *1925*
         Here and at 54.35 Rezia has at least two other sisters, whereas at 73.15 and 73.30 she is 'the younger' of two, and there is a reference to 'her sister' at 124.22. *Holograph* has no analogue here, as it does at 54.35 (see textual note).

29.29   Yet, after all, how much she owed to him later]   *1925*;
Yet how much she owed to Peter Walsh later   *1929*;   Yet
after all, how much she had owed to Peter later   *Holograph* (twice).

Wright adopts the *1929* reading 'because it avoids the
ambiguous pronoun reference of the original sentence',
adding 'It is unclear whether Woolf herself ordered the
revision'. But the deletion of 'after all' (to make room in
the line of type for 'Peter Walsh') is surely no improvement, and no real ambiguity existed, for the context
showed that the reference was to Peter, not to Breitkopf.
(There is greater ambiguity in the preceding two paragraphs with their feminine pronouns.) In the present
editor's opinion *Holograph* offers the best and most characteristic reading in the form of the verb ('had owed') –
the 'had' was perhaps accidentally omitted in the proofs
and not restored. Virginia Woolf may have substituted 'to
him' for 'to Peter' in order to avoid the jingle of 'Peter'
and 'later'.

41.14   already, I am not late.]   *this edn, Holograph*, already. I
am not late.   *1925*

46.37   'Here's my Elizabeth']   *this edn, Holograph*; 'there's
my Elizabeth'   *1925*
cf. 53.19–20, which this passage echoes.

54.19   Elise]   *1925*;   Elsie *Holograph*   (four times).
Virginia Woolf may have overlooked a transposition
error – or accepted it as a happy accident.

54.35   sister]   *Wright, Holograph* (twice);   sisters   *1925*
It is hard to see how the reading 'sisters' here and at
18.29 could have come into being except in response to
Virginia Woolf's typescript, or remain in the proofs without her acquiescence. She may have contemplated giving
Rezia an additional sister in later passages. If so, she
failed to carry out her plan, so it seems best to allow
weight to consistency and to *Holograph*.

61.1   Kinloch-Joneses]   *Wright*;   Kinlock Jones's   *1925*
For consistency with *1925*'s spelling at 61.1.

71.12   confidante]   *Wright*;   confidant   *1925, Holograph*
Both the masculine and feminine forms of the word
have been in use in English since soon after 1700 (*Oxford*

English Dictionary), so if Virginia Woolf wished to indicate by her spelling that she was not using a French word
there was no need for her to do so.

75.10   cheek] *A 1925*; cheeks *1925*
A logical emendation by the American copy-editor
without authorial direction. No analogue in *Holograph*
('She put down her hat, & kissed him.').

78.9–10   He only wanted to help them, he said.] *1925, Holograph*; He only wanted to help them, she said. *Wright*

78.36   and it went] *A 1925, APR*; and went *1925*
APR and *JR* give the passage in which this occurs as
follows: 'in a vase, upon which the sun struck directly,
signalling from Evans. It went'. The intention of Virginia
Woolf's alteration in *APR* and evidently in the Hogarth
Press proofs (she did not alter *JR*) was correctly executed
by *A 1925* and incorrectly by *1925*.

83.9   Holmes and Bradshaw] *Wright, JR*; Holmes Bradshaw *1925*; his torturers *A 1925*
APR and *JR* read 'his torturers', for which Virginia
Woolf substituted 'Homes [sic] & Bradshaw' in *JR* (she
did not alter *APR*) and evidently in the Hogarth Press
proofs also, where she either omitted the '&' or wrote it
so indistinctly that the printer overlooked it.

84.24   this sense; in fact his sense] *this edn, APR*; this sense;
in fact, his sense *A 1925*; this sense; his sense *1925*
The purpose of Virginia Woolf's alteration in *APR*
(she did not alter *JR*, nor, evidently, the Hogarth Press
proofs) must have been to avoid the collision of the two
senses of 'sense', a collision emphasized by the resem-
blance of 'this' and 'his'.

84.28–29   true belief which is her own – even now engaged] *this
edn*; true belief which is her own – is even now engaged *1925*
The second 'is' of *1925* is superfluous and syntactically
incoherent after the words that precede the passage between dashes ('a Goddess even now engaged'). It is probably a printers' error induced by the 'is' in 'is her own'. In
Holograph the construction, which bears out the emendation, is 'who is even now engaged (. . .) even now en-
gage [sic]'.

85.7   Conversion] *Wright, Holograph*; conversion *1925*
85.25   patients']   *A 1925*; patient's *1925, APR, JR*; pa-
              tients *Holograph*
                    As Sir William has many patients, it is probable that
              Lady Bradshaw means all his patients rather than one
              single (generic) patient, and that *A 1925*'s copy-editor
              made a correct emendation of an error that Virginia
              Woolf overlooked.
87.10   fifty-five] *1925, Holograph* (fifty five); fifty-one
              Wright
                    Wright emends in order to correct the inconsistency
              with 62.27–8 (Peter, 'who was two years older than
              Hugh, cadged for a job. At fifty-three he had to come and
              ask them . . . '). But the reader may feel that the four extra
              years for which Hugh has 'been afloat on the cream of
              English society' add something to the portrait. (Cf. Ham-
              let's flexible age, as discussed by A. C. Bradley, *Shake-*
              spearean Tragedy (1904), Note C.)
89.13   never read a word of poetry herself] *1942*; never read
              a word poetry of herself *1925*
103.16   no woman could possibly understand it] *Wright, JR*;
              no woman possibly understood it *1925*
                    Wright points out the conection with 'But could any
              man understand what she meant either?'
107.15   How detestable] *A 1925*; How destestable *1925*
                    'Context demands that this conjunction [i.e. 'But'] ap-
              pear as part of Miss Kilman's response to Elizabeth, not
              as a transition word in the narration of their dialogue'
              (Wright). But is not their dialogue an unspoken one? Cf.
              Holograph (deletions not recorded except in one case): 'It
              was rather pointless, somehow Elizabeth felt. Every now
              & then Miss Kilman made a remark; and then nothing
              happened. She had never felt that before – that sudden
              misery. She was looking at the table, – She saw Miss
              Kilmans hand open & shut & it became wrought into
              her misery; that nothing mattered. She took her gloves.
              [And *deleted*] Miss Kilman said, 'I have not quite done.'
              Elizabeth waited.'
124.1   remained to him] *A 1925*; remained him *1925*

131.28–29   'How heavenly it was to see him. She must tell him that.'
That was all.] *1925*; How heavenly it was to see him.
She must tell him that. That was all. *Wright*. See note
on 132.10–11.

132.10–11   'Heavenly to see you. She must say so!'] *1925*; 'Heavenly to see you!' She must say so. *Wright*
Wright objects to the quotation marks around reported speech; but they serve to distinguish between the
substance of Clarissa's letter and Peter's reactions to it.

145.17   Wilkins] *1947*; Wilkin *1925*

157.9–10   went through it first, when she was told, suddenly] *A
1925, APR*; went through it, when she was told, first,
suddenly *1925*

161.8   in red] *1925*; in pink *1947*
Wright, comparing 141.25 ('in her pink dress'), 144.16
('in the pink dress'), and 165.35 ('in her pink frock'), com-
ments, 'Woolf simply overlooked the error in factual details.' However, 'red' should perhaps be allowed to
remain. It may indicate that Sally sees the dress as red, or
that the dress is bright pink, not pale pink. Even if 'red'
is a mere error, it is one created by the author, not by the
printer, and that she did not change the word is a matter
of some interest.

165.10   humbugs,' said Peter] *A 1925*; humbugs,' said Richard *1925*
A mechanical error of Virginia Woolf's (probably in
typing from her handwritten manuscript), caused by the
proximity of 'Richard' in 165.8. Emended by the American copy-editor without authorial direction.

165.16   fifty-two to be precise] *1925*; fifty-three to be precise *Wright*
Wright emends for factual consistency (Cf. 87.10 and
note), but his discussion of Peter's and Clarissa's relative
ages is hardly relevant to this passage, Clarissa's age not
having been mentioned since 30.6–7 and 37.10.